T H E

BROKEN HEART

THE
BROKEN
HEART

N.J. GALLEGOS

NEW YORK   LOS ANGELES

Jacket design by Rejenne Pavon
Jacket Copyright 2023 by Winding Road Stories
Interior book design by A Raven Design
ISBN#: 978-1-960724-17-5 (pbk)
ISBN#: 978-1-960724-16-8 (ebook)

Published by Winding Road Stories
www.windingroadstories.com

1

He stopped, drawing in a breath of night air, and savored its crispness. No choking humidity this time of year. Muscles quivered with unspent energy, and he fought the urge to crack his knuckles—channeling his impatience into physical activity. He might have given into such urges when he was younger, more cocksure, but experience was life's best teacher and making untoward noise could give away his position. Lord knew it had happened before… more than once. Not tonight. Cocking his head, he listened, carefully containing the exhilaration that—still, even after all these years—threatened to overwhelm him. As he held stock-still, the forest moved around him.

Minute snaps and crackles. Twigs, dead leaves, pattering footfalls of all manner of creatures. Skittering insects, four-legged mammals; some hooved, others with delicate paws. Nothing substantial like the clomping of his fleeing prey—gusty exhalations, thin whistles from narrowed, abused airways. Wings fluttered, snug within nests. Something crunched through a carpet of foliage—too far away to be of any interest to him.

He knew they weren't *her*. Brow furrowed—where *was* she? Moving eyes only, he scanned his surroundings. Perhaps behind that that moss-covered boulder, cowering in fear? Or had she pressed her battered body against the forest floor—ignoring the crawling legs of rogue spiders whispering against her soft cheeks—hoping she'd be overlooked, and he'd give up the chase? Not a chance, he'd search until light bled through the horizon. Nothing stirred in his field of view, but he didn't rely wholly on sight and sound—like any adept predator, he had other tools in his arsenal. Nostrils flared and a damp soil aroma rushed in, reminding him of earthworms wriggling in the dirt after a fresh rain but on the heels of that? A sharp tang on his tastebuds that also tickled his tender nasal mucosa, something one might mistakenly attribute to the surrounding trees and foliage if they didn't know better.

The man knew better.

Fear. It was the scent of pure, unadulterated fear. It rolled off the women in waves, lingering in the air and like a prized hound's nose or a flickering snake's tongue—he easily detected it. She was close.

Awfully close.

Lips twitched and curled, exposing his pointed incisors. Muscles coiled. Tensed. He waited.

Snap!

There!

Head whipped towards the disturbance and body followed. Silence was no longer a virtue and he crashed through branches and bushes, eyes firmly on her retreating back. Tattered fabric from her shirt snagged on passing branches fluttered here and there, acting like Hansel and Gretel's breadcrumbs in case he lost sight of her—unlikely. She'd taken a nasty tumble earlier, right after she broke free from him. With every stride, he drew closer, enjoying the lurch of her shoulders with every agonized step, clearly favoring the right leg. She shot a furtive look behind her, eyes rolling in their sockets giving her the appearance of a terrified bovine, and saw him, inching ever closer. A sob spilled out, followed by a plea that traveled to his ears by the headwind they both ran against.

"Please! Stop. Just… just… let me go." She sniveled back a glob of snot, a nasty, sucking sound. "I won't tell anyone. I promise." Legs slowed yet, she still ran, or at least, loped along as well as someone could with a bum leg. But the begging? The bargaining? That signaled one thing.

Lost hope. Fleeing her predator wasn't going to happen and she'd come to *the* horrifying realization all the women inevitably did:

She was about to be caught—all because he had to scratch an insatiable itch.

His knife glinted in the moonlight and flashed, its point unzipping her skin, releasing a litany of sweet screams, along with blood, so warm cascading over him.

Such beautiful pleasure contained in suffering.

2

I studied the menu, a task made infinitely more difficult thanks to the inane conversation of my "friends." They're more than mere acquaintances, but we didn't exactly share friendship necklaces and braid each other's hair.

Reuben? Or tuna sandwich? Maybe a big salad of please-shut-the-fuck-up? I thought, keeping my face neutral.

"I don't know if I've told you, but I've been doing KETO!" Amber said, tossing a perfectly coiled chunk of hair over her shoulder.

Eyeroll. She only mentioned it a few times a week on Facebook, like deepthroating tablespoons of coconut oil was healthy or something.

"Keto isn't even good for you," Jenny scoffed. "That's why *I* do Paleo."

Amanda had the right idea. Sitting directly across from me, Amanda's eyelids appeared heavy thanks to her half-guzzled martini, and she was in her own happy place. The lucky bitch. I *longed* to order a Moscow Mule or a glass of red wine. Not being able to drink during these once-monthly

"Moms' Lunches" had to be a human rights violation of some kind.

But at least I could still eat carbs and I planned on rubbing it right in Amber and Jenny's macros. Extra fries… I'll just take an extra dose of diuretic to offset the salt content, so Dr. Yang didn't chastise me at my next appointment. Tuna sandwich with extra fries confirmed, I set the menu down and leaned back in my chair. My oversized sweatshirt shifted; a loose thread snaring on my still-healing incision just below my breasts. I glanced around the table.

The diet twins had moved on to debating the merits of essential oils, while Amanda—with a bone-dry glass in front of her—picked at her teeth with the plastic sword the bartender used to spear three olives.

I ceased to exist for the moment—either they'd gotten used to the whirring noise under my clothing, or they decided *not* to notice. I snaked my hand out and tugged at the fabric, wincing as it rubbed against the driveline. The smallest movements hurt like hell, but what did I expect? It had only been a few months since my surgery, when Dr. Yang turned me into a human version of The Tin Man. *If only I had a heart!*

"You doin' okay, hon?" Amber asked, her face pinched into an expression that I was all too familiar with—a cocktail of pity and a dash of thank-God-that-didn't-happen-to-me. Amber's eyes flitted to the bulk of my chest and widened, like she'd purchased a ticket to a circus freak show, and I was the first attraction on deck.

Step right up! Take a gander at the bionic woman, Casey Philips, more machine than human! Here she is, next to the airheaded bimbos! At least Amber didn't gawk, unlike most of the general public. But like a great many things recently, I've accepted this was now my life.

"Sure. Just had to adjust," I answered. Why couldn't this

water be vodka instead?

Amber nodded. "How's Owen doing these days?"

As if she didn't know. I've heard the whispers from the other parents. At the school play last week, when I walked in with a well-sauced Jack, even the most gossipy of conversations halted. Always a reliable way to know people were telling tales about the *incident*. That's how Owen's principal put it, almost hissing the word. *The incident.* A rather kind descriptor for what had happened.

"Fine," I replied, plastering my face with a fake smile that burned the corners of my mouth.

"We just hope he's getting the, uh—" Jenny paused, as if searching for the appropriate word. "Well… *help* he needs?"

"Yep." I picked up my phone, ending the conversation as abruptly as it began. I'd already recounted *the incident* for Owen's psychiatrist ad nauseum and was sick over it. Sometimes at night when I couldn't sleep, I saw the poor bird. Tiny bones that looked like toothpicks sticking out of its wings and its body… stomped to pieces. Flattened. Small smears of blood on the sidewalk. The principal had taken pictures, adding them to Owen's permanent record. No doubt the pictures would resurface in twenty years when Netflix recorded a docuseries about my son, the serial killer.

"Casey…" Amber started. She had the faintest furrow between her eyebrows.

"What?"

"Well, we were talking." Amber twirled her massive diamond engagement ring. "We love *you* but—"

"Oh my God, we love you so much!" Amanda burst in; her words ever-so slurred.

Amber shot Amanda a glare. "Right. And… well… we—"

"Just tell me." There was no use of pussyfooting around it. And while I didn't want to talk about any of this, I couldn't blame them for being concerned. A wave of nausea rolled through me and like I did several times a day, especially when the topic of Owen was at hand, I popped a Zofran under my tongue. Sweetness bloomed and I felt better almost instantly.

Jenny cleared her throat. "Um. We don't feel comfortable with our kids around Owen anymore. You know my little Madison is… fragile." Fragile… that was one way to put it. Madison cried anytime a butterfly so much as fluttered her way.

"Nothing against *you*, Casey. You're great." Amber added.

"No offense, Casey, but your kid's scary as fuck," Amanda exclaimed, armed with liquid courage. I smelled the gin on her breath from across the table.

"AMANDA!" Amber admonished. Her perfectly manicured fingers clutched invisible pearls around her neck.

"What? He is! He curb-stomped a bird to death at recess in front of the whole class and laughed about it. How would you describe that other than scary as fuck?" Amanda protested, crossing her arms in front of her ample chest.

"Well, still! My God, drink some water, you lush," Jenny said.

I stood up and grabbed my purse heavy laden with pill bottles and extra batteries for my machine. "It's fine, I understand." And I did. Owen scared the fuck out of me too, but mothers don't have the luxury of speaking about their children in public. Especially if their reviews were less than glowing. "Listen, I'm not feeling well. I'm gonna get my food to go. You know how tired I get," I added. The one perk of being chronically ill and on the transplant list? I could offer vague excuses to get out of most situations.

"Text me! Kiss Eleanor's cheeks for me!" Amber called out. I offered a weak wave and walked over to the waiter.

Time to abort this gathering with my extra fries.

There was something to be said for eating one's feelings.

3

—————

R eaching into the takeout bag, I extracted a fry and popped it in my mouth. Greasy goodness. The van was still in park, not yet ready to shift into drive for the trip home. Or as I sometimes thought of it, my gilded cage. Jack wasn't expecting me home for another hour or so, not that he would be in any condition to read a clock by the time I arrived.

Other than the total embarrassment of having my friends shun me, lunch didn't go as badly as it could have. The early exit meant I avoided the traditional photographic pissing contest every lunch devolved into. Not that I didn't enjoy showing off Eleanor. I did. My daughter had reached the adorable six-month age where she was all fat rolls and gummy smiles. Plus, she'd finally grown into most of the clothes I received at the baby shower, so I was constantly snapping pictures, texting them to the gift-giver as a thank-you receipt. It sure beat writing a million thank-you cards.

At last month's lunch, I nearly died of shame when Amanda swiped my phone and perused the photo gallery, announcing to the table, "Guys, Casey only has like four pictures of Owen."

"No, I don't," I lied. "I have them in a different album. Amanda, give that back. I'm waiting for a call from Dr. Yang." I wasn't, but Amanda didn't know that.

Once home, I studied my photo gallery. Owen was in more than four photos but... not by a lot. At least ten. Maybe. And each photo looked like either a mugshot or a movie poster featuring a murderous child. Like *The Bad Seed* or *The Good Son*.

I felt like a bad mother, but I couldn't muster up the gumption to take any more photos of Owen. He had a *way* of looking at me. Of looking *through* me, piercing the phone's lens. And I hated to agree with Amanda on anything but—

Owen *was* scary as fuck.

"Can't argue with that," I said aloud and stuffed another fry in my mouth. The boring black purse shoved up against my side shook and I swallowed the fry prematurely, cringing as it scraped down my esophagus. Wiping my greasy fingers on my jeans, I reached inside and rummaged for my phone, locating it underneath a bottle of Coumadin, or as I liked to think of it, my rat poison.

The screen read: Dr. Yang's Office.

Fuck. What was wrong now? My thoughts raced to last week's round of routine blood work. Dr. Yang very rarely called with good news.

"Hello?" I answered, picking at an already ragged cuticle.

"Casey Philips?" Dr. Yang asked, like she did each time, probably for some HIPAA reason. It wasn't like Jack was going to answer the phone. He'd gone with me to exactly one appointment, ever the supportive husband. Each time I sat in her office, I stared at the empty chair next to me, trying to ignore the ragged hole in my soul.

"Speaking." I ripped a piece of skin off and a bead of

blood welled up. More than normal thanks to my rat poison —my INR must be up.

"It's Dr. Yang." As if I didn't know that already. "I'm calling about your blood work from last week." Dr. Yang sighed. Great, a sigh. "Your electrolytes were fine; your INR was 4.5 so hold your Coumadin for the next two days and…" She paused. Dr. Yang notoriously opened with the good news, closed with the bad. Shit. "Unfortunately, your kidney function continues to worsen. Some of that might be dehydration. For the next five days, I want you to hold your Lasix. I'll have you come in next Monday for repeat blood work. With any luck, your creatinine will improve but…" She paused again, in that infuriating way doctors often did. "If it doesn't, you'll need referral to a nephrologist." Her tone brightened. "It so happens that my wife is one and she's excellent. And I'm not just saying that, either." She chuckled.

"Wait, a nephrologist? Like dialysis?" I panicked. Things just kept getting better and better, didn't they? First my heart up and quit, now my kidneys?

"Just as a precaution *if* your creatinine doesn't improve. And we're not nearly to the point of dialysis, don't worry." Easy for her to say, her wife was a nephrologist and could probably fix her kidneys in their living room if they were an issue.

I closed my eyes and pinched the skin of my forehead, hoping to ease the developing tension. "Okay. I'll see you next week, Dr. Yang." I'd stop taking the Lasix tomorrow; it would be rude of me to waste food when kids were starving in Africa.

"Goodbye, Casey." Dr. Yang hung up, leaving me alone with my racing thoughts.

As expected, when I arrived home, Jack was passed out on the couch. ESPN blared in the background. I turned the TV off, hoping to stall the impending migraine. He'd shifted at some point during his coma and upended a mostly empty can of Pabst onto his lap. Despite my annoyance, I smiled meanly, thinking of him waking up to a cold, chafed crotch. Served the prick right.

The smile dropped from my face.

Shit… where was Owen?

With the TV off, I became acutely aware of how quiet it was. And quiet in a household with two children, one infant and one psycho, *that* was *very* concerning.

"Shit," I muttered, dropping my purse, and hurried as fast as my body would allow to the kitchen.

Empty.

All the chairs were pushed in around the table where a spilled bowl of Cheerios congealed on the wood. Probably Owen's mess but I couldn't completely rule Jack out, especially depending on how many empties were stuffed in the recycling. Out of reflex, I glanced at the countertop, at the knife block, still safely locked within a thick plastic container. All knives were accounted for. Thankfully. After the bird *incident*, I'd purchased the box and only I knew the combination of the lock, 09-02-17: Eleanor's birthday and length in inches at birth.

I started up the stairs, huffing and puffing, my legs screaming as I reached the top. Just last year, I could have dashed up them with a full load of laundry. But now? I was lucky if I didn't pass out, and it took me an alarming amount of time to catch my breath.

The hallway was still too quiet, apart from my wheezing. I struggled to slow my breathing, to calm my beleaguered nerves, and I pushed open the door of Eleanor's nursery, expecting to discover blood splashed all over the pastel-yellow walls. What would I say to the police? *Sorry, I left my daughter with my alcoholic husband and my son murdered her. Have you heard about the bird* incident *at Appleton Elementary? That's my little Ted Bundy.*

For the briefest of moments, I *saw* blood slowly dripping down the wall next to the crib and when inhaling, I tasted iron on my tongue. Eleanor was in her crib, onesie dyed crimson, her tiny back unmoving.

Oh no.

I blinked.

No blood. Eleanor laid on her stomach in her Christmas onesie patterned with Santa's face, breathing just fine. But… just to be safe, I checked on her, earning a tired grunt. She promptly fell right back to sleep.

Eleanor's being safe alleviated a great deal of anxiety but there was still the mysterious case of what-the-fuck-had-Owen-gotten-up-to?

Beheading stuffed animals, as it turned out.

I barged into Owen's room without knocking and found him sitting on his dinosaur bedspread, a dreamy, far-away look in his eyes as he worked on decapitating a Care Bear—Tenderheart, if I wasn't mistaken. A litany of other animals—sans heads—littered the floor at his feet.

"Owen! Stop that right now!"

The peaceful, almost meditative air about Owen shifted in an instant. His eyes hardened, taking on a flinty cast and a thundercloud rolled across his features. He tipped his face upwards, and I recoiled at his sneer. A splash of ice cascaded through my veins.

"Fuck you, cunt." He practically spit the insult out.

"OWEN! Shame on you! Where did you even learn that word? You can't say those things, you know that!" I admonished him, knowing it fell on deaf ears. He didn't give a shit—about anyone or anything.

He shrugged. And had I not just heard the venom he'd spewed; I would have thought he was like any other little boy. He *almost* looked like an innocent six-year-old, concerned about collecting dinosaur figurines rather than curse words. Sandy-brown hair flopped across his forehead with the barest hint of a cowlick in the front. Dark brown eyes, inherited from his father, flashed with a steely anger. Unlike his father (whose good qualities waned by the day), Owen's eyes didn't sparkle with good humor or merriment. His eyes projected a lifelessness that I'd never seen in another child. A future already extinguished. Anytime I met his gaze, it made me shiver. I could only imagine how much worse he'd be as he got older. And stronger.

"Because of your foul language and—" I looked over the ruined stuff animals, at a Teddy Bear staring up at me, feet away from its body, white cotton-candy stuffing spilling from its neck. "And this mess, you are grounded. No TV until I say so. No video games either. Until you learn your lesson." Fat chance of that.

Ever repentant, Owen muttered, "Fucking bitch."

Motherhood was great.

6

Tuesday. Taco Tuesday.

Taco Tuesday was my mantra during Owen's psychiatry appointments. Since I couldn't pound margs or sling shots of tequila, I needed *something* to look forward to. Since Jack still expected me to perform my wifey duties: cooking, cleaning, and childrearing, I might as well make something that brought me a morsel of joy.

Taco Tuesday. I glanced around the waiting room. No capering cartoon characters or exam tables that looked like a whale in this office. Dr. Logan preferred a more… aseptic motif. Atomic bomb blasted desert chic: muted browns interspersed with an anemic sand shade. Maybe it was fashionable or there was some scientific reason—blah earth tones soothed troubled children. If that were the case, I'd buy a truckload of sand for Owen's room. Turn it into a giant litter box. Another woman across the waiting room from me thumbed through an outdated *Us Weekly*. Sans husband. Or partner, one couldn't assume sexual orientation these days. She could be a single parent, but the woman turned the page (perhaps to the latest *Real Housewives* scandal, per the cover), and I caught a glint of gold and diamond, left ring finger. *Somebody* was in the picture. Presumably.

Although, *assuming made an of ass of you and me*, as my Grammy Eleanor pontificated around the dinner table. Then she'd lean back and slurp her coffee, having imparted a great truth. I had to admit, my grandmother *was* historically correct about most things. Shortly after announcing our engagement, Grammy invited me over. A homemade pecan pie (my favorite) sat in the middle of the table, two slices missing. Only one bite in and Grammy pounced. I hadn't even swallowed my first mouthful.

"Casey… are you sure about this?" Her wrinkles deepened and settled into a frown.

I forked another bite of sugary goodness in my mouth, buying myself time. Was I sure about Jack? I *thought* so. Was he perfect? No. But who was? At least he wasn't an ax murderer!

"Grammy, yes. I'm sure." Even as the words left my lips, I knew they weren't altogether true. But most people had reservations before committing to someone for the rest of their life… didn't they? It was completely natural. At least, that's what I told myself.

"Okay. I just wanted to make sure," Grammy said, giving me her patented "I-know-you're-lying-to-me-but-I'm-going-to-let-it-go" expression. She'd let the subject drop and instead launched into a monologue about how that old bitch Susie was rigging the BINGO numbers down at the Knights of Columbus.

Against my better judgement, I ignored the nagging voice in the back of my mind begging me to reconsider. If only I'd heeded Grammy Eleanor's advice, given the matter more thought before jumping headlong into marriage.

Everything would be different.

I wouldn't be sitting alone while my scary as fuck son

(Amanda had a point) got his *treatment*—not that it was worth a tin shit.

No Jack though… that meant no Eleanor. A tightness crept through my chest and tears prickled.

But it was simple math, wasn't it?

No Eleanor.

No LVAD.

No shitty Terminator jokes from Jack.

"Mrs. Philips?"

Dr. Logan peered at me through thick framed glasses, a weary expression on his face.

"Yes?" I studied his face closely. Good news? Bad news?

"Can you step into my office?" Dr. Logan said, gesturing towards the door. Golden cufflinks glittered at his wrist.

"Of course." I kept my voice even, but alarm bells were going off. Flashing red and blaring sirens, filling my skull. What new, horrible information did Dr. Logan have? Clutching my purse, I walked into Dr. Logan's office. I swallowed and winced. Bone-dry. The rows of books lining Dr. Logan's wall, so orderly and *prestigious*, blurred. Doubled. Tripled.

Fingers rested on my chest, feeling the machinery underneath. The whirring sounded like it always did—a roaring tinnitus one learned to live with.

Just panic. That's all.

I set down heavily and inhaled.

"Mrs. Philips?"

"Yes?" His eyes were wide behind his glasses. Probably shitting his pants, terrified I was going to keel over in his office. Psychiatrists didn't deal with dying people, a fact I'd gleaned from extensive *Chicago Med* binges. Sometimes, I imagined myself on set. Clad in perfectly tailored scrubs with MD monogramed over the pocket. Hair pulled back in a ponytail, functional *and* germ conscious. It *almost* was me;

I'd even taken the MCAT and everything. But then I'd ignored Grammy Eleanor, like an idiot.

"Are you feeling… okay?" His face was pinched, begging me to just say *yes*.

"A little short on air but…" I took in a heaving breath. "Fine."

"Good." Visible relief. Dr. Logan's eyes were back to their normal size. He took his seat across from me and peered at me. Cleared his throat. "Today's session was…" A thin hiss escaped his lips. "Enlightening."

Enlightening. Great. "Okay…" Where was he steering this? Softening the blow before slapping me, I guessed.

He nodded over steepled fingers. "As you know, I evaluate Owen in different ways. Your standard talk therapy of course. What does he tell me and why? That sort of thing. Observation is also extremely useful." Dr. Logan pointed with his chin, and I followed.

A large glass window looked into a playroom of sorts. Assorted toys were strewn about and—

Owen? My eyebrows shot up. His face wore a scowl, and he dead eyed stared *into* me. Yeesh, talk about spooky. "Can he…?"

"See us?" Dr. Logan filled in. He shook his head. "No. It's a two-way mirror. We can see *him*."

"I see." This knowledge didn't stop the heebie jeebies capering through me.

Dr. Logan opened a large Moleskin notebook. On the front was Owen Philips in bold block letters, written in Sharpie. Prim printed words lined the page, packed margin to margin. It looked like he was copying *War and Peace* longhand or slaving over a manifesto like the Unabomber. Not good.

Not good at all.

Pages ruffled as he perused the exhaustive catalog of

Owen's depravity and finally located what he'd been looking for, midway through.

"Mrs. Philips? Some of what I do is observe how they act when they think no one is watching." He frowned. "Although… I have an inkling that Owen has his suspicions that he's being observed, but…" Dr. Logan shrugged—*what can you do?* Feeling Owen's eyes boring into me earlier, I *knew* he knew. He just didn't care.

"Certain toys and objects are set about. What do they gravitate to? The green toy ray-gun? Dolls? And how do they interact with it?" I could only hazard a guess at what Owen might have done now. Christ.

"Sure, you pick his brain, so to speak."

"Well… I wouldn't say exactly that, but… yes." Dr. Logan shifted in his chair and his back cracked. He averted his eyes. "Frankly, he displays *very* disturbing behavior. Sometimes I think this therapy is a game to him or a test of sorts. He thinks, *can I pass off as normal?*" I knew what he meant. No one else in my life realized what Owen truly was. Jack dismissed it. *Boys will be boys*, he said. But I saw it firsthand, felt the swirling darkness gathering within my house.

"I know what you mean. I feel like he's messing with me all the time." Playing the part of the innocent little boy with the grandparents, all smiles, and hugs, never stepping out of line. My stomach dropped every time he tiptoed towards Eleanor and planted lips on her soft forehead, much to the grandparents' delight. So close to her soft spot, one devastating blow and she'd be dead. "Such a good big brother!" they called out and at that, Owen turned, meeting my gaze, his eyes cold and dead, a sinister grin plastered on his face.

Dr. Logan nodded. "He's charming and manipulating when it serves him, I've seen that firsthand." He twiddled with one of his cufflinks: a gold H. Hermes, like on the purses the women on *Real Housewives* lugged around. Cleared his throat. "What… exactly is his relationship with Eleanor? How does he treat her?"

Oh shit.

I understood why Dr. Logan was concerned though. I harbored similar reservations.

"I do my best not to leave her alone with him. At all." Except last week. *But never again*, I vowed.

"Casey." Casey… he never called me by my first name; it was always Mrs. Philips. Using first names was just another sign that the conversation was heading down a dark road. "Keep her away from him. At all costs. I worry what he might be capable of." His head drooped. "Therapy isn't a miracle cure. Especially not in Owen's case. Some issues aren't—"

"Treatable?" I cut in. "You're saying… you don't think Owen will ever get better?"

He nodded.

"He'll only get worse?"

Another nod, this one curter.

"What kind of worse?" I asked, certain of the answer. He'd already asked in the form of a question, like on *Jeopardy*. Alex, what is, *"How does he treat Eleanor?"*

"Escalation," Dr. Logan replied. "He might test the waters, pinch Eleanor, inflict pain just because he enjoys it. And I don't say this to scare you but… I've read case studies on children like him. Owen displays the first hints of antisocial personality disorder; except we can't diagnose it in children. We call it a Conduct Disorder instead, and once they turn eighteen, *voila*, antisocial personality disorder." He pinched the bridge of his nose and shut his eyes. "Sociopaths. Murderers. Rapists. But he'll play the part of the perfect All-American boy and put on a front that distracts from his true nature. He's *already* learning how to manipulate adults around him."

A million different scenarios played out in my mind: Owen crying alligator tears when it suited him, how he deftly maneuvered his parents against each other, as if playing both sides of the chessboard... the list ran on and on.

"Yes, he does," I agreed. Dr. Logan was spot-on thus far.

"He's the worst kind of dangerous. A charming budding sociopath. Able to fly under the radar, get away with things. Avoid suspicion to weave his way in closer to the most vulnerable. Smart." He leaned forward, grasping my forearm. His palm was warm against my skin. Involuntarily, his gaze settled on the bulk of my chest, then flitted upwards to meet my eyes. I fought back an urge to say, "Hey my eyes are up here!" just to lighten the mood. Historically, Dr. Logan didn't find humor in most things, having had his sense of humor excised during medical school.

"Please, keep him away from Eleanor."

"I will," I said.

And I would.

7

His skin crawled under harsh fluorescents that rendered his coworkers' skin simultaneously jaundiced and anemic. Even his sharp cheekbones and stunning brown eyes were muted by it, taking him down to a paltry 6 from a 10—something that irritated him to no end. He wasn't common like the plebs around him. Tapping his feet, he raked fingernails over his forearms, inhaling sharply at the sting of pain when he breached the top layer of skin. A faint hiss escaped his lips. Doug, his cubicle mate, gave him a look.

"Just allergies," the man said with a shrug, folding his arms in his lap. Eyes cut to the clock hung above the hallway leading to the breakroom, the bathroom, and the parking lot —places he enjoyed as opposed to the claustrophobic cube he was forced to inhabit forty hours a week.

Only 2:10. Five minutes since he last checked. He released a gusty sigh.

"You good?" Doug asked, turning his face towards him. Doug's computer screen reflected on the lens of his glasses. The frames looked straight out of the Unabomber's police issued sketch.

"Fine," he replied evenly.

Doug rolled his eyes. "I could blow my fucking brains out; this day is passing by so slowly." As if Doug had any room to bitch. A job that normally took an hour took Doug twice as long, three times if not properly caffeinated. The man had already finished his work for the day and busied himself by appearing occupied, which consisted of loudly clicking his mouse, intermittently sighing, and stroking his brow, with an extra heaping of wrinkling his forehead while scrolling through pages of already completed documents. With nothing work-related to distract him, he felt like a heroin addict jonesing for a fix—desperate to check his phone and see how his fishing forays were panning out. Scrolling through Tinder last night netted him more than a few matches and as was his custom, he fired off introductory DMs filled with empty compliments and irresistible, yet witty one-liners. He *had* to have a nibble by now. Fetching a look at Mr. Henley's door and finding it closed—the inner shades drawn signaling he was either engaged in a meeting or watching porn—he pulled his phone out and tapped in the passcode. Checked his inbox. A faint smile curled his lips.

Got one.

Mercedes. He leaned back in his chair, allowing smugness to run through him. It was like shooting fish in a barrel, he really ought to write a book on how to reel 'em in and become a millionaire.

Step One: Women with certain names often bore fruit, especially anyone named after a luxury car. Only poor people went with such ridiculous monikers, thinking it conveyed class and prestige—trailer trash in other words. Girls who grew up in a single-wide invariably had daddy issues, making them easy marks.

Step Two: Peruse their profiles, keeping eyes peeled for certain phrases and key words. Women who proclaimed, "not looking for hookups/friends-with-benefits/a quick bang" usually were searching for just that. A classic case of *the lady doth protest too much*. Women bemoaning, "Are there any nice guys left out there?" laid out their desperation to find a mate for all to see like someone laying down a winning Royal Flush in poker. Anyone could play the part of a nice guy…. for a while anyway. He kept his eyes peeled for profiles advertising for six-footers or above, shorties need not apply. Shallow bitches like that *loved* his 6'5" frame.

Step Three: Examine their pictures. Caked on makeup, artificial nails, and skimpy clothing were practically the starter kit of women who typically fell prey to his charms. They wore their low self-esteem like a badge of honor and how easy it was to swoop in, peppering them with compliments and love bombing. They ate that shit up.

Miss Mercedes met all the criteria. Fancy car name, admonishments to not even click on her profile if your dick was six inches or less, decrees of *I hate drama* (oh she *loved* drama), and fake eyelashes coated with mascara.

His profile had been carefully curated and his photos usually sealed the deal. Him shirtless on a trail—six-pack on display—a dog at his feet; no one had to know he'd adopted it from a shelter expressly for this picture, returning the yellow lab the next day citing irreconcilable differences. Another of him wearing a suit and tie, the sleeves pushed up to reveal muscular forearms, an attractive stubble decorating his rugged jawline. His favorite? A perfectly photoshopped pic of him reclining in a private cabana on a gorgeous white sand beach, clutching a sweating bottle of Dom Perignon.

And judging by Mercedes' flirty banter and the racy selfie she'd attached to the DM—her standing in front of a bathroom mirror with tousled hair, duck lips, and a lacy black bra—

He'd located his next victim.

8

Taco Tuesday: the only thing keeping my sanity going, other than my anti-depressant, and I suspected that cute little white pill might be a placebo anyway. I pulled the van into the garage and parked next to Jack's prized Camaro which was currently covered with a tarp. Glimpses of bright blue paint peeked out from under the covering, glimmering under the automatic light overhead.

Owen unsnapped his seatbelt (assuming he'd snapped it in the first place, truthfully, I didn't check) and hurtled out of the car, through the door to parts unknown. Probably off to fashion his toothbrush into a shank, or something equally awful.

I gathered my things: purse and a small bag of groceries. I started to walk up the three steps leading to the house and paused. Head on a swivel, I glanced around the garage, taking in dusty corners filled with cobwebs, boxes containing holiday décor, and Jack's corner where he stored all his tools.

Amongst other things.

I might have been the only living, breathing person in

the garage, but I'd long discovered Jack had other women contained within.

There was the car, of course.

Jack spent far more time with *her* than anyone else in the house, lovingly running his fingers across her waxed exterior, slowly replacing old parts with new. On more than one occasion, while washing dishes or cooking dinner, I've heard Jack's voice, barbed and rough with the faintest of slurs call the vehicle, "a stupid cunt" and "a stuck-up bitch." Maybe that was where Owen learned all his profanities. I ran my hand along the hood as I walked towards Jack's tool bench, marveling at the cool metal under my palm. Any jealousy I held towards the car for stealing my husband's time had long evaporated, replaced by admiration. It was a shame I didn't know how to drive stick. Maybe one day, with practice, assuming I lived that long.

I set the purse and grocery bag down on the bench.

I'd need both hands to examine Jack's *other* woman.

Rows of drawers beckoned, some containing tools while others boasted assorted parts with names I could only hazard a guess at. Not that it mattered; I knew exactly what I was looking for.

Last drawer down, off to the right. Hooking my fingers under the handle, I pulled and peered inside. As expected, a half-gone bottle of whisky, its glass clean and dust free, unlike the sheath of papers nestled next to it topped with an inch of fluffy grime. Liquor and papers didn't interest me though.

I shot another glance over my shoulder, just in case Jack had learned apparition like Harry Potter, but I had the space all to myself. Perfect. Grasping the whisky bottle, I tipped it to the side and groped underneath the paper stack. Fingertips made a trail within the filth, meeting rough paper —*not* what I was looking for. Reaching further, something glossy rasped against my skin and using my fingers like a pincer, I gripped it and pulled. Like the booze bottle, it was relatively free of grime. Still, I blew on the surface, disrupting a few dust particles (all the better to see you, my dear), and brought it up to my face.

Perhaps at one time, Jack had the photo within a frame, maybe on his dresser, or even his nightstand—a place of honor for any teenage boy. Blonde hair tumbled over petite shoulders, perfectly coiffed. Bright blue eyes, full lips, perfectly straight, white teeth. Clear skin. She could have been an actor in a Neutrogena commercial, splashing water on her immaculate complexion with reckless abandon. Although this wasn't my first viewing (more like twentieth), my eyes were drawn to her chest. A C-cup, if not a D. With a frown, I looked down at my chest. Solid B-cup, on a good day. At least the LVAD gave the illusion of a bust.

Turning the photo over, I read the inscription, although I knew it by heart.

To Jack,
I will love you forever.
Tara

Apparently not, I thought. Things might have turned out a hell of a lot better if Tara had. There was a large black fingerprint, whirls, and swirls, near her face. That was new since my last viewing and even though it wasn't funny in the slightest, I snickered. Here was proof that Jack had been manhandling his prior paramour.

Your honor, I submit into evidence: Tara's glamour shot. See this fingerprint? Quite clearly it belongs to Jack Philips, as his wife has dainty hands and his children do not possess meaty paws. This is striking evidence that Mr. Philips is NOT over his ex!

"Asshole," I muttered, returning the photo. Briefly, I

considered dumping the whisky in the sink but thought better of it. What was the point? Then he'd know I found his hiding spot and… did I really give a fuck anymore?

32

9

While hamburger meat browned on the stovetop, I fed Eleanor dinner.

"Here comes the plane!" I said in a high-pitched tone—my talking-to-animals-and-babies voice. A pea tumbled to the table before the spoon landed in Eleanor's waiting mouth. "Vroooooom, what a good landing!" I exclaimed. Funny, how much the vrooms sounded like my LVAD motor. I almost didn't even notice the noise anymore, just like one grew used to insects trilling in the night when camping. At first, I'd thought the sound would drive me mad, a modern-day retelling of *The Tell-Tale Heart*, except *my* heart was the problem—not the old man's, the one with the cloudy pale blue eye. Months of constant whirring conditioned me though, and now I barely noticed it.

Eleanor let out a squeal and clapped as if to say, *more peas! More peas!*

"You silly girl! Do you like peas? Or do you just like Mommy pretending to be an airplane?"

"Blargh!" Eleanor replied.

I grinned. "I'll take that as a yes to both." I dumped the rest of the peas on Eleanor's tray, knowing that after dinner

I'd be picking smashed peas from each crevice of the highchair. "Don't stuff those in your nose! I don't feel like another ER visit," I admonished. Although, taking my kids in would be a first. At this stage in life, I practically had a frequent flier punch card. On the tenth visit, you get a brand-new heart! ER staff probably groaned when they saw my name pop up on the board. I was what was widely known as a fucking disaster.

Meat perfectly browned, I poured seasoning in the pan and stirred. Stole a glance at Eleanor—picking up the peas one-by-one with chubby fingers—and looked at the kitchen clock, a black-and-white cat with moving eyes and tail.

7:05.

Late… again.

Jack got off work around 4:30, later during tax season, and the commute to his accounting firm only took ten minutes—with traffic. Either he'd died in a horrific car accident on his way home (doubtful since the police hadn't called) or he was at the bar.

Again.

Distantly, I heard the garage door opening. Speak of the Devil and he shall appear. As I spooned taco meat into shells, the door banged open.

"Daddy's *finally* home!" I called out to Eleanor. Nothing like some passive-aggressiveness to spice up the night. Jack grunted and shambled past. A cloud of malodor trailed behind him: stale sweat, cheap liquor, and a hint of cigarettes. Trailer trash chic.

Completely ignoring me, Jack exclaimed, "There's my little girl!" He picked Eleanor up and she screeched with unabashed delight. "Who's my sweet girl? Who is Daddy's favorite?" Each uttered 's' was slippery. Not quite a slur but headed there. Maybe one or two more drinks and he'd be firmly within sloshed territory.

"Maybe Daddy's *favorite* girl can ask Daddy if he's going

to eat dinner with the family or did he already drink his supper?" Given that Eleanor hadn't even spoken her first word, it was quite the tall order. I smiled sweetly at Jack's glare and finished setting the table. Sour cream, cheese, hot sauce, and all the fixin's were ready to go. No Corona though, alas.

"Eleanor can tell Mommy that Daddy already ate and will be out in the garage," Jack replied. Back he went, slamming the door behind him hard enough to rattle the cat clock. Part of me felt relieved I didn't have to endure his sullen attitude, in addition to his obnoxious open-mouthed chewing that made me want to murder him but… another part felt slighted. Out to the garage to take nips from the bottle, tinker with his car, and undoubtedly, fondle the photo of Tara and himself.

I sighed. When did everything go so wrong?

Of course… I knew the answer to that.

All roads ended with Jack.

10

J ack didn't make an appearance until after I'd showered —a chore since I had to secure everything within a shower bag, including the driveline, carefully zipping all the parts within—and was in bed, tucked in with a bodice-ripping romance novel.

"Hey babe," Jack said, giving me a lop-sided grin. Once, that grin acted as foreplay, making my stomach flip-flop. The first time I'd seen it, I positively swooned over the deep dimple that appeared on his left cheek, even in the dim lighting of the bar. Nowadays, it didn't have the same effect. He hadn't lost his looks, not completely anyway, but instead of seeing a handsome man who might have been a model in another life—

I saw a predator.

"Hi." My greeting was flat. Bland. Impersonal. Anyone with any sense would have heard my tone and realized *Danger Will Robinson! Danger!* Do not pass Go.

Not Jack.

I returned to my book, immersing myself within a world where men were men and each one had a massive cock and a heart of gold. If only. I'd just reached the part where the heroine, a princess under the thumb of her asshole king father, submits to a Fabio lookalike knight.

Jack slipped under the covers, leaving his dirty clothes in a heap in the middle of the bedroom. Why put them in a hamper? Especially when his personal maid and cleaning fairy flitted about. His stench hadn't improved and had grown sharper, flavored with a hint of motor oil. Would it really kill the man to take a fucking shower? I pictured the caked-on grime rimming his fingernails, marking up the freshly laundered sheets and gritted my teeth. *Don't say anything, let it go, just chill out, it's not that big of a deal.* As drunk as he smelled, he ought to drop off quickly, leaving me with my fictional characters and a world where postpartum cardiomyopathy didn't exist. A much better world.

Moving with a speed that was eerie, Jack sidled next to me, his sweat-slicked skin pressed tightly against me. Sharp whisky clouds washed over me, sending up a wave of nausea, and like a bad dream, his hand ran up my inner thigh.

Fighting to stifle a scream, my world crumbled.

It was happening again.

No, no, no. Not again.

"Don't you FUCKING touch me!" I screamed, leaping up from the bed as quickly as my LVAD allowed. The whirring increased in volume with the sheets and covers off. My book flew across the room, thudding against the wall, and the bookmark ejected like a pilot from a fighter plane cockpit. My legs shaking, I ran to the bathroom, slammed the door, and locked it. Only then, did I feel safe. Of course, the damage was already done, wasn't it? Looking down, instead of seeing my sternum and breasts, I saw my LVAD. My eyes filled with tears, I held my head in my hands and—

Remembered.

11

I stared at the green plush rug in front of the tub, becoming absorbed in every fiber. Sniffing, I wiped tears with the back of my hand, and like my therapist taught me, took in a massive deep breath, and held it until my head swam. Released. I repeated the ritual until my nerves calmed some and my hands no longer shook like leaves.

PTSD. That's what it was. Like I was a shell-shocked war veteran with a litany of kills weighing on my conscience.

"Seriously?" I'd asked Pat when she brought it up. "PTSD? But… isn't that a bit… I don't know… excessive?"

The slight woman with graying hair cut in a bob peered at me, the end of her ballpoint pen touching her bottom lip. "Not at all. Anything can cause PTSD. It's not always what's depicted in the media. You know that classic scene where a soldier comes back from war and a backfiring car sends them into a tailspin? Yes, it is *that,* but it's far more than that. Any traumatic event can lead to PTSD. Car accidents, shootings, the death of a loved one, and—"

"Rape." I kept my gaze on the carpet, memorizing the

pattern, and placed my hand on my chest. No LVAD then. Not yet.

"Rape," Pat agreed.

Silence loomed between us.

"I can't stop thinking about it," I said, the words tumbling from my mouth like a hurried confession—which it was.

"That's normal. It's a trauma response," Pat said. She tapped her pen on the open notebook in her lap. The page was mostly blank, but Pat's sharp handwriting filled the top few lines. "Sometimes, talking about the incident is helpful. But only if you feel comfortable."

I considered. Did I want to talk about it? *Could* I even talk about it? Would recounting the story wound me more, taking the metaphorical knife and twisting it?

No, I didn't *want* to talk about it.

I *needed* to talk about it.

Pat watched me through thin-framed glasses. Bifocals. Behind the glasses, her gray eyes were kind. Sympathetic. The fact that she was a woman… that helped. There was something faintly Fairy Godmother about her and I bitterly wished Pat could wave her wand around and bippity-boppity-boo, change everything back to normal. Her eyes crinkled as she favored me with a reassuring smile. "If you want, we can just sit here until you're ready to talk. Or, if you want to talk about reality TV, I'm game. *You* are in charge here. We do whatever makes *you* feel comfortable."

I closed my eyes, took in a ragged breath that burned my throat and started speaking. Once the words came out, they poured out like a dam bursting.

"Monday Night Football. A weekly tradition with the guys. He goes every week." Jack didn't give a shit about football, at least, as far as I knew. I'd never washed any football jerseys and Jack didn't swear undying allegiance to any team other than Budweiser. "I think he goes because it's a socially acceptable way to get shit wasted." I *knew* that was most of the lure. Another thought had crossed my mind. Watching men ramming each other to assert their dominance? The way they lovingly patted each other's asses in those obscenely tight pants that perfectly showcased thick gluteal muscles? Seemed *awfully* homoerotic to me.

"Owen dropped off quickly, which was a miracle in itself. So, I went to bed early. When I woke up, he was already on top of me." The reek of bargain booze and stale peanuts filled my nostrils. I'd never forget *the* smell. "I asked him to stop."

I told her how my words came out a whisper as his hand fumbled between my legs, pushing my panties to the side and without preamble, he'd rammed into me, the dry friction sending a surge of pain through my pelvis. Grunting on top of me, drops of sour sweat dotting the T-shirt I'd earned in a local 10K, his thrusts grew shorter, more erratic until he'd shuddered, dumping his load directly inside of me before promptly passing out on top of me in celebration. His dead weight anchored my body into the bed, pinning me down, trapping me. Jack's dick softened inside me, shrinking from its actual size almost as if it wasn't there, too lazy not to outstay its welcome.

"Oh yeah, dear, it was great for me too!" I'd thought, laying in the wet spot, stuck staring at the ceiling since I wasn't exactly able to move. A deeper part of me felt used… like an object, a human flesh light who existed only for a man's pleasure. The words "cum dumpster" occurred to me and I grimaced. Unfortunately, the term struck close to home… that was all my husband thought of me.

Pat took a sip from her mug, pursed her lips together. Paused. "Consent. I'm hearing a lack of consent. And how does that make you feel?" What a typical shrink phrase, *how does that make you feel?*

The next morning, Jack sauntered downstairs, his

normal, hungover self. Either he didn't remember the previous night's encounter, or he chose to forget. Maybe Jack thought he deserved free use of my body? Funny... I couldn't recall Jack paying my father a dowry for my hand in marriage as if I were nothing more than something to be owned.

"It made me feel like property. A human sex doll. Used. Disrespected." Worse? The next night, he made *another* pass at me. "Hey baby, the weatherman said we were gonna get six inches" and he grabbed my crotch. With a sour stomach, I brushed him off, rolling my eyes. Six inches... he *wished*. Something between us had irrevocably changed, whether Jack realized it or not.

I sighed. "I tried to put it out of my mind. Hoped that I would be able to let it go." Make it become nothing more than a bad memory. I let out a rueful laugh. "Obviously not, right? Since I'm in here chatting with you?"

"Well..." Pat smiled and the wrinkles bracketing her eyes deepened. "I think *everyone* could use therapy, me included." Therapists needing therapy, like that old question: who was the town dentist's dentist? "Honestly? From what you've said, Jack needs this a hell of a lot more than you." Maybe they could toss Owen in, and we could qualify for a family discount!

"Ain't that the truth," I'd replied then, in the cozy confines of Pat's office.

And even now—huddled in a little ball in the master bathroom, my only comfort a fuzzy bathmat probably covered in E. coli—I knew my family was in trouble.

What I didn't know was what to do about it.

nother doctor's appointment.

At least it wasn't with my OBGYN, Dr. Yakoff. Dr. Yang was leaps and bounds ahead of Dr. Yakoff who acted as if I utterly bored him, reacting with indifference to each medical malady I developed. Why did the illustrious Dr. Cameron have to move to Idaho to deliver babies in the mountains?

I fidgeted with the Coban wrapped around the crook of my elbow. Underneath the blue wrapping was gauze, snug against the phlebotomist's pinprick. I wasn't allowed to peek yet, remembering the admonishment of thirty minutes of pressure, but I hoped it didn't resemble a maxi pad on a heavy flow day. It shouldn't—I'd held the Coumadin per Dr. Yang's recommendations. Wrenching my attention from my arm, I surveyed the waiting room.

Prints of hearts decorated the walls. Most were artistic renderings but there were several anatomic hearts—one I recognized from my anatomy and physiology atlas in college. *Did all cardiothoracic surgeons have similar waiting rooms?* I wondered. Other than me, all the patients likely held AARP Memberships and were first in line at Golden Corral for the early bird special. Save for a purple-haired woman who had to be in her seventies, I was the only one without silver threading my mane.

"Casey Philips?" A young woman with form-fitting scrubs clutching a clipboard stood by an open door that led to the examination rooms. I stood up, very carefully. My incisions had entered a crusty phase of healing and the driveline continuously chafed them. "If you'll follow me?" the woman said, turning. Ever obedient, I followed.

The hallway was long, reminding me of the one from *The Shining*, except the carpeting wasn't bizarrely patterned and looked relatively new. As I plodded forward, despite my bone-dry mouth, I swallowed, producing a clicking noise. Pat would have a field day with me, if she could read the emotions roaring through me. I had a vision of a PTSD anonymous meeting, metal folding chairs arranged in a circle. "Hi, I'm Casey, and I'm terrified of hallways in doctor's offices!" I'd get *so much* sympathy from war vets with missing limbs, gunshots constantly firing in their heads.

Dr. Yang's artistic hearts were much preferred. I'd seen worse.

And just like that, I was reliving that first OBGYN appointment—when *everything* changed.

———

THE OBGYN OFFICE was plastered with professional photos of babies. Like Anne Geddes' elaborately staged babies in buckets but lower budget. The hallway was wallpapered with birth announcements and Christmas cards. I remembered claustrophobia closing in as I plodded to what felt like my doom, past all the babies that seemed to follow me with their eyes. Judging. Which was fair. Lapsed Catholic upbringing popped up, marinating me in guilt (which was probably the point) and since that damn plus sign appeared… I'd been considering my… *options*.

One of the many reasons I voted the blue ticket.

Options.

Peed in a cup which somehow felt degrading; urine heating clutched plastic. A thread-barren gown, open in the back as the nurse instructed. Cold, coarse paper against my bare bottom. A knock, a two millisecond wait, and the doctor came in.

"Wait… where's Dr. Cameron?" I asked, clutching the fabric around my neck.

He'd given me a look then—an inclined eyebrow and a paternalistic expression on his middle-aged face. I hated him on sight. Opening his mouth made it worse. "Mrs. Philips. I *apologize.*" Grease dripped off the word. "My receptionist must not have told you. Dr. Cameron sold her practice to me last year. Winters without skiing every weekend must have really taken their toll." He paused, as if to say, *what do you expect?* "Anyway, I'm Dr. Yakoff, your new OBGYN." A meaty hand (that would soon be plumbing the depths of my vagina) extended and on instinct, I took it, where he proceeded to crush my fingers in his grip.

"Pleasure," I muttered, feeling nothing of the sort.

He plopped down on the rolling stool and opened a tan file. *My* chart. "You've had a positive home pregnancy test?"

"Yes." Those agonizing minutes, waiting for the stick to determine my fate. For lack of anything better to do, I'd studied the packaging. A happy, smiling couple staring at a plus sign. If they wanted truthful advertising, a teenage girl on the verge of a mental breakdown would be more appropriate.

Still absorbed in the chart, Dr. Jackoff (the name came to me in a flash of brilliance) didn't look up. "And that… would make you gravida two, para one."

"Para what?" I asked.

Arched eyebrow coupled with a twitch of his lips upwards. Contempt. "Para: How many living children do you have?"

Prick. Why not just say that? But no, gotta show off the degree. "One."

"Last period?"

I cast my memory back. Dad's birthday. About three months ago.

Shit.

"Three months ago?" My periods were never regular, so I hadn't thought much about missing one… or two. Three was where I got concerned.

Then came the exam, my feet in the stirrups, a watchful nurse chaperoning. Cold jelly, thick fingers (not in a good way), followed by swabs. Dr. Yakoff leaned back. "We can do the ultrasound right now; I can get the tech in here." He waved a finger and the nurse picked up the phone, murmuring something I couldn't hear.

"Wait. I wanted to see what…" Swallowed. "See what my options were?"

Dr. Yakoff waved a hand. "We can talk about that during the ultrasound. Two birds, one stone." Another knock (with a respectful five second wait). "Come on in, Sarah!"

A thin woman in blue scrubs wheeled a machine in and parked it, engaging its little brakes. "Mrs. Philips, I'm Sarah. I'll be performing your ultrasound." A quick smile and she turned, rummaged, and emerged, clutching a rather phallic wand. The other hand unrolled a sheath of plastic—that bore a striking resemblance to a condom—down the probe with an ease that reminded me of the one porn I'd watched in college. Copious jelly dripped on the tip—a woman's touch I very much appreciated.

"Mrs. Philips, your *options*." The doctor's words wrenched my attention away from Sarah.

"Yes. Options."

"Based on the first day of your last period, you're about twelve weeks. Three months," he quickly interjected, as if he tired of fools asking how much time that meant. "A medication-induced abortion is off the table. Only appropriate for 77 days." Another pause. "Which is about eleven weeks. You'd require a D & C performed in an Operating Room with anesthesia."

I'd expected as much, according to my frantic Google research.

"Mrs. Philips? I'll be inserting the probe now. It might be a bit cold—sorry about that. When I tell you, take a deep breath and try to relax your pelvic muscles," Sarah said, taking a seat.

I did as instructed, wincing while Sarah inserted the wand. Once snugly inside, a picture formed on the machine's screen: rapidly changing shades of gray and black that coalesced into a figure.

My baby.

As if aware it was being observed, it kicked its little legs out like an Olympic swimmer. I held my breath as the ultrasound tech tapped a variety of buttons and centered a line over its rapidly fluttering heart. "156 beats per minute, perfectly normal," Sarah announced.

"Can you… do you know…?" I started, unable to wrest my attention from the screen.

"The gender?" I heard the warm smile in Sarah's voice. "We usually can't tell until about 16 or 20 weeks but sometimes…" Sarah trailed off.

"What do you think it is?" I asked. A flurry of emotions flooded me. A boy? Like Owen? Even the risk that a child like him might happen again… no, I couldn't bear the thought. The poison within the Philips' bloodline *had* to be located on the Y-chromosome.

But a girl…

Dr. Yakoff interjected, nearly forgotten in the corner of the room, "I'll be in my office. Once you're done with the sono, Mrs. Philips, get dressed and the nurse will show you where to go. So, we can discuss…" The door opened. "*Options*." The door slammed, plunging the room once more into darkness.

I looked from the monitor to Sarah who shook her head and said, "Listen, I'm not supposed to do this and this early on, I might be wrong but, see this?" Sarah pointed with a gloved finger at an amorphous blob roughly at the crotch region of the fetus. "Looks like a little hamburger?"

"Sure," I said, pretending to see.

Sarah smiled. "It's a girl."

Options were off the table, just like that.

I was having a baby girl.

13

A knock interrupted my train of thought and memories of Dr. Yakoff's office dissipated into the ether. Dr. Yang breezed in, followed by a cloud of perfume, her white coat fluttering behind her. "Good afternoon," she said, giving me a curt nod. She clutched a sheath of papers.

"Hi, Dr. Yang," I replied, squinting to make out what she held. Little bursts of red and black spotted the top page. In my experience, red was bad, black was good when it came to lab work. And taxes.

"Before we get to your labs, I need to examine you," Dr. Yang said, removing a black, futuristic stethoscope from one of her white coat's pockets. At a prior visit, Dr. Yang proudly told me it was a newer digital model, capable of amplifying sound forty times, and could be linked to a computer program to further examine heart sounds. Very fancy and probably expensive. The doctor listened to my lungs. "Deep breath in… and out." Moved on to my heart, or rather, what passed for my heart these days. "May I?" Dr. Yang asked and I nodded. My gown opened, exposing my bare chest (save for the black harness I wore that looked absurdly like suspenders, the LVAD's two batteries snug in holsters as if I were an old-timey gunslinger), and Dr. Yang's delicate fingers probed the machinery. She murmured to herself, "Driveline looks good, incisions well-healing." Satisfied, Dr. Yang gestured for me to close the gown. "Now, your blood pressure." The first time, I'd been surprised, expecting my blood pressure to be taken as it had ever since I was a little girl at the pediatrician's office. Not so with the LVAD. Using the blood pressure cuff and a handheld machine (Dr. Yang said it was called a "doppler") held against my radial artery, she puffed the cuff up and listened, until a constant noise was heard. "Blood pressure is great. And how have you been feeling Casey?" she asked, taking a seat behind her desk.

How was I feeling? Like ten pounds of shit in a five-pound bag. Sleep had been non-existent; getting comfortable with a machine in your chest was a fool's errand. But… I had to admit, I did feel better. "Feeling okay. I don't get nearly as out of breath as I used to. You know, *before*." Climbing up a flight of stairs before the LVAD was akin to the Bataan Death March I'd learned about in school, huffing, and puffing, fighting the black dots dancing in my vision. I'd even passed out a few times… not that I disclosed that fun fact to anyone.

"Good. That's great, actually!" With an audible sigh, Dr. Yang pulled a paper—seemingly at random—from the stack she'd brought in. "Your labs are looking better. Well… *mostly* better." Great. I gleaned from that *mostly* that there was bad news. "Your INR is therapeutic, so you can resume your normal dose. And remember, no leafy green vegetables." No worries there, I loathed spinach with a passion. "Electrolytes are normal. BNP was fine, so you're not retaining any fluid." *But… where is the but?* I thought. Dr. Yang extended a finger. "But…" There it was, right on schedule. "But… your creatinine continues to worsen. I'm afraid if a new heart doesn't come along soon… we will be talking about dialysis within the next month or two."

Dialysis. Awesome. It would pair perfectly with the LVAD. With any luck, I'd at least be able to secure a handicap parking placard to hang from the minivan's mirror. Catching my glum expression, Dr. Yang quickly added, "Don't worry. You've moved up the UNOS transplant list and are very near the top. There's still time."

Sure… I had *nothing* but time.

Until time ran out.

14

I'd just left Dr. Yang's office, letting the front glass door shut behind me when my cellphone rang. "Fucking telemarketers," I muttered, digging in my purse for the damn thing. Once located, I glanced at the screen and ice trickled through my veins.

Appleton Elementary School—

Never a great sign. Calls from Owen's school had become more and more frequent, and never once had it been good news.

"Hello?" I answered, steeling myself.

"Mrs. Philips?" Deep baritone with the faintest hint of a posh British accent. Mr. Wilson then, the principal. *Really* not good if he was calling.

"This is she." Shit... what did Owen do this time? Normally his teacher called if there was a problem. Only after the bird... *incident*, had Mr. Wilson made the call himself.

He cleared his throat before speaking. "Owen, I'm afraid, has been involved in an altercation of sorts." Oh, an *altercation*. What joy. "It seems that Owen stole the class hamster from its cage and took it out to the playground.

Timmy Reynolds says that he saw Owen with a large rock in one hand, the hamster in another. Naturally, Timmy intervened and well… we had to send him to the hospital."

"The hospital?" The words burst out. "What exactly did Owen do?" The hospital? Oh, this was *not* good. Not good at all.

"Well… Timmy got the hamster away from Owen—unharmed I might add." Thank God. I'd always had a soft spot for animals, which was exactly why we didn't have any pets. Not with Owen around. "But… Owen… attacked him. Mrs. Reynolds informed me that he suffered a broken nose and multiple… bites."

Bites? "Wait… Owen *bit* Timmy?"

"Oh yes. Several times," Mr. Wilson answered very matter-of-factly.

"Christ," I said.

The other end of the phone was silent and for a moment, I thought the call dropped. Then, Mr. Wilson's words filled the void, "Listen… I'm going to have to suspend Owen for the next week and I'm convening a special meeting of the school board to discuss… *expulsion*." Expulsion? And leave Owen with me all day? Oh fuck. "You're going to have to pick Owen up. I had the school nurse look at him, but he did suffer minor injuries from the *altercation*." Great… first the *incident* and now there was the *altercation*. The gossips were going to have a field day with this—Amber, Jenny, and Amanda included.

"I'm on my way," I said, pushing the unlock button on my key fob. Sliding into the driver's seat, I considered driving to the airport instead, high tailing it to a sunny Mexico beach with bottomless margaritas and sparkling blue waves. Leave Jack to deal with his demon spawn.

But, as much as I wished I could leave, I wouldn't.

Who would protect Eleanor if I did?

15

Owen wore a sullen expression along with his tattered blue backpack when I arrived. Faint bruises peppered his face, the largest of which was around his left eye, already deepening into a thundercloud purple. On my way, I called Owen's pediatrician who advised me to go to the ER. For once, it wasn't me on the stretcher.

Per usual, the ER was a madhouse. After checking in at the desk, a harried middle-aged woman took down Owen's details, and we settled into two uncomfortable chairs.

And waited.

Luckily, there was no shortage of entertainment.

In the corner, a mounted TV played mindless *Fox News* drivel which I refused to watch, and with phone in hand—more as a prop than anything—I watched human drama play out. A crying teenager held a bloody towel to her face seated across from us, her sobs providing a soundtrack to the ensuing chaos. Then, a flurry of activity near the front door and a mass of people in scrubs followed by burly security guards tossed a young man with facial tattoos on a stretcher—sanguine geysers spraying from his chest—and hustled him to the back.

"Excuse me?!" I turned my head. A woman sporting a Karen haircut rushed to the desk, clutching the hand of a toddler who appeared completely fine if not for a snotty nose. "We were here first, why did *he* get to go back before us?" Um, maybe the fact that the poor man was mere inches away death had something to do with it. With a mean glee, I watched the encounter play out. This was way better than reality TV.

"Ma'am, I think your child's ear infection is much less important than someone shot in the chest. Take. A. Seat," the receptionist said through gritted teeth. "If you don't, I'll have security escort you out." Displeasure crossed Karen's face and she opened her mouth, thought better of it and snapped it shut, and with as much indignity as she could muster, took a seat with her germy child.

About an hour later, they called Owen's name and placed us in a treatment room in the back. A triage nurse came in, dutifully taking down medical history and allergies. "Jordan, your nurse, will be in soon, followed by the doctor. They're a bit busy right now with a critical patient." No doubt the young man with the gunshot wound, somehow receiving care before the kid with a cold. Alone again in the treatment room (twice in one day, unfortunately not a record for me), I turned to my son. "What happened? And I want the truth."

A flash of displeasure. Owen crossed his arms across his chest. "Timmy got in my way."

I cringed. "From what Mr. Wilson told me, you stole Hammy from his cage. What were you going to do with that hamster?"

Coal-black pupils bore into me, sending a shiver down my spine. "You really want to know?" Owen's lip curled in a sneer.

"Yes, I *really* want to know. That's why I asked." I really didn't want to know.

Owen rolled his eyes, and I fought the urge to slap him across his smug face. "I wanted to hear what he sounded like when I bashed his skull in. That's all."

To that, I had no response.

16

The nurse—*Jordan*, my brain whispered—came in some time later, holding a small cup with two white pills inside. "Tylenol, ordered by the doctor," Jordan said, feeling my gaze on her cargo. Her eyes widened in recognition. "Hey, I think I've taken care of you before. Haven't I?"

She wore royal blue scrubs like everyone else in the ER, but Jordan's face was imprinted on my mind. One of my saviors that swept in as I choked on dry land, fluid filling my lungs, drowning me. The panic, the certainty that *this was it*. Death. No longer an abstract idea, the knowledge that sure, one day I *would* die but not *today*. From my position on the cot, gasping and clawing at my neck, the ER's hallway blinked in and out of existence as my brain starved of oxygen. Lights flickered, as they did during storms when thunder roared before the brilliant lightning strike was no more.

"You're going to be okay," a nurse said, squeezing my hand. A name tag, Jordan, flashed in my field of vision. Bustling movement to my left, a dim consciousness that *something* was happening just out of sight. Rough hands gripped my head, and on my skull, a band snapped—

59

painful but distant—and a mask descended, covering my nose and mouth. A rush of air pushed into me, rocketing down my airways.

And—

The frightful pressure around my heart let up and my vision cleared.

"For the fluid overload," came from somewhere near my head, a deep, pleasant voice.

The room sharpened into focus and my labored gasping eased. A woman, brunette hair gathered in a messy bun, stood in the center of the chaos, calmly relaying orders, her eyes never leaving me. The Meredith Grey of the ER—the attending. An open red crash cart sat in the corner of the room; several drawers cracked. Jordan flitted into view, clutching a needle, and before I knew it, the IV was in. After the initial mad rush, the mood calmed and only Jordan remained in the room, pushing medications through the IV, adjusting drips. Watching me like a hawk.

How could I forget her?

"Yup. You saved my life," I said. And *she* had. I saw the doctor again, but only for a few minutes, before she was called away after a blood-curdling scream echoed through the ER. Jordan did the brutal work of keeping a human alive. Feeling sheepish, I asked, "You still remember me?"

Setting the medication cup on the counter, Jordan turned towards me. "How could I forget? You were so sick." Leaning back against the counter, she remarked, "I thought you were going to die. You had *that look*."

That look? I didn't doubt it. Desperate gulps of air, breathing through what felt like chunky chicken noodle broth, my heart racing in my chest.

"If you don't mind me asking, what happened?" Jordan's kind brown eyes rested on my face. "I didn't know if it ended up being pneumonia or ARDS or what."

So, I told her.

17

My elation at having a baby girl was short-lived. Shortly after the initial appointment, I started vomiting. And vomiting. And vomiting. "Morning sickness," Dr. Yakoff said dismissively. Sure… *morning sickness*, except instead of only happening in the morning, it happened *all the fucking time.* Puking day and night, no matter what I ate or didn't eat. The wind blew from the southwest and that made me vomit. Mercury in retrograde made me upchuck.

"Dr. Yakoff gave me pills, telling me some *could* cause a birth defect but… the chance was 'negligible'," I said miming quotation marks with my fingers, remembering how instead of gaining weight, the numbers on the scale ticked downwards, requiring a hospital admission for IV fluids, until I could hold down the bare minimum: dry toast.

Jordan nodded. "Hyperemesis gravidarum. I had it during my pregnancies too. Fucking horrible." She wasn't kidding.

After my fifth month, the morning sickness (what a joke of a name) abated, but another entity took its place: preeclampsia. Another bodily betrayal. My blood pressure skyrocketed, my kidneys dumped protein into my urine, and my red blood cells—once so good at carrying oxygen with their cute little donut shapes—tore into ragged pieces that looked positively moth-eaten under a microscope.

"Preeclampsia," I said. "I hadn't even heard of it before then. But Dr. Yakoff assured me that many women dealt with it and did just fine." Wrong again.

Jordan's face twisted. Fear. "Whoa. You didn't develop eclampsia, did you?"

Eclampsia, another *charming* condition, if it were to develop, would have wracked my body with devastating seizures, baking both my and Eleanor's brains into an oatmeal mush. "Luckily, no. During my third trimester, my liver joined in the dysfunction though." I remembered Dr. Yakoff's furrowed brow as he looked over that latest round of blood work. Liver enzymes sky high, their values highlighted in red and bold enough that I could read them from way across the desk. "HELLP syndrome," I said, parroting Dr. Yakoff's diagnosis. I'd been a medical student's wet dream then, a hodge-podge of horrible disease processes that worsened at a startling rate.

"They took me for a C-section at 36 weeks." A planned but emergent procedure, an oxymoron if I'd ever heard one. "Remove the baby and all the issues often miraculously cured themselves." Or so Dr. Yakoff said.

Jack donned green hospital scrubs, looking ridiculous with a lunch lady bouffant cap pulled over his thinning hair. He held my hand from the other side of the sterile curtain near my head, careful to keep his eyes averted from my abdomen, splayed open like a Thanksgiving turkey. Notoriously squeamish at the sight of blood, he once fainted in the kitchen after accidentally fileting his palm while struggling to open the thick plastic packaging of one of Owen's toys.

I didn't have to see Dr. Yakoff's blood-streaked, white-gloved fingers. I *felt* them dancing around inside me, rearranging my innards and scooping giblets out. There'd been a horrid tugging sensation from deep within me that the epidural couldn't mask and even now, my pelvis ached just thinking of it.

But the loud cry that filled the room—Eleanor's first vocalization—brought tears to my eyes, making all the pain and sickness worth it. Delicious warmth flowed through me, likely a rush of hormones at hearing the cry of my newborn, but I knew it was *love*. No matter how grueling the pregnancy had been—it was worth it.

I had a daughter, a little girl.

Of course, I didn't tell Jordan *everything*.

I didn't say how my next thought was of my son.

And how fear clutched me in its steely grip since.

18

The rest of the ER visit went swimmingly. An APN, Ashley, got us in and out quickly, after a negative CT scan of the brain. No broken bones, luckily. I wouldn't have been upset about a nice brain bleed taking Owen out for the count, but alas.

Once in the van, I turned, my machinery shifting painfully against my skin, and met Owen's eyes—frigidly cold and blighted. Suppressing a shudder, I said, "Listen, Owen. You *can't* be doing this! Animals are living, breathing creatures, and what you're doing is…" I groped for the right word. "Wrong," I said lamely.

Owen crossed his arms over his chest, obscuring the T-rex shirt he'd picked out that morning. So… childlike, like a kid about to throw a tantrum because they couldn't have ice cream for dinner. The expression on his face was anything but. "To *me*, it's not wrong. It's fun. Who cares about animals?" Pausing, he gave a sinister smile, and a primitive intuition filled me. *Predator. Danger!* "Who cares about anybody," he said, rolling his eyes, voice oddly monotone.

"What do you mean, people don't matter to you?" I demanded, my hands involuntarily balling into fists. Not that this was a revelation to me, but hearing him say it aloud —so casually, as if he was chatting about his favorite cereal —was alarming.

"They don't. No one does. Not Dad. Not you." He laughed, a chilling inhuman sound, and I tensed. "And *definitely* not Eleanor. Who needs a baby around anyway? They're super stupid."

With every fiber of my being, I resisted the urge to slap Owen across his face. A tempest of emotions whirled within me: fear, stark raving fear for my daughter's life, and something red and hot, anger augmented by a mother's love. Slapping Owen—and fearing I might not stop at that— wasn't appropriate, I'd only be stooping down to his level.

While driving home, making my way to suburbia, I worried, wrapping my mind around the idea that the very existence of my son threatened that of my daughter.

19

The man flopped onto the sofa; its worn cushions protested. He raked a hand through hair soaked with sweat. Today's workout? Four miles on the treadmill, throwing a few sprints in, just to keep his body well-tuned when late night hunts went wrong, then the weight room for upper body work: pecs, delts, and biceps. Having endured such torture at his own hand, he figured he earned some TV before showering. Channel surfing, he eventually landed on reruns of *The Office*, surprise, surprise.

Only minutes after Jim did his signature face to the camera, his phone vibrated. Fishing it from his pocket, he read the notification, and whooped.

"Alright! I still got it!"

One message from Brittany. He'd hit her hard with compliments (mostly about her hair, a gorgeous brownish red shade that reminded him of those old Herbal Essences commercials where the women acted like they orgasmed from shampoo and conditioner) and showed appropriate interest in her activities. Their last message, he really worked her over—talking about how much he loved talking to her and how he was dying to hear her voice in person. "But only if you feel comfortable," he'd said. Women loved that shit, to feel comfortable and respected.

Her message read:

Want to meet up for a drink, handsome? ;)

"Looks like Eugene gots himself a date!" he announced to the empty apartment as he typed a reply to Brittany. He hoped to meet for drinks next week, then maybe?

Just maybe, they could deepen their relationship. Their bond.

He smacked his head and chuckled. "Gotta sharpen that knife too." Number one on his to-do list after Mercedes. He'd stabbed her more times than he could count, and the blade was dull.

A loud rumble cut through the slow rhythmic pattering of rain on asphalt. Rumble became bone rattling crash that filled the air, followed by a profound, chilling silence. Acrid scents of flame and burning flesh rose, flavoring the atmosphere. A utility pole shifted from its formerly ramrod straight position into an awkward angle only seen when tragedy abounded. The pole, however, fared far better than the motorcycle laying at its bent base. It resembled a crumpled yellow accordion; shattered almost beyond recognition; errant pieces normally hidden away exposed to the elements.

The hog was a prize pig compared to its former occupant. Its rider had been a handsome brown-haired man, whose eyes crinkled at the corners every time he smiled—though that smile never truly touched his eyes. They were steely. Cold pits. He'd been a man who—in life —had a laugh that sounded as if it originated from the tips of his toes. When burbling up from his throat, it was a joyful sound to most who heard it.

Excluding a *significant* number of women.

Initially, they leaned in, happy with his attention and

affections. But soon, they found his jangling tones of laughter cruel and barbed, assaulting their ears. Too often, it was the last sound they heard before succumbing to his darker desires.

The man's formerly pink, soft flesh dimpled and sizzled, resembling hamburger meat—the sort of meat that came from slaughterhouses contaminated with rancid shit, infecting little kids with deadly E. coli. Those poor children, their tongues dancing with delight as they munched on an innocent hamburger, with no clue they'd end their week in a pine box after succumbing to septic shock. Things were not always as they seemed.

Minutes ticked by indifferently, not caring one whit about the suffering that dominated the man's world. Rain pattered on, intensifying into a downpour that extinguished the growing flames greedily licking across his skin. The flames seemed almost sentient, intent on sinking their burning tendrils into exposed flesh. Gobbling, feeding.

Consuming.

Gasoline glugged out of ruined tank onto the road; most of the amber fluid coalesced into a puddle under the ruined figure. Rain fell in thick sheets—a real corker of a storm—keeping further predatory blazes at bay. A pregnant, bloated moon hid behind a thick ceiling of storm clouds, its pale ghost barely visible in the sky.

The man lay motionless in a heap, steam rising off his charred body, dissipating into the humid night air. He'd mercifully succumbed to unconsciousness. Not that this was altogether surprising, since his head—rather than the expected oval—had assumed a grotesque watermelon shape, a painful consequence of forgoing a helmet while riding. His skull fractured in several places, producing a hole that communicated with the outside air. Gelatinous pink brain oozed out with languid slowness. Warm, vital brain matter greeted cooler air, producing a faint steam, like freshly baked bread pulled from the oven. The adage, "You need that like you need a hole in the head" didn't apply here. In fact, the slow leakage of brain prolonged the man's life, acting to relieve the skyrocketing intracranial pressure building in his head, not dissimilar to what a skilled neurosurgeon might do with the appropriate tools. Rudimentary. Easy. A second-year neurosurgery resident could do it, assuming they weren't all thumbs: grab a drill, burr a hole through the skull and relieve the pressure. Except tonight, instead of skilled hands, a pole and the unforgiving highway surface accomplished that feat. Had he not devastatingly cracked his skull open, spilling himself over the asphalt, he would have died rather quickly as his brain herniated. The centers controlling his breathing would have gone dark, his diaphragm halting its familiar rhythmic dance, and the man would have gone to the great beyond.

But that's not what happened.

Brain dripped on pavement for nearly half an hour, an accompaniment to the raindrops, but each time the grey matter struck the ground, it made a dull wet *smack*—the world's most ghastly metronome. Each smack signified a loss of the man's core being.

Smack… there went grade school.

Smack… forget ever using a fork again.

Smack… goodbye first kill.

21

The soft yellow glow of a single headlight bathed the grisly scene in stark light. Left headlight was a dark husk in the dim hours of the early morning, unseeing. A new bulb was an extra expense Jane couldn't afford. The car desperately needed an oil change, a fact Jane well knew.

Jane was headed to her job, cleaning for a local flea bag motel—off the books, of course, no W-2 for her, thank you. She'd been drowsily thinking about the day ahead of her. Another day spent peeling used condoms off bedspreads that hadn't been washed since the Reagan administration. *What fun!* Her gaze landed on a sight that chased away thoughts of double-decker toilet pranks and she took in the scene that popped into view, illuminated by her one working headlight.

Sleepiness departed abruptly, leaving an icy fear in its wake.

For a brief second, Jane considered gunning it, letting the accident melt away in her rearview mirror. Let someone else make the call, someone who didn't have outstanding parking tickets and less than savory past. All it would take was a hotshot rookie cop taking down her name after calling the accident in and running it through the database, his tone smug. "Mrs. Herrera, did you know you have over $1,000 in outstanding fines from parking tickets? Oh, and we also see from your records that you used to turn tricks? Can you come down to the station to talk?"

Right foot imperceptibly applied steady pressure on the gas pedal just as her eyes alighted on a pale streak on the pavement.

A body.

A badly battered one, at that.

Jane pumped the brake pedal, bringing the car to a lurching stop. The sight of the man's brain matter sitting innocently on the pavement brought her morning slug of coffee back up her throat. Scrambling, Jane got her seatbelt unlatched just in time and threw her door open, acidic, half-digested coffee joining brain on the asphalt. She wiped her mouth with a clammy hand that trembled against her pallid lips. *Great, now she'd gone and upchucked, undoubtedly leaving her DNA on the scene.* Now she *had* to make the call for help. She grimly pictured a crime scene technician sampling the java puke and triumphantly proclaiming, "Yep, that's Jane Herrera, alright!" They'd made leaps and bounds these days with science, she had no doubt they'd be able to track her down. She'd watched plenty of crime shows, switching on the old TV sets within the hotel rooms, cleaning while watching Elliot Stabler nail some pervert to the wall after crafty lab work revealed some vital truth.

Shakily, she pulled her cellphone from her pocket—a necessary expense since her son suffered from asthma and horrid peanut allergies. She anxiously awaited the call from the school: a terrified school nurse telling her that her son was in the throes of anaphylactic shock because some kid forced a PB&J down his throat.

Her quivering index finger keyed in 9-1-1.

"9-1-1, what's your emergency?"

The dispatcher coolly recorded the information provided by Jane, fingers flying over her keyboard. Each stroke of the keys activated the services needed: police, fire department, and EMS.

Persistent raindrops acted as a low bass rhythm in a song, soon accompanied by high-pitched sirens of emergency vehicles. First to arrive was a police officer who asked Jane only cursory questions after assessing the man briefly. He did *not* run her name through any database, much to Jane's relief.

The man still had a pulse—slow and steady—and he was breathing, thus, the officer didn't need to apply any of his limited lifesaving first aid. Privately, the officer suspected it would be kinder if he pulled his firearm and put the poor guy out of his misery. He'd do it for an injured dog in the same condition, but his opinion amounted to shinola.

The fire truck and ambulance arrived together, as expected, since they were housed in the same building. The emergency call had rousted them from warm beds. Paramedics rushed to the man's side, gloved hands probing his neck for a pulse and one medic pressed a stethoscope against his torso, assessing the man's breathing. They slapped a collar around his neck to prevent spinal injury, which was the least of the man's problems since his brains were currently chilling on the pavement—looking more and more like a spilled, congealed slushie from 7-Eleven.

He sported assorted scrapes and bruises, nothing too exciting for the medics, they'd seen far worse. A large weeping burn had bloomed over his stomach, but luckily, the rain had put the culprit fire out quickly. Based on the mechanism of the accident, he probably had a few broken ribs, but if one ignored his misshapen head, one might suspect he'd suffered a rather minor accident.

The paramedics performed all their tasks with efficiency

but didn't operate with the same level of haste they often did with a critically ill patient that stood a chance.

They knew the guy was soon to be a dead man. Hurrying a few seconds here and there wouldn't magically knit his head into a shape resembling normal or return ruined brain to his skull unharmed.

Firefighters roped off the scene and more police officers arrived. Some took pictures and others hashed out measurements. All showed a morbid fascination with the residual brain at the scene—not that it was the first spilled brain they'd seen, not even the first brain that month! They all too vividly remembered last week's scene: a 16-year-old kid whose last meal was a shotgun shell. The back of his head had exploded outwards, skull demolished, leaving brain smattered on the wall, white flecks of skull peppering the pink tissue.

His brain lingered on the pavement, long after the man departed in the back of the ambulance. And there it would remain until someone either scooped it up with a shovel and tossed it off the road, or hungry animals discovered a gourmet treat.

22

High-pitched beeps from the call pager woke up the senior resident, Marshall. Bleary-eyed with foul breath as if a baby dragon took a massive shit in his mouth, he squinted at the page: LVL 1 TRMA. MTRCYCL, HEAD INJURY, EXPOSED BRAIN, ETA 10 MIN. The great, unknowable being who sent out these trauma alerts seemed to take absurd pride in randomly deleting letters, a fact that chaffed Marshall to no end. God forbid they used the vowels needed for motorcycle!

"Hope you got to spend some extra time with your kids with all the time you saved deleting those letters, you stupid fuck," he grumbled, lurching off his lumpy cot in the call room. Knees cracked as he struggled into an upright position.

Various other underlings summoned by their pager's insistent tones gathered in the hospital's trauma bay: several battle-hardened nurses who Marshall thought could easily double for prison guards given their sunny dispositions; a smattering of residents from various specialties; an anesthesiologist; and two pissant med students stood in the bay—all waiting with varying degrees of patience. The medical students wore rapturous expressions; an expression not echoed by anyone else. Marshall rolled his eyes, remembering the simple-minded pleasures of students. He knew they were hoping to get a chance to perform CPR or maybe, gosh just maybe, one might get to shove a gloved finger knuckle deep in the patient's asshole to check the holy rectal tone for a spinal cord injury!

The automatic double doors leading into the ambulance bay whooshed open, belching forth paramedics hauling the patient in on their stretcher. They'd inserted a plastic tube into his throat and one medic calmly pressed the bag, supplying bursts of air every five seconds. Efficiently, but with little haste, they transferred the man to the trauma bay cot. With the airway already secured, the anesthesiologist exited, presumably returning to his Sudoku workbook with a steaming cup of coffee with a nip of Bailey's Irish Cream nestled inside (a very poorly kept secret known to all on the surgical team). During routine surgeries, Marshall often observed the gas-passers day trading or reading the newspaper instead of meticulously monitoring the patient.

Marshall—being the most experienced resident on the surgery service—performed his examination of the patient, dutifully starting with the A, B, C's: Airway, Breathing, Circulation. While he explored every nook and cranny, even peering underneath the man's scrotum and spreading his ass cheeks, nurses flitted about starting IVs and placed the patient on the monitor. A cacophony of beeps soon filled the room, different tones and pitches denoting oxygen saturation and heart rhythm.

Having completed a full head-to-toe assessment, Marshall dispatched one of the medical students to page the on-call neurosurgeon, figuring he needn't wait for a CT scan if he could examine brain personally with his eyeballs. Privately, Marshall considered the man a colossal waste of time and said as much to the senior nurse standing next to him, "What kind of idiot gets on a motorcycle in the middle of a rainstorm without a helmet?"

She gazed at the Marshall over her glasses. "An organ donor, obviously!" and let out a cynical laugh. Marshall supposed it took a certain kind of idiot to go around ruining hard earned sleep for exhausted doctors trying to catch a few z's amid stupid pages from floor nurses asking if the patient could have a stool softener—an urgent matter at 3 a.m. when patients were deep in dreamland and *not* straining on the commode against a boulder of a turd.

"Let's get him in the scanner," Marshall said, proclaiming the patient stable. Well, as stable as anyone could *be* with more brain outside their body than in. Into the CT scanner he went, where he was scanned stem to stern, revealing only a few broken ribs. No accompanying collapsed lung which disappointed the two medical students to no end, based on their crestfallen expressions. Marshall knew they'd feverously hoped they'd get the pleasure of watching him railroad a chest tube into the poor sucker's torso. Typically, Marshall enjoyed the procedure as well but not when it interfered with his beauty sleep.

Marshall sent the more annoying of the students on a coffee run and waited for the neurosurgeon to make her appearance. He idly wondered if underneath her scrubs, the neurosurgeon had a rockin' bod.

23

The neurosurgeon sauntered in, clutching a steaming cup of hospital grade sludge. Even in rumpled scrubs with no makeup, Marshall thought she was a knockout but heard she played for the other team. *What a waste*, he thought. She'd already perused the scans in her private office and delivered her verdict after a cursory examination of the patient.

"He's totally fucked," she proclaimed; tact never being her strong suit. Leaning over the computer monitor, her scrub top gaped in the front, providing Marshall a momentary thrill, and she pointed to the obvious gap between the man's skull and the surrounding air. "You don't have to be a genius to know that most of this guy's brain is still lying on Route 98 somewhere." She scrolled upwards, revealing another view of the pulverized brain. "And see here? He already herniated. The guy has no meaningful reflexes of life. He's toast."

She briskly stood, meeting Marshall's eyes, a knowing look on her face like she'd felt his eyes crawling over her cleavage moments before. "You can call neurology to perform the official brain death exam, but I recommend seeing if this guy is an organ donor. Get the ball rolling on that. That's about all he's gonna be good for at this point." She took a long pull of her coffee and grimaced. "Thanks for the oh-so-interesting consult." Sarcasm colored her words, not that Marshall minded. She'd just confirmed his suspicions.

He sighed, not relishing the day ahead of him, chock full of conversations with the gorked patient's family. They were always full of tears, protests, and lots of *stupid* fucking questions like:

"What about all those movies where people just wake up and get better?" As if some fictional character knocked out by a falling clock who temporarily lost their memory was the same as someone who ended their day with less brain than they started out with.

The med student brought Marshall his coffee and he got to work.

Police couldn't locate any close family for the man. His next of kin were dead and extended family wanted nothing to do with him, each essentially telling the police, "Fuck off" as politely as possible before hanging up.

The man's driver's license displayed a red heart, signifying he was an organ donor. Marshall suppressed a smirk each time he read the man's name: Eugene Bartlett. What kind of nerdy-ass name was *that?* The poor dude probably plowed into the pole because he'd grown tired of being called Genie-weenie in the locker room. Nah… Marshall preferred thinking of him as "the patient." Less secondhand embarrassment that way. Fucking awful name.

One of the staff neurologists performed the brain death exam and delivered his verdict. His colleague waited an hour and performed her exam with identical results.

The guy was toast, just as the neurosurgeon said:

T-O-A-S-T.

The organ transplant team eagerly swirled about the

room, reminding Marshall of vultures waiting for the final death shudder of a previously proud beast, their talons at the ready to tear through the dead but willing flesh to secure precious organ meat. The two medical students stood in the back, thrilled, wriggling like excited puppies. Based on their delighted expressions, Marshall could tell that were thrilled about Genie-weenie's demise since it meant they got to watch some cool shit.

He couldn't blame them; his first organ harvest had been exciting too. But by now, it had grown far too routine.

The man's organs were removed without ceremony—a rather boring four hours for the medical students whose initial excitement gave way to a bone aching fatigue. By the end, their shoulders were hunched forward, eyes dull and unfocused.

Surgeons harvested multiple organs, including the liver, kidneys, lungs, corneas, areas of unburned skin, and the pancreas. Scalpels gleamed under the fluorescent Operating Room lights, a deep anti-septic smell baked into every surface of the room as the blades danced, severing vital connections. The organs were in pretty good shape, in Marshall's opinion. The lungs were perhaps a little contused from the rib fractures, but a cystic fibrosis patient wouldn't turn their nose up at 'em.

The most impressive organ by far though, was the heart. After completing his surgical residency, Marshall was heavily considering applying for cardiothoracic fellowship and paid rapt attention when the transplant surgeon plucked the heart from the man's chest. It was shaped more like a fist than the traditional Valentine's heart in popular culture and possessed more whitish coloring than one might expect. It weighed 11 ounces, as announced by one of the scrub nurses who'd plopped it on a scale—deceptively light for its size.

Back in undergrad, in a mandatory anthropology class

that was snooze-inducing at best, Marshall learned that many cultures theorized the heart served as the vessel for the human soul. But to the harvesting surgeons, the man's heart wasn't notable in the least. It was the expected size of a grown man's heart, of normal color, and most importantly, it hadn't sustained any damage in the accident. *Those* were the only facts that mattered. It was a heart good enough for UNOS, the organization that handled organ transplant matters. The heart was destined for a lucky soul on their transplant list, a veritable lottery win for its recipient.

Unless, of course, another catastrophe erupted; perhaps the plane transferring the heart ensconced in its cooler would suck a bird in its engines, hurtling a perfectly good heart—not to mention several human lives—straight into the ground at breakneck speed.

The heart, though, made it to its destination without incident.

24

<hr>

My thoughts chased themselves and sleep was thin. Not that sleep was *ever* good. Having a mechanical heart meant finding a position of comfort was impossible, especially for someone who'd always preferred sprawling out on their stomach. Cracking my eyes open the next morning after that fitful doze felt terrible, like a wicked college hangover after innumerable shots of tequila. Bringing my fists to my eyes, I rubbed vigorously, praying to rid myself of the sandy gritty feeling clinging to my eyelids. Once content, I lurched up, cringing when one of my LVAD batteries alarmed, signaling it was nearly kaput. The first time it went off, I practically had to be removed from the ceiling fan by firefighters. By now, I was used to it. Exchanging the battery, I thought of my morning cup of coffee, the ten minutes of my day when I wasn't continually harangued. Then, I groaned, remembering my to-do list.

First, to the wretched party store for supplies for Owen's upcoming birthday next month, his 7th. After vetoing his requested party themes (war, why encourage him?) or cowboys and Indians (racially insensitive), we'd agreed on a

85

pirate theme. A very tame, not weapon-ridden, pirate theme.

"Still, no reason I can't enjoy my coffee," I muttered. Alcohol, while difficult to resist sometimes, was far easier to forgo compared to my caffeine. I needed one vice! Stuffing my feet into slippers, I made the perilous journey across the bedroom, complicated by strewn about clothing—Jack's. His discarded pajama pants snagged my foot and I nearly fell face first, pinwheeling my way to balance by only the grace of God. "Dammit, Jack!" Not that his behavior would change, even if I asked nicely. My concerns always fell on deaf ears. With 100% certainty, I knew that thousands of black hairs from his three-day-old stubble covered the bathroom vanity, as they had since the beginning of time.

"Asshole," I muttered, kicking the pants away from me. Flannel bounced away and an ear-splitting screech shattered the relative silence, causing me to jump back, nearly tripping over Jack's pajama pants *again* and I bumped my hip on the nightstand, which helped steady me but hurt like hell. A sharp hiss escaped my lips, and I clutched my side. Thanks to my Coumadin, I'd have a nasty bruise there come afternoon.

Cocking my head, I tried to pinpoint where that *awful* noise was coming from. It was deafening, reminding me of a smoke alarm but worse. Battling ringing ears, I rushed towards the clangor. Before long, it would wake the kids, and would completely ruin my coffee date with myself.

Right on cue—Eleanor loudly inhaled over the baby monitor and sent up a blood-curdling cry. Not to be outdone, Owen screamed "FUCK" from his bedroom at the top of his lungs, voice bright with glee, happy to participate in such chaos. I groaned. Why did school have to be closed today for parent-teacher conferences, of all days? I'd gladly allow a tax hike if it meant Owen was out of the house more.

A revelation seized me, and my breath caught in my throat.

It couldn't be?

Could it?

Following the screech, I heaved an *Us Weekly* magazine off my bedside table. Several tubes of cherry Chapstick rolled, two off the table but the other rolled into a violently shaking, shrieking pager. I hadn't even realized I'd set it down there. When was the last time I even carried it with me? Weeks? Months?

After my LVAD placement, they'd placed me on the transplant list, and like a shitty consolation prize, awarded me a pager. Dr. Yang staunchly instructed me to carry it everywhere. And I did. At first. Each day, I dutifully clipped it to my jeans immediately after dressing. I'd felt like equal parts resident doctor and time traveler from the 90s. Part of me felt a certain smugness, so certain I'd get a heart in no time.

Optimism only led to disappointment; I soon learned.

The pager, for months, didn't do a damn thing.

In fact, it seemed somehow *delighted* in its own obstinate silence. After the first month, I became certain the pager had achieved sentience and made a hobby of destroying my mental health, which wasn't great to start with. The longer the mass of plastic and circuitry remained dormant, the more I forgot to carry it, let alone cart it out on rare trips out of the house. At some point I must have decided—unconsciously—that I was over with, finished. No heart was coming for me, the universe had deemed it so.

But here was evidence to the contrary. The pager's black casing vibrated, making a racket against the nightstand, and bright green lights blinked on and off, in addition to the shrill noise.

A heart.

It was actually happening! More than half a year spent

on the transplant list—not a long amount of time for those in good health but a *lifetime* for me—and I'd worked my way up the ranks by having the good sense not to die in the meantime.

A line of black text rolled across the screen, backlit by a sickroom green color that always reminded me of the hospital emesis bags they handed me on my many ER visits. Words flickered across the screen, rolling together like gibberish... or an unfamiliar language.

Could this be... *a mistake?*

I blinked and rubbed my eyes with the heel of my hand, fighting to regain composure—a task that required strict focus. Like Pat taught me, I took a deep breath, held it for several seconds. Released.

My mind cleared.

Eyebrows furrowed as I read the unspooling text: `proceed immediately to the hospital, a heart has become available.` My forehead wrinkles ironed themselves out in sudden understanding.

"YES!" I shouted and let out a whoop of joy, not giving a tin shit if the noise disturbed the kids—they were already awake anyway. My hands shook and I dropped the pager with a dull *thud* on the carpet. Leaving it there, I sought out my phone on the bedside table—plugged in and charging—and snatched it up, fingers trembling as I dialed Jack who was just arriving to work.

"Jack! I'm getting a new heart!" The words spilled out of me, letters stumbling over each other. Happy tears tracked down my face and I smiled.

Maybe, just maybe, my luck was changing.

25

L ike Cinderella arriving at the ball, I stepped out of the van at the hospital's receiving entrance and plopped down in a waiting wheelchair. A handsome young man clutched its handles, wearing the maroon vest signaling he was a volunteer. I'd met plenty of them during my many hospital stays. This one was probably in his early 20s, based on his smooth unlined skin with hints of a tan. Ryan, per his nametag. Ryan's dashing good looks sent a momentary thrill through me, adding to my mounting excitement—he even resembled a young Paul Walker! Posters of the movie star wallpapered my girlhood bedroom and much to my mother's chagrin, I wore out my copy of *The Fast and the Furious*. Twice. Most of my go-to masturbatory fantasies involved Paul—not that anyone knew that… especially not Jack. While Jack wasn't hideous by any stretch of the imagination, he'd grown doughy and sported a dad bod. A heartthrob, Jack was not.

But Ryan…

Even with LVAD churning, my heart fluttered. Thick strands of blonde hair threaded with chestnut brown tumbled onto Ryan's forehead and his ice-blue eyes met mine as I turned in the wheelchair to further ogle him. Unlike Owen's emotionless, coal-dark eyes, his danced with merriment. He flashed me a bright white smile which I returned shyly. Heat filled my cheeks. No one could fault me for window shopping. I was heartless—although not for much longer—not dead.

"Welcome to the hospital, ma'am. Where might I push you to?" Ryan asked with a smile, dimples adding a dash more hotness. Jack was off parking the car, and hadn't I earned some harmless flirting with a boy who reminded me of girlhood crushes? Of better times. Jack was *no* Paul Walker. Even better? Ryan could spirit me away from my husband—for a little while anyway.

I answered, "I suppose if there isn't a spa around here, the pre-op surgical area will do."

The wheelchair lurched forward, its left wheel emitting a thin, high squeal, making me wince. My day thus far was filled with noise. Thankfully, it petered down into a faint hiss as the wheelchair gained steam. Ryan chatted as he pushed. "You don't look very nervous. I would be a *wreck* if I had to have surgery! You look…" he paused, as if searching for the right word, "…well… *happy*, I guess."

I chuckled. The worse thing that ever happened to Ryan was catching a cold or getting kicked in the nuts during recess. Poor kid probably couldn't fathom the idea of chronic illness, with a packed schedule of endless appointments, surgeries, pill after pill after pill. Ryan didn't have a clue. "Oh, I'm nervous. My stomach's tied up in knots. I'm more so relieved. Honestly, I'm still in a bit of shock this is even happening."

Ryan nodded and directed his focus to navigating through the hordes of humanity. I took in the passing surroundings, seeing them through new, appreciative eyes. The sheer ordinariness of the day had a magical quality, making everything and everyone oddly bright. The knowledge that someone's heart was about to become mine filled me with nervous anticipation. Was someone else— maybe in the operating suite next to mine—receiving an organ from the same donor? It was possible.

Harried people dressed in scrubs rushed about while others—most wearing plainclothes, but I spotted some white coats in the bunch—waited in a long line at the coffee kiosk generically named The Coffee Bean, and grim-faced patients walked the halls, each wearing muted blue gowns tied in the back. We whizzed by an elderly man dressed in a smart cardigan and a bowler hat reading the newspaper. I caught a glimpse of the headline: "X-Killer Still at Large." I gave myself an imaginary pat on the back, at least I wasn't murdered before getting my heart. Not that I could count myself completely safe from that fate, living with Owen and all. Chasing those thoughts away, I smiled upwards at Ryan. No use in dwelling on *that* stuff when I could lose myself in those baby blues, so unlike Jack's dark eyes. An ocean of hotness.

Ryan returned my smile. "I mean, people usually aren't *this* excited unless they're about to have a baby or something." He gave me an appraising look, eyes lingering on my bulky midsection. The wheelchair slowed. "And you don't look *that* pregnant."

My bubbling good humor evaporated, disappearing like Jack's cache of booze on Superbowl Sunday. Smile melted into grimace. The very atmosphere surrounding us changed, as if a cold front had suddenly raced in, blotting out any trace of warmth. Ryan looked panic-stricken. If I weren't so pissed, his sheer alarm might be amusing. He backpedaled, both verbally and literally, shoes squeaking against linoleum. "What I meant to say was… uh—"

I cut him off—my tone sharp and cutting—in a stark contrast to my general affable nature. "No. Getting pregnant is what *caused* this whole mess." I opened my jacket as if to flash him my boobs like a Mötley Crüe groupie, instead, revealing a white T-shirt with a plunging neckline. Ryan's blue eyes involuntarily gravitated to my chest; his greedy eagerness quickly giving way to surprise. Then, to shock. Ryan's expressions flickered through the spectrum and despite myself, I felt a delightfully evil sort of amusement watching his reaction.

"Wha—what is that?" He asked, eyebrows up near his hairline.

"Oh, this old thing?" I said, gesturing downwards with my chin. "That's my 'heart.' My *real* heart was donzo." I held the jacket open a bit longer, giving him a real eyeful of pale sternum speckled with puckered pink scar tissue. And my bustling LVAD, which tended to surprise most people. Its *whirrrrr* became louder momentarily, then muffled once more as I let the jacket fall into place. "*That* is why I'm here. My heart went kapoot shortly after my daughter was born. Said 'sayonara' and rode off into the sunset. A one in one thousand chance and *that's* the lottery I pick the winning number on. So, this lovely little machine acts as my heart and—today of all days—a heart became available for me." Watching Ryan's jaw clench and unclench, trying to process this stunning turn of events, I wondered: How *had* my new heart came to me? Suicide? Murder? A run-of-the-mill accident, completely random and devastating? Something worse? As I pondered, Ryan looked away from my lumpy torso. He glanced around, as if looking for rescue, then forced his eyes up to my face. Based on Ryan's squirming, I'd nailed my desired expression of you-are-a-pure-and-utter-imbecile.

"Soooooo. You're getting a heart, then?" Ryan looked hopeful, like a student trying their damnedest to answer a difficult exam question.

"Bingo," I said flatly.

Ryan audibly gulped and rushed back to the chair,

grasping the handles again. Redoubling his pushing efforts, we were soon traveling at a brisk pace just short of a slow jog. We didn't speak again until reaching the pre-op desk. Ryan stopped the wheelchair and engaged the brake. I took my time getting out, gathering all my belongings which included a black bag filled with battery packs for the short time I still had the LVAD, and a small overnight bag packed with the essentials: a toothbrush along with a travel-sized mint toothpaste, a pair of pajama bottoms, and a book. Ryan grasped my elbow and let out a gasp.

"Is everything okay?" I asked.

"Yeah, sure." Ryan avoided my eyes and dropped my arm as if he'd touched a piping hot stove burner. He surreptitiously wiped his hand on his khaki pants. Rubbing cooties away. Interesting.

"Thanks for the lift," I said.

"Don't mention it. Good luck." He called behind his retreating back. I watched him go, his broad shoulders rippling underneath the dumb vest he wore. Ryan might have been gorgeous, but he was an idiot, just like the rest of them.

I gave my name to the young woman behind the registration desk who, after consulting her computer, led me back to the pre-op area with a friendly smile. Neutral prints of sand dunes, tropical trees, and oceans adorned the walls. My eyes lingered on a photo of a sport car roaring down a road lined with trees. Maybe, after the surgery, I'd learn to drive stick and take Jack's old Camaro out, watching highway melt away underneath my wheels. Leave hubby at home.

Once in the pre-op area, time took on a hurried quality. Staff moved as if taking part of a well-practiced dance—regimented yet chaotic. I changed into an ugly green hospital gown with a flimsy tie on the back, leaving my buttocks hopelessly exposed to cool hospital air. Luckily, I'd be on my back and wouldn't have to worry about mooning anyone. Tucking my hair into a surgical cap, I caught sight of my reflection and chuckled inwardly. I might as well be slinging sloppy joes in the school cafeteria.

Next, was signing the requisite forms that released the hospital from liability should I drop dead on the operating table (a real possibility given my shitty health) or should I find myself maimed from an unfortunate medical complication. Just last week, I'd watched a special on TV about negligence occurring within hospitals. Surgeons leaving towels or tools inside people. Removing the wrong organ altogether. The program mentioned a surgeon who had accidentally removed a kidney instead of a spleen. Talk about a real fuckup.

Hope for the best but prepare for the worst: That was my motto.

Sitting on the stretcher, watching the ticking minute hand, I waited, for my surgery to start or my husband to show up. I'd stared at the ceiling until I was cross-eyed, finding no hidden patterns. I did find a dead fly carcass though. Five minutes before the start time, Jack rushed in, panting, clutching a brown, grease-spotted bag.

"You seriously went and got a hamburger instead of spending time with your wife? I could literally die today! These could be our last moments together. Christ." Not that I particularly cared about spending time with him, but it *was* sort of offensive. I was supposed to be the light of his life.

Red-faced, he said, "Listen babe, I was hungry. I haven't eaten since breakfast." Wah. I hadn't eaten since last night, which was fortuitous for my surgery. Jack fell into lockstep once an orderly started pushing my stretcher to the surgical area.

"This is as far as he can go," the orderly said, pointedly looking at a thick black line on the floor dividing those authorized from mere mortals. Jack bent over, kissing my unready lips. Even through two sets of closed lips and an overwhelming scent of fried onions (he'd eaten at least one onion ring), I detected a ghostly whisky undertone. Dark circles drooped from his eyes and Jack's shoulders slouched forward, his head jutting forward like an elderly man. Standard hungover look.

My lips pursed.

"I'll see you soon, babe, and I'll bring the kids. I love you," Jack said. He squeezed my hand and dropped it. I crossed the line into authorized personnel and just like that, I was on my way.

26

They pushed my stretcher into a sterile, cold Operating Room. A strong smell of antiseptic hung in the air as scrub nurses hustled and bustled about, all careful to keep a disapproving eye on the medical students in the back of the room who were notorious for fucking up the sterile field. An anesthesiologist bent over me, most of her face obscured by a mask, but she had distinctive dark brown eyes that I recognized immediately: the same anesthesiologist I'd had for LVAD surgery. I couldn't remember her name to save my life. Luckily, heart transplant surgery didn't entail a pop quiz. The woman greeted me warmly and clutched a face mask that faintly smelled of medicinal bubble gum. Mask descended, covering my nose and mouth and it was like Dubble Bubble straight from the package. Overpowering.

"Can you believe they pay me to pass gas?" she said, her eyes crinkling in the corners at her own wit. It was the same shitty joke she told me before LVAD surgery, and I'd barely mustered up a thin-lipped smile then. Maybe this is how you die—a whiff of bubble gum, an awful, overused joke, and then you get dropped into wherever you end up next, as if you're being processed like some filled-out form by a secretary who can't wait to punch the clock.

There was another flurry of movement, then Dr. Yang walked into my field of vision, bending over near my ear, murmuring well wishes and assurances. After taking deep breaths from the mask—marinating in the sugary reek—my head was pleasantly swimming, and Dr. Yang's words of encouragement sounded like they were beamed in from Mars. I dreamily watched the anesthesiologist hook up a syringe of milky white medicine to my IV tubing. *Propofol*, I reminded myself, the name sounding funny and make believe. Michael Jackson preferred this same medicine for sleep, ignoring the fact that it was meant for general anesthesia and *not* as a sleep aid, according to a documentary I'd recently watched. "Count backwards from twenty for me, Casey."

Blood rose to my cheeks. Not that I'd had many surgeries in my life, but I always felt ridiculous at this whole bit. When I was a teenager, I'd suffered from an appendix rupture and still—sick as I was—remembered the secondhand embarrassment of counting aloud, terrified I'd miss a number. I was also vaguely offended. Who couldn't count backwards from twenty? Even Owen could do it, if he were allowed to punctuate the countdown with intermittent curse words.

"Twenty… nineteen… eighteen… sevente—" The white sedative hit me with the ferocity of a freight train, immediately slurring my speech. My breathing slowed. Vision wavered and reminded me of the moments before succumbing to sleep. The hard edges of the operating room softened and blurred. A dark curtain descended, and muscles slackened. Warmth pervaded my body as complete blackness and nothingness settled over me.

I drifted off.

Into oblivion.

27

Casey felt nothing as the anesthesiologist inserted a curved laryngoscope into her mouth, slipping a piece of plastic between her vocal cords, nor did she feel the sharp bite of Dr. Yang's scalpel gliding over her chest. The sharp blade left a dark red trail across her pale skin, creating more highways in Casey's atlas of marred tissue. Creating future scars. Thankfully, Casey experienced nothing of the hours Dr. Yang spent dissecting her way through delicate muscles through hosts of sensory nerves that would scream in agony had Casey been conscious.

Not to say the surgery was completely uneventful.

Something happened.

Later the matter would be hotly debated by the doctors present in the OR during a quality review of the case. Any adverse outcomes or sentinel events were discussed ad nauseum and Casey's incident was no exception since patients shouldn't move of their own accord during surgery.

Everything had been textbook up until that moment: no surprises. Routine without the slightest hint of trouble.

That all changed when it came time for Casey to receive her new heart.

A life-changing moment for anyone, to be sure. But in Casey's case, it was completely life-altering… not that she had any idea of that.

At least… not yet.

The room hushed as one of the senior nurses reverently plucked the donor heart from its bath of cool saline and handed it to Dr. Yang. Both handled the organ as if it were a priceless, sacred artifact revered by a forgotten culture. Dr. Yang placed the heart into the hollow of Casey's chest cavity, cocooned by healthy, spongy pink lungs. When the donor heart made contact, Casey's body violently twitched, muscles in her arms and legs—meager as they were—bulged as she strained. Her eyes shot open, and she bucked on the stretcher. Tendons stretched under the skin of her wrists, prominent as she struggled. The medication infusing in her IV appeared as useless as sugar water. A horrid choking came from Casey's mouth, and she gagged on the tube thrust down her throat, eyes wide with panic and fear. A muffled scream erupted from around the rigid plastic stuffed down her airway, a noise made infinitely worse because it might mean the patient felt every bite of scalpel, every severed nerve ending.

Agony, in other words.

"What the fuck? Anesthesia, are you gonna give her more juice or what? She's moving!" Dr. Yang yelled at the startled anesthesiologist, broadly gesturing a slim gloved hand at Casey who continued to gag, tears and snot streaming down her face.

The anesthesiologist hurried, drawing up and slamming a syringe filled with Propofol into Casey's IV tubing. Gloved fingers whirled a few knobs on the machine, producing small tweaks in Casey's inhaled anesthesia concentration. She shot back at Dr. Yang, "Hey, I'm giving her perfect anesthesia. She shouldn't be moving! *You* probably stimulated a nerve in her thoracic cavity or something!"

"That's crap and you know it!" Dr. Yang said, her tone haughty, "I wasn't even—"

As suddenly as it occurred, the struggling ceased and Casey stilled; the incident quickly forgotten as the surgeon went to work patching in the new heart, marrying foreign tissue to native. But *it* was brought up later, at the root cause analysis meeting involving all those present in the OR— barring the pissant medical students—conducted under the watchful gaze of the hospital CEO, chief medical officer, and other various suits. Hospital review boards tended towards anger any time a patient woke during surgery, fearing lawsuits for pain and suffering. Both anesthesiologist and surgeon reacted as anyone else would, blaming the other in an age-old pissing match between the two specialties, like an eternal Bugs Bunny and Daffy Duck argument, but instead of Wabbit Season, no, Duck Season it was:

It's surgery's fault!

No anesthesia!

Surgery!

Anesthesia.

Who knew why the patient moved? But it sure wasn't their fault, each argued passionately.

The root cause analysis proved inconclusive, essentially the whole matter chalked up to an unfortunate incident that everyone hoped the patient wouldn't recall later. Because *that* proved very expensive for hospitals. But as it turned out, *neither* doctor was at fault. Casey had enough medication flowing through her veins and vented down her lungs to put down a horse, and Dr. Yang hadn't inadvertently poked a sensitive nerve.

No. Nothing like that.

Casey had sensed *something* as the donor heart encountered splayed flesh, left open to the cool circulated OR air. Not that she recalled the fleeting sensation once conscious. Whatever she felt had been visceral, a natural reaction to something utterly putrid. When the foreign tissue touched Casey, a sharp pain lanced through her very core, followed by a dull, budding dread. Something inside her… was… *repulsive.* Abhorrent. Wrong. Something more awful than feeling the dead, cold skin of a treasured loved one after pulling them ashore following a fateful dive, hope and any feelings of happiness sucked away, leaving suffering in its wake.

But just as quickly—

There was nothing.

28

The rest of the surgery passed without further dramatics.

Casey's brief wake-up episode punctuated an otherwise routine, textbook surgery with a moment of unremembered sheer terror. Heart now in place, Dr. Yang spent hours painstakingly placing sutures around new vessels, peering through magnifying loupes that made her appear part woman, part microscope. After admiring how beautifully Casey's anatomy melded with the donor heart—each connection carefully married—surgeon and nurses removed all instruments from Casey's chest cavity, counting and re-counting. Casey needn't worry about Dr. Yang's surgical towel cozying up to her liver or strangulating bowels in a few years' time. The counts were right on each time. Everything foreign had been removed—other than the new heart, of course.

Each set of eyes in the OR turned towards the donor heart. No, *Casey's* new heart.

It sat, inert, with not a flutter or thump. Still.

The thick muscle that once beat strongly and reliably within someone else's chest, was unmoving. Not a quiver. A sense of anticipation permeated the room—a sort of hush before the storm. The cluster of medical students in the back wriggled like children who desperately needed to use the restroom, a nervous energy radiating off each of them as they anxiously wondered if the new heart would take. Would it restart? Seasoned vets shared a certain apprehension as well, having scrubbed in on many such cases, aware complications could, and often would, occur. Dr. Yang shuffled under the guise of stretching her legs but she too worried. Most times, the heart restarted without incident, but… *what if it didn't this time?* Things were much different with Casey compared to her other patients. As awful as it was to admit aloud—and Dr. Yang never would, except to her wife—the stakes were much higher. Casey was young, with many years of life yet to be lived. Much more tragic if she died on the table. Heart surgery on an octogenarian who'd used and abused their body for more than half a century with a laundry list of medical conditions? If they died, it wasn't exactly a massive shock. Losing a young woman… a wife… a mother… *that* would cut far more deeply.

Harsh fluorescents overhead shed their artificial light on the organ, highlighting bluish vessels that—with any luck— would soon fill with Casey's blood. Dr. Yang crossed blood-stained gloves in front of her sterile blue gown and stared at the perfusionist technician ensconced in the corner of the OR. The loupes dangled from Dr. Yang's scrub cap, no longer required. The technician sat next to a large machine —the cardiopulmonary bypass—which served as Casey's heart and lungs. Several monitors attached to the machine beeped and occasionally alarmed, all reporting different parameters that the tech understood but were near indecipherable to most in the room. An obscene amount of tubing wound from the machine to Casey's immobile figure, most of it containing blood circulated through Casey's body.

Blood leaving the machine was oxygen-rich and fed all of Casey's tissues; blood returning to the machine was used-up, ready for replenishment. The machine was a medical marvel and had supported Casey through the entire surgery.

And the time had come to remove it.

Casey only had one course of action.

The heart—*her heart*—had to restart, simple as that.

Dr. Yang could help her along, but she was a mere surgeon—not God. But this was the part that made many feel immortal—bringing life to the lifeless.

The perfusionist turned after jotting down a few notes on a clipboard, locking eyes with Dr. Yang. "It's about that time?" She asked the surgeon, not waiting for a reply. She'd already turned back to the machine, her hands poised and ready to twist the appropriate knobs and dials.

"I think it is," the surgeon agreed with a curt nod of her head, the ties on her surgical cap rustling in the air conditioning. Loupes bobbled. Dr. Yang held her hands out without uttering a word and the lead scrub nurse knowingly slapped two gray tools into her waiting palms. The choreographed dance of a heart transplant proceeded into its final—and one might say—most heart stopping step: restarting the heart. And while she wasn't God, Dr. Yang was a master of her craft and required her lifegiving tools. The power Dr. Yang held in her hands at that moment frightened her… she literally held a person's everything in her mere mortal hands.

There was a sharp whine as the cardiopulmonary bypass machine slowed. Dr. Yang held the gray implements in her hands; a fist wrapped around each. They tapered down at the ends to a round metallic paddle that looked oddly like a soup spoon, except this utensil bristled with electricity at the touch of a button. "Charge to 5 Joules," Dr. Yang commanded.

A nurse turned a dial and called out, "5 Joules, set for

defibrillation." High pitched beeping rang out as the machine charged.

"Is everyone clear?" Dr. Yang looked around the operating room, ensuring no one laid a finger on Casey or—God forbid—on the heart. Having a patient wake up briefly during surgery was bad enough but blasting someone in attendance with electricity was *one* real big fuck up.

"CLEAR!" A chorus of voices rang out. The loudest among them came from the useless medical students in the back who were so far from the table they practically needed binoculars to see the action.

"Defibrillating at 5 Joules." The paddles in Dr. Yang's hand sputtered with energy against either side of the still heart.

CA-THUNK.

All eyes in the room homed in on the heart.

It remained inert and quiet.

"Charge to 10 Joules!" The surgeon called out, voice calm and seemingly, unconcerned.

"Charging to 10 Joules, set for defibrillation." The nurse called back. High pitched beeping followed.

"Everyone clear?"

"CLEAR!"

"Defibrillating at 10 Joules!" Dr. Yang pressed the paddles against the red muscle.

CA-THUNK.

Nothing.

Dr. Yang muttered under her breath, letting out a string of curse words in both English and Chinese. A bead of sweat dripped from her temple as she directed the nurse, "Charge to 30 Joules!"

The nurse's eyes widened, and she paused for a moment, as if giving Dr. Yang time to change her mind. Her hand hovered over the dial. "30 Joules... Doctor?"

Dr. Yang's surgical mask moved, her face spreading in a

wide, wry grin the fabric mostly concealed. "You know, you're right, 30 isn't enough… we need more juice. Set it for 40 Joules!"

Eyes widening further, the nurse complied, twisting the nob over to 40. "Charged to 40 Joules, set for defibrillation."

Beepbeepbeepbeep.

"Everyone clear?"

"CLEAR!" the choir chimed—loudest again from the back, from those who had no chance of being shocked to kingdom come.

"Defibrillating at 40 Joules!"

CA-THUNK.

A deafening silence filled the room, unbroken by the beep of monitors, people clearing their throats, or shuffling of tired feet. The quiet permeated the OR. One might have thought the world had stopped spinning momentarily, so encompassing was the stillness. Another might conjure up thoughts of misty tombs that may or may not be empty, especially as the witching hour crept ever closer. Eyes danced over the dark red muscle, all hoping and willing the heart to move. Hoping for *something*.

"Shit, charge to 50—" Dr. Yang started, sweat darkening her scrub cap.

Beep… beep… beep… came from the monitor, pointed blips marched across the screen, steady and strong.

The new heart muscle rose and fell, responding to the electricity, like a dead car roaring back to life after being jumped. Applause rang out in the OR, starting in the back where the medical students stood clustered, their elation palpable. Even the seasoned vets took up the gesture, all in attendance clapping vigorously. "Great job team! We have ourselves a working heart," Dr. Yang said, a grin hidden behind her mask.

A collective sigh of relief filled the room.

The new heart pulsed in Casey's chest cavity, the

powerful muscle squeezed in time, working without a hitch! Circulating blood coursed throughout her body, perfusing organs. The surgery was a veritable miracle of modern medicine! For a moment, not that she would never admit it to anyone—not even her wife—Dr. Yang *felt* like God. She'd taken a donor organ that had traveled from states away—motionless in a bath of ice-cold saline, safely nestled within a cooler that looked like it contained a construction worker's lunch if one ignored all the stickers plastered on the outside proclaiming Human Organ For Transplant—and gave a mother a second chance at life.

The waxy, white sternum she'd sliced in half at the beginning of the surgery was rewired shut over the newly beating organ, coming together with a snap. Staples with fiendishly sharp teeth sealed the overlying skin—closing the once open thoracic cavity. Nurses applied dressings to the repaired skin and tended to the various tubes snaking from Casey's body. Once satisfied, they pushed Casey's stretcher to the PACU for recovery—another cold, sterile room lined with non-descript drapes that smelled of Band-Aids.

Casey spent a lot of time in the PACU, not yet wholly back within the conscious realm. Her brain basked in a Propofol-aided sense of calm, enjoying the extra dose received after the accidental wake-up. The anesthesiologist (whose nametag incidentally read "Dr. Dignan") sat by her bedside, diligently noting Casey's vital signs in a paper chart for several hours. This was highly atypical. Once the endotracheal tube was out, and the patient was semiconscious, the anesthesiologist usually jetted off to the lounge in search of the holy gas-passer grail: coffee, crosswords/sudoku, and a warm locale to check up on their stocks. But post-heart transplant patients were much trickier than patients with a hot gallbladder or a routine appendectomy. Naturally, this translated to more hands-on care and time spent at the bedside, but Dr. Dignan spent even more time with Casey, unconsciously repenting for the incident during surgery, even though she firmly believed—and rightly so—that she wasn't at fault.

For Casey, the time passed in a blurry haze—her mind fuzzy from the anesthesia and pain medications. She was dimly conscious of a faint burning ache in her chest, a pain that would crescendo, becoming a ripping, tearing agony once the pain medications wore off.

Once Dr. Dignan felt satisfied with Casey's recovery from anesthesia, they wheeled her to her room in the Cardiovascular-ICU, where a team of nurses greeted her. They worked efficiently, managing all the tubes snaking out of her body: multiple IV lines; a central line sutured to her right inner thigh; a chest tube draining scant blood from her chest cavity; and a catheter draining urine from her bladder into a bag that looked like it contained lemonade if one didn't know any better.

Casey rejoined the realm of the living.

29

Groggily, I watched a hoard of nurses descend upon me. Their movements were swimmy, fuzzy. An older woman barked out orders—obviously the Winston Churchill of the CVICU—while underlings bustled about doing her bidding. One organized an obscene number of cords into orderly rolls that made the perfectionist in me a little hot, while other hands slapped stickers on my torso and limbs, hooking me to more well-organized cords. After they gave me a thorough once over, they allowed my family in. Lucky for me, as they walked in, my pain medication started wearing off, making the visit grueling. A sheen of sweat broke out on my brow, but I tried to keep a stoic face. Jack clutched Owen's hand and juggled a large vase filled with red roses; a task that would have been infinitely easier if Owen weren't trying to break free of his father's grip, presumably to wreak havoc. Owen's eyes widened, clearly enchanted by the chiming and beeping, taking in the sharp clean edges of the machines just begging to be touched, all the switches flicked, especially any towards the OFF setting. Bonus points if they were life support.

Jack had been about to hand over my flowers, when a

sour-faced nurse swooped in, intercepting the vase like she dabbled part-time as a football safety, citing a-flowers-were-not-allowed policy—the rule probably buried deep within a staff handbook from the 80s—and promptly confiscated the roses as if they would cause my heart to explode within my chest, like a reverse Chestburster from the *Alien* franchise.

My parents followed closely behind Jack, my dad cradling a sleeping Eleanor in his arms, bundled carefully in a blanket with yellow ducklings marching across it. Both husband and parents had bags under their eyes, skin pale and waxy under the harsh hospital lights, adding five years to their faces. Jack had developed new worry wrinkles overnight around his eyes and I felt absurdly touched at how distraught he'd been over my surgery… although his being hungover certainly didn't help matters. The leftover anesthetic was clearly making me emotional.

Everyone exchanged warm words of love and encouragement—other than Owen who was dying to push the button marked Code Blue and required forcible restraint from Jack and Eleanor who lacked the capacity to speak—each taking extra care to avoid my myriad tubes and lines, approaching each hug and kiss with caution. Shortly after Owen made a frantic grab at the tube draining my bladder—no doubt hoping to tear his recovering mother's urethra in half—the one and only flower Gestapo marched in, telling everyone it was time to leave or as she put it:

"My patient needs rest and recovery, so beat it."

I offered up a weak groan, just to keep up appearances, but was secretly thrilled. My eyelids were heavy and felt as if Dr. Yang stitched weights to them. Whole body hummed with dull pain, feeling almost feverish while—oddly enough—the center of my chest felt ice cold. Not the skin but the tissue deep *inside* of me.

I pushed my call light. Immediately, a nurse bent over

me. "Are you in pain, Casey?" I nodded and she flitted off, returning with a syringe filled with clear fluid.

"Morphine," she said. A pleasant lightheadedness seized me, brain floating above the clouds, and the pain dulled to almost nothing, other than the pit of ice at my core. As I drifted off to a Morphine-assisted sleep, I giggled, thinking that they'd fucked up, gone and implanted a snow-cone where the heart should be. And stitched weights to my eyelids, best not forget that! I always tended to run hot, favoring ice cubes and fans in the summer so I took an odd delight at the cold.

Which was good… since I'd feel it for the rest of my life.

30

The seasons turned while I recovered. Leaves curled on the trees, transforming into brilliant shades of orange, yellow, and red. The first of them fluttered to the ground when it came time to remove the chest tube from my thoracic cavity. The surgical resident instructed me to hold my breath and deftly grasped, then pulled the tube out. I imagined they briefly glimpsed my newly re-inflated lung, spongy pink tissue engorged with air and then the hole was sealed with a thin black suture.

Slowly, I was being knitted together, good as new.

Chest tube removed; the next day marked my first intensive round of physical therapy. A young woman had come by the day previous and had me sit up in bed, performing gentle exercises that reminded me of geriatric water aerobics sans swimming pool. While it hadn't been a complete cakewalk, the exercises were easy, and I figured that I'd sail through physical therapy. Alas, what had been labeled physical therapy previously was gentle calisthenics that even Stephen Hawking could probably do. *Real* physical therapy—which I soon realized—was an exercise in agony, complete with copious amounts of trembling and wheezing like an elderly woman afflicted with horrid emphysema. My task for the first session? Using a wheeled walker to complete a circuit of the physical therapy room, avoiding foam blocks strewn about that acted as quaint little roadblocks. At the outset, the task seemed laughably easy, but after five steps with the walker; the effort qualified as Herculean. I might as well have been tasked to clean the Augean stables or kill the Hydra! Lungs burned with every raw inhalation, muscles between my ribs flaring in fiery torment with each movement, quadriceps and hamstrings shook like a newborn foal's. The head physical therapist watched me closely, her eyes glittering with the barest hints of malice as I puffed and scraped my way around the room, collapsing in a heap on one of the chairs after finally completing the circuit. As I sat there, panting, and trying not to pass out and/or vomit, I imagined her in an SS uniform instead of the hideous polo that made her look like a lesbian PE teacher with an anger management problem. Somehow it made me feel better.

Part of me wanted to cry for mercy while crumpling to the floor and the old Casey might have done just that. But something stopped me, bolstering my flagging strength. I'd grown tired of playing the victim, tired of being the amiable wife and mother expected to roll over and take whatever abuses were heaped upon me.

Things were going to be different from now on.

I became absolutely convinced that the physical therapist—Olga, how fitting of a name—in a previous life might have enjoyed a flourishing career as an Auschwitz guard. Olga outfitted herself in a polo shirt with Physical Therapist stitched in yellow above the left breast pocket, which was lined with ballpoint pens and a laser pointer Olga wielded to express her displeasure. One of her favorite pastimes was pulling the laser pointer out and shining it in arcs on the floor where she wanted us to walk. "Walk! Walk! Walk!" she screamed and had I had strength, I might have screamed at her. But I was fighting for breath and couldn't waste any. The bitch certainly picked the right field since she obviously derived a sick pleasure out of watching people sweat, shake, and nearly die. Bonus points if she made us puke.

After that first session, a nurse popped in to check on her exhausted patient. The RN's eyebrow raised as she took in my hair, matted to my forehead with hard earned sweat. "Seems that Frau PT really did a number on you today, huh?" I let out a braying laugh at that, even though it caused a sickly stitch of pain to radiate through my chest wall. The nurse giggled. "Yeah, you're not the only one who thinks Olga's a bit of a slave driver. One patient said that she looked like a male gym teacher in a skirt, and another compared her to Hitler, but *he* said that Hitler might have been nicer." She gave a shrug. "Be happy you're not outside today with the Frau—sometimes she takes y'all outside. It's much too chilly for that today. It's the kind of cold that sticks to your bones. I had to break out the ice scraper for the first time."

She handed me a small Dixie cup full of medications of varying shapes, sizes, and colors, and pushed an unopened water bottle across the bedside table. I gamely gulped down the meds. The largest—and most important—lodged in my throat, causing me to choke and sputter. Chugging the rest of the water, I felt the pill dislodge and inch leisurely down my esophagus, scraping tender tissues on its way—slowly—to my stomach.

The nurse gave me a sympathetic look. "That Tacrolimus can be a bitch, can't it?"

I barked out a hoarse laugh, earning another spark of pain between my ribs. Shit. "Yep. Good thing I only need to take it for the rest of my life, right?" Wasn't that the truth? The nurse offered up a courtesy laugh, but I could see she'd already mentally moved on to the other million tasks of her day: mindless charting, ferrying pills to other patients, and probably planning dinner for an ungrateful husband, if her glittering wedding ring was any indication. A woman's work was never done, a fact I well knew.

Leaning back, I reclined on a pillow I'd nagged Jack to bring from home. Hospital pillows tended towards a flatness that made pancakes jealous and I cringed thinking of all the blood stains laundered out of them—not to mention other bodily fluids. Yuck. My pink pillow from home smelled strongly of pine and—oddly enough—freshly baked bread. Not that I'd ever baked bread in my life unless Pillsbury biscuits straight from the can counted. The scent, rather than making me think of home, suggested carefully constructed television sets: *The Brady Bunch* living room, the kitchen from *Leave It to Beaver*. Fake. Plastic. Homes that operated as a gilded prison instead of a sanctuary, no matter what the chortling studio audience might think.

I wrinkled my nose at the cloying pine scent as it tickled the fine hairs inside my nostrils. A telltale prickling took root inside the bridge of my nose, and my eyes filled with tears. An incoming sneeze—most unwelcome. Sneezing after heart transplant surgery was akin to a vigorous torture session by a merciless dictator—one who found water boarding far too humane. One simple sneeze sent fresh flares of pain throughout my chest cavity, and a succession of them? Absolute murder. Prickling gave way to stinging, as if hundreds of fire ants bit my tender nasal mucosa, latching on with tiny pincers. Gritting my teeth, I squinched my eyes shut, willing it away. The building sneeze teetered on a grand precipice. Would it? Or wouldn't it? Just when I thought I'd hit the point of no return, the sneeze loosened its grip and vanished.

Thank God.

Funny, how a sneeze lasting two seconds caused *hours* of suffering.

Of course, I'd been suffering for a long time now, all due to my husband's two second orgasm. Jack's quick spurt of jizz had set off a devastating cascade of consequences. Someone really ought to put a photo of me with my LVAD on brochures advocating against teenage pregnancy. It *was* a hell of a cautionary tale. Ruefully, with a thin smile, I thought, *use condoms, kids*. Maybe after I healed up, I could film a PSA they could air during PrimeTime.

Thankfully, the sneeze had gone—not that it couldn't come back. It probably *would* come back, but I felt a simple pleasure displaying *some* mastery over my body. There was a great deal I hadn't been able to control in my life, a distressing fact to someone who tended towards a Type-A thinking style, who abhorred the sensation of losing control. Flying induced horrendous panic attacks—not that I'd flown in years owing to my *condition*—since I was completely at the pilot's mercy. What was stopping the pilot from suicidally nosediving the plane into a craggy mountain range after a fight with their spouse? It happened more often than people liked to admit. Giving up that control set off a deep anxiety within me, leaving me feeling helpless. Growing up, I had always been a bit meek, never the thrill seeker. Famously, my father bragged that I would never say *boo to a goose*—whatever that meant. Canadian geese were practically the devil with wings, so I didn't think saying *boo* to them was a smart move.

No more of that, I resolved. No more going with the flow, allowing other people to govern me.

I was done with that shit.

Having nothing but free time—except for my murderous physical therapy sessions—I had *plenty* of time to muse. Ponder. Staring around my room, at the mounted TV that boasted an alarming amount of evangelical programming—to be expected since it was a Catholic hospital—all I could do was think.

And think I did.

How *much* had I missed in life because of circumstances beyond my control? So much.

My train of thought always came back to Eleanor. And Owen.

It wasn't exactly Sophie's choice—I knew who I'd pick, every time.

Eating my snack—Jell-O with floating pieces of pineapple—I seriously considered the idea of divorce. Sure, I'd *passively* thought about it, even daydreamed about it, but… now the concept was tangible and within reach. Ditch Jack, give him full custody of Owen, and I'd take Eleanor. Sort of like *The Parent Trap* except there was no adorable set of twins played by Lindsay Lohan. But life didn't quite work out like that.

Still, I'd think of something.

Unfortunately, some things were completely out of my control, a fact I well knew but I thought my luck was finally changing for the better. All I had to do was work hard during my recovery, take my meds diligently, and hope that my new heart minded its P's and Q's. Absentmindedly, I rubbed my chest with both hands, as if to warm myself from the outside-in. The chill must have settled in my chest, just like the nurse had said: sticking to my bones.

31

My team of physicians deemed me medically stable—medical stability being inversely related to how many tubes protruded from one's body—and I was discharged from the high-tech CVICU room to the rehab floor. Despite my protests that I didn't *need* rehab—I wasn't some invalid elderly woman with a hip replacement, and Frau PT, as much as I hated her, had made me much stronger—they relegated me there.

And as it turned out, each day I learned just how clueless I was.

Being on the rehab floor meant that instead of the one slavedriver, Olga, I had many. The blonde-haired, blue-eyed Aryan Auschwitz princess led a group of physical therapists, all intent on putting me through hell in the name of recovery. More therapists equaled more torturous fun! My stamina was completely shot from my cardiomyopathy, and I'd morphed into an unrecognizable weakling. With my LVAD, I hadn't exactly pushed myself to my physical limits, so I hadn't realized *how* deconditioned I was. The difficulty of clutching a seven-pound dumbbell and walking up several steps was unreal—I used to run 10K's without stopping for fuck's sake! Each day I ended up bathed in sweat, rivulets cutting ragged paths down my face, turning the back of my hair into a tangled rat's nest. Running a brush through the severe snarls brought me to my knees.

While I abhorred the unrelenting pain coursing through my body each session, I found the challenge oddly enjoyable and, most of all, I delighted in the fact that my body—for once—wasn't fighting me tooth and nail every step of the way.

As if the physical therapy/torture wasn't bad enough, I had another fun hoop to jump through: mandatory talk therapy sessions focusing on my new heart and second chance at life. As Dr. Yang explained in my CVICU room before I moved to the rehab floor, "It would be criminal to only concentrate on your body while your mind is undergoing a massive change, too." It sounded like some new age bullshit to me, but I wasn't really in the position to refuse. I didn't have MD after my name. Not that I was *opposed* to therapy, I had spent an inordinate amount of time in Pat's office, but that was for a specific issue. But if I wanted to return home someday—even if my home *was* a prison in disguise—I had to comply. Jump through the hoops like a poodle performing for the circus.

Plus, I missed my comfy bed and down comforter. I missed holding Eleanor who rewarded me with smiles that were all gums, filling me with love and joy. But whenever anyone asked, I sure put on a show, saying how much I missed my *whole* family. I'd become much more proficient in lying.

Twice weekly for one hour, I met with my assigned therapist—Jim—in his office. The ugly beige-colored walls in his office were plastered with stereotypical shit: posters of kittens dangling from their front paws on a clothesline with the caption, "Hang in there" and a poster of the ever-so-helpful mantra, "Today is the first day of the rest of your life." I rolled my eyes when I saw the posters for the first time and repeat viewings contributed to murderous fantasies starring my hands, wrapped around Jim's throat, throttling the life from him. Jim was no Pat, that much was clear.

I stared at that damn picture of the kittens hanging from the clothesline, "Hang in there," during the sessions, hate prickling my eyelids. Anytime I read the puke-inducing motivational sayings, my anger grew, as if someone was feeding coal to a rage-furnace within my body, stoking it lovingly, never allowing the flames to falter. As if the posters weren't bad enough, Jim's office didn't contain the stereotypical reclining couch seen in every therapy scene ever on TV.

Pat had one—not that I sat in it. I figured owning one would be mandated by law or, at least, by their professional societies. Could you really call yourself a shrink without one? I wasn't sure. Instead, each session I relegated myself to a plaid easy chair tucked in the corner. The fabric on its arms was thin and worn through, crisscrossed with patches of light gray that didn't match the original color. I imagined multitudes of patients worriedly rubbing fabric as they relayed their deepest anxieties and fears to Jim the toad. I was drawn to the mismatched patches, raking my fingertips over them during sessions, testing the limits of the patches' integrity. The easy chair was located directly underneath yet another obnoxious poster; this one featuring a smiling sun wearing sunglasses with a speech bubble proclaiming, "There are brighter days to come!" Double puke.

And Jim himself? *Completely* repugnant. He sported thick Coke-bottle glasses that made his rheumy eyes double their size behind the lenses. His scalp was in a constant state of active sunburn or peeling from prior sunburn. Jim kept the few remaining strands of his hair combed over the top of his head—trying and failing miserably to conceal an ever-expanding bald spot. The shoulders of his shirts were littered with white dandruff flakes and an ample belly strained against the buttons. Each session, I expected one to pop off with the force of a bullet firing from a gun, possibly into my eye. Worse, was the way he *looked* at me, as if I were a fascinating specimen he wanted to study in a jar, fondling whenever it pleased him. Jim was mostly a dweeb, but he reminded me of a shrewd ferret, always watching, waiting to pounce on smaller, weaker prey.

Another thing? Jim didn't seem to give a tin-shit about my new heart, instead preferring to delve into my childhood —almost as if he hoped I might tell him a sordid tale of daddy slipping his hand somewhere naughty. I quickly grew tired of my sessions with Jim and feared my eyes might get stuck staring at the back of my skull after oft repeated eye rolls. Naturally, I invented stories just to fuck with his head. My favorite fabrication involved my high school best friend, a hot tub, and some "experimentation." I didn't delve into the details of said "experimentation," instead electing for vagueness so Jim-the-perv could imagine whatever his dirty little heart desired. How his eyes gleamed as his pen flew across the page of notes. I was certain that he was sporting at least a half chub in his khakis, hilarious since I had never been with a woman. Men were *so* disgusting.

32

On waking, my entire body ached like a rotting tooth. Overdid it at therapy? Organ rejection? Depression? Impending death? Whatever it was—my mood was sour the second I climbed from the bed and my feet encountered the freezing linoleum floor. I clogged my toilet after a nice BM which was embarrassing, and I found a hair-tie in my hospital-prepared lunch of a tuna melt. On a mostly empty stomach, I submitted to another grueling day of PT and—unfortunately for me—Olga didn't delegate to one of her underlings, who tended to be less severe than their malevolent leader. I imagined the hateful bitch screaming at prisoners of war in a dusty camp yard to *pick up the pace!* as they dropped dead from hunger and typhus.

"C'mon, Casey, LET'S GO! Weakling! You'll never get better at this rate!" she shouted. Sweat poured down my face and my eyes filled with hot, furious tears. WEAK? Me—WEAK? What was weak about surviving through a horrid pregnancy, heart failure, living with a machine plumbed into my chest, and coming out on the other side, intact and better?

I left the session seething, thighs and arms shaking. I

couldn't believe the bitch had *THE NERVE* to call me weak. If Frau intended on igniting my fuse... well, she'd succeeded! I returned to my room, fuming, raring to take my rage out on somebody. *Anybody*. Luckily, my idiotic husband came through—for once.

Cellphone rang and JACK appeared onscreen. "Hello?" I answered, glaring at my post-physical therapy snack of Fig Newtons and apple juice. More fuel for me to clog my toilet.

"*Hon*... do you realize you didn't order Owen's cake for his birthday?" His voice dripped with disdain, as if he couldn't believe he'd had the bad luck to marry *such* a dumb bitch.

A tendril of red-hot irritation squeezed my heart, blanching away some of the cold that had taken residence within. Who the *fuck* did he think he was??? Anger flared—hot and poisonous—erupting from me like a volcano of repressed emotions. It was stronger than anything I'd ever experienced but... part of me enjoyed it, basked in it. I screamed into the phone, spit flying and splattering on its glass front, "Maybe you didn't realize, *hon*, I'm in the fucking hospital! Did you remember? I had an LVAD after you knocked me up and my heart failed? Got a heart transplant? Ringing a bell?"

My knuckles blanched white as I gripped the phone. "Tell me, when would I have time to order a cake for him, *dear*? Maybe in between getting my ass kicked by the physical therapist and taking all these fucking pills? Or, you know what? Maybe I can have Dr. Yang order it! I'm sure she's not busy! Perhaps you didn't get the memo I nearly fucking died? But no, you're just a selfish prick who doesn't think of anything other than yourself." My chest heaved and my cheeks burned. Here Jack was, bitching about me not doing something for Owen—and not because it affected Owen. No, Jack was pissed he had to lift a finger and didn't have his lovely wife who doubled as his personal secretary/slave to perform such menial tasks.

Jack sputtered a reply that I didn't hear, and I abruptly hung up. I had *nothing* more to say and listening to him flounder just pissed me off more. My only regret was that my hang up wasn't as dramatic as I would have liked had it been on a landline. Pressing end call was *way* less satisfying than slamming the receiver down. One of the many drawbacks of technology.

On the plus side, least I didn't have to stare at Jack's stupid fucking face tonight, as I was still relegated to PT and talk therapy hell. I thought of Jack's deeply flushed cheeks, spider veins crisscrossing his nose, loose skin dangling from his neck and chin from too many nights of boozing, and that dull, bovine expression in his glassy eyes. No thanks. Once, I thought he was one of the most handsome men I'd laid eyes on. My knight in shining armor, ordering me a drink after I'd failed miserably to grab the bartender's attention. Can you believe he even had abs at one point? Abs! When we'd first slept together—cuddling, basking in post-coital bliss—I couldn't resist running my fingers along his chiseled stomach. I didn't get close enough for such activities now, and I didn't want to caress the keg he sported under his clothing.

Back then, Jack had a certain sad aura about him, evident in the way he stared at the ceiling, deeply lost in the depths of his own mind. Silly me, I thought Jack was a tortured soul, like a misunderstood artist, and it only increased his attractiveness in my mind's eye. Now, knowing what I knew, I wondered if he hadn't been picturing Tara writhing underneath him instead of me the whole time.

Not that it mattered anymore.

33

After Jack's call, I swaggered into Jim's office for another dull therapy session, full of energy and indignant, fiery wrath—not dissimilar to how Napoleon strode into war meetings. I flopped down on my designated plaid seat—gray patches and all—and without preamble, launched a scorching tirade. Jim's eyes grew wider with each word, making him look even more idiotic than he already appeared daily.

"I'm the one that must sacrifice, give, give, and oh, give some more! Did you know I went to college? Yes, I did! I didn't go just for the MRS degree like so many of those empty-headed bimbos. I majored in biology and chemistry. I wanted to *be* something. I could have been a doctor. I had the grades and the drive, but my stupid ass had to fall for Jack. I got suckered in by his brown eyes and steady stream of bullshit, '*No honey you don't need to work, just take care of the house and children. I'll be the breadwinner and you can be my little housewife. Later, you can go to medical school.*'" I gestured broadly at the massive scar on my chest. "Look how well that's worked out for me! I birthed a kid that is a complete sociopath. Don't give me those shocked eyes, Jim—the kid *is* a little asshole, and everyone knows it. He doesn't have a kind bone in his body and he's probably responsible for eradicating the local dragonfly population single-handedly. Do you know what it's like to want to hug your child and have them scream, pull your hair, and spit in your face? Call you a cunt? It makes you feel like absolute shit and a failure! How could your DNA fuck a kid up so spectacularly?" Spittle flew from my mouth, barbed words dripping like sulfuric acid. Flecks of saliva struck Jim's cheeks and forehead, but in his astonishment, he made no move to wipe his face.

"And then I'm supposed to just sit, all prim and proper, the perfect little housewife while my husband sneaks around with his friends, drinking and carousing. I found a business card in his pants pocket with a number written on the back —the bitch wrote, *'call me! Trixie'* with a heart next to her name! Trixie? Seriously? You can't tell me she wasn't a prostitute. Who names their daughter Trixie? It had to be a stage name." Trixie. I remembered how my stomach turned when I pulled the card from his back pocket. She'd dotted the i with a heart—which somehow—made it *that* much worse. "The asshole has some nerve taking prostitute's numbers, coming home late from his stressful job of number crunching, reeking of booze while I sit at home minding his delinquent son! Oh, I also found a picture of his ex—Tara —hidden in the garage. Does he stare at me and picture her? Did he fuck me and imagine he's screwing her? It's fucking bullshit, JIM!" Jim startled at the mere mention of his name, clearly perturbed at being brought into the discussion. A mean thrill bloomed in my gut at Jim's shocked expression.

With a sheen of sweat budding on his forehead, Jim started, "Well, I… uh… I think—"

"FUCK WHAT YOU THINK, JIM! You're not even a psychiatrist, you don't have a medical degree or a PhD.

What the fuck did you *do*—complete an online certification? You're a fucking hack. All you care about is stories about incest and lesbian fantasies. I hope you know; I made *all* that shit up, just to mess with you. You don't *even* matter. You're a dweeb, Jim. A fucking loser."

"That's… that's… a bit… harsh," Jim said, his eyes downcast, his gaze on his trembling fingers in his lap.

"Get used to it, buddy. Life is fucking harsh. In fact, in case you didn't know, life can be a real bitch! I sit at home, keeping house for a husband who has slipped into alcoholism—a functional alcoholic for the moment, at least —minding his demonic spawn, and what thanks do I get? Oh, that's right—one night he comes home drunker than a fucking skunk and forces himself on me! How is that for gratitude—spousal rape! And guess who gets knocked up during this lovely interlude? ME!" I thrust my thumbs into my chest for emphasis and continued, "ME! Then my body and health went into the shitter. The whole pregnancy was torture! If it weren't for Jack, I wouldn't be sitting here now looking at that stupid expression on your face. I wouldn't have had to live with a machine in my chest and wouldn't have some dead person's heart beating in my chest! But here I am, living the fucking dream! And he jumps my ass for not ordering the little shit a birthday cake while I bust my ass in the hospital? I swear to God, I could just murder that fucker where he stands. The fucking pig." I slammed my fists on the coffee table, punctuating the end of my rant. A vase filled with fake flowers tipped on its side with a *clack* near Jim, causing him to jump, nearly upsetting his full cup of coffee. He reminded me of a terrified mouse cringing in a tomcat's shadow. The air between us was full—pregnant even—with a scorching rage. The ambient temperature of the room felt as if it'd risen several degrees. Quite honestly, I was *enjoying* this: raising my voice, not bowing down to the societal pressure of being a good girl.

I didn't care that Jim squirmed with discomfort. I didn't even *see* Jim.

Nor did I see the boring, beige walls, and didn't once glance at the poster depicting a thunderstorm that proclaimed, "Only YOU can weather the storm." A dull red haze overtook my vision, growing in intensity, pulsing with grim strength. A hot hate consumed me, tearing through each part of my body, infusing each cell with a searing heat that begged for release. Each nerve ending was aflame, exposed, and tender, but in the pit of my chest, a stinging, inhospitable chill reigned.

As always. I clenched my fists so tightly my fingernails gouged bloody crescent-shaped wounds into my palms, cuts that would sting like a bitch once I eased my grip, blazing with indigent fury each time I washed my hands or used hand sanitizer. Not that I noticed then. Muscles bristled with pent-up energy and if Jack were here in front of me, in this state? I would gladly smash them straight into his smug face and would savor the feeling his nose made splintering under my fist, just like I'd savor delicacies served up during a five-star meal. Feasting on his pain, dining on his cries of dismay and outrage. A cruel smile stretched across my face; teeth bared in a predatory grin like a coyote watching its prey struggle after a good mauling. My nostrils flared, as if I scented blood in the air, and I felt powerful, completely unlike myself. But in a way, I was beginning to feel completely like myself.

Ding!

Jim had bent himself into a shape closely resembling a pretzel in his chair, his legs drawn up into his lap. He rubbed his hands against each other mindlessly. Eyes loomed large and swam behind Coke-bottle lenses as they darted about the room, as if searching for the life preserver on a sinking ship. Beads of sweat rolled down his forehead, mingling with my saliva. "Um… that was the timer that signals the end of our session," Jim said. He swallowed hard, his Adam's apple bobbing. His eyes shone brightly—fear and trepidation. Jim shrunk back in the chair as he spoke—any further and the fabric may well have swallowed him whole, perhaps off to another dimension, a destination that would suit him just fine, I suspected.

And just like that, my rage burned itself out.

It'd rampaged like an out-of-control forest fire, consuming everything that stood in its path but as quickly, extinguished once encountering a barrier. In this case—a simple timer. The tinny *ding* cleared the red mist swirling dangerously in my vision. I blinked and came back to the mundane office with my tedious therapist. I looked down, surprised to find my fists tightly clenched; knuckles blanched white. Uncoiling my fingers with a dull creak, my tendons ached as they stretched back out.

Jim stared at me, fear rolling off him. I felt like a perceptive predator, aware of my prey's every emotion and thought. The office air tasted sour, flavored with his apprehension. His mouth opened. Paused. Reconsidering his decision to speak, jaw snapped shut, teeth audibly clicking. Even with my ire back to baseline, I enjoyed how uncomfortable Jim was. "I guess we're done then, huh? Saved by the bell!" I remarked sweetly to Jim. Words were pure honey and nectar, all saccharine. "Thanks for listening!" Without waiting for a reply, I sprung up and left the office.

No doubt he was happy the monster had gone.

34

J im held his breath until the door swung shut behind Casey and—seeing he was truly alone, away from *her*—he exhaled a sour breath. Weariness settled over him, rendering his limbs leaden. He felt like a man of 65 rather than a meager 45. His hands shook from residual adrenaline, and he fumbled for the pack of cigarettes that he'd hidden in his desk for *just in case*.

Officially, he'd stopped smoking three years ago after endless nagging from his wife—both for his health but mostly, due to the rising cost of their health insurance thanks to his smoking habit—but he left a pack of smokes inside his desk drawer for emergencies. *Just in case.* He'd only dipped into the stash twice—once after receiving the news of his father's death and the other after learning one of his favorite patients jumped from a twenty-story building immediately after their session. While no one had died this time, the aftermath of such a horrendous session seemed like a perfect *just in case* scenario to Jim.

It took a few tries to set the match aflame, thanks to his shaking fingers. Once the match was lit, he touched it to the cigarette's black circle, thrilled when the tip caught fire. Jim took a deep drag, and it flared like a burning coal—hot and red. Precious nicotine suffused his beleaguered nerves with a calm he sorely needed, bathing them with poison that masqueraded as a friend. Index and middle fingers holding his cigarette ceased trembling, leaving him feeling almost serene. *Almost.*

Another deep inhale of sweet tobacco, Jim's eyes rolled back with pleasure. Thoughts wandered from the frightening storm that was Casey Philips, to a conversation he'd had with one of his colleagues, Rob. Both had been deep in their cups, a decanter previously filled with amber whisky nearly empty on the table between them. Each had two fingers left in their glasses, and Rob lit up a cigarette. Jim had waved off the offered pack of smokes with regret— this wasn't a *just in case* moment—but he relished the thick smoke that wafted over, enclosing him in an inviting cloud of secondhand exposure.

They'd been talking shop, sharing stories of their utterly fucked up clients, without revealing names of course, ever mindful of HIPAA. They'd moved on from Jim's patient with persistent delusions that he was the second coming of Christ to one of Rob's patients who was sure that she'd been Marilyn Monroe in her other life, before being tragically murdered by the CIA and/or Bobby Kennedy, depending on the day. Rob talked about how her eyes darted all over his office, searching for hidden cameras and listening bugs planted by the government, confident the feds were always watching.

"People are fucking nuts!" Jim cried out, laughing over Rob's horrible impersonation of his patient singing Happy Birthday to JFK like Marilyn Monroe in her breathy, sexy voice. Jim's second coming of Christ patient was a fuckin' nut too but at least he didn't sing… at least not yet.

Their stories always started out lighthearted and humorous, the shared humor of those toiling on the front lines with patients who could benefit from committal to some sort of asylum—not that such places existed anymore. They were like boys at a sleepover who started out with age-appropriate cartoons and pizza, ending the night with flashlights upturned on their faces, the words, "It was a dark, stormy night," preceding every ghost story while R-rated horror movies played in the background. Every therapist had ghost stories of their own.

Rob took a long drag, cigarette tip glowing a deep red ember. It almost looked like an eye to Jim, especially in the gloomy room. He then exhaled a series of smoke rings, finishing with a proud smile. Even in his champion smoking days, Jim never mastered the skill himself and felt a thin thread of jealousy course through him. A foreboding look settled over Rob's face. "Did I ever tell you about my patient who drowned all three of her kids in the bathtub?" He paused, waiting for Jim's reply.

"God, no! That's pretty fucked up," Jim answered, his interest piqued. He slugged his remaining whisky down, enjoying the flower of heat erupting in his esophagus and the pleasant buzz in his skull that followed.

"Yeah. She was a piece of work. You know what she reminded me of? Like a drone from a scary movie, a pod person? *Night of the Body Snatchers* or something. It was like *something* had sucked out the very essence that made her human. Sure, she looked human enough, but she had no *life* behind her eyes. They were dead, just like her kids." He paused and gave Jim a shit-eating grin at his little quip. "It gave me a case of the creeps to look directly at those eyes. They were like bottomless pits you could lose yourself in. She talked like a robot, no emotion in her voice *at all*. Not even when she talked about drowning her kids—which she did—in grisly detail. No remorse, no sadness. Shit, she wasn't even happy about it! Just nothing. Flat. But do you know what the absolute worst part was, Jim? The thing that

I still think about at night when I can't sleep? Not that I *want* to think about it, mind you."

Jim shook his head. "No, what was the worst part?" The skin of his arms was tight, broken out in the cold creepy crawlies. Someone had once told him that anytime he got goosebumps, it meant a goose walked over where his grave would be. Jim suspected that he was going to be buried on a farm.

"Her smile, man. She had this smile on her face that could have been pretty under any other circumstances. Believe it or not, she *wasn't* a bad-looking woman, *even* if she drowned her kids. Which is fucked up, but you get it, right? Sometimes people are just good-looking, even if they're complete monsters. I mean, shit, women threw themselves at The Night Stalker even when he was in prison!" He shook his head. "But her smile reminded me of an animal caught in a trap, chewing off its own leg to get free. I saw a badger like that once with my dad as a kid, and that's the *exact* look. The badger had its teeth bared in a hideous grin, even as blood spurted from its leg stump. It's a look—a smile—that says, *don't fuck with me.* Would you mess with an animal that's willing to gnaw its own leg off to continue living? Because that's what she did. She drowned her kids so *she* could live, as messed up as it sounds. It was all there, in that godforsaken *smile.*"

Rob's eyebrows knitted together as he spoke, his normally vibrant eyes taking on a flat appearance. "I sometimes worry that smile will be the last thing I see before I die. It was *that* awful. It wasn't something from this earth. I can tell you that much." Rob held up his glass of whisky and —with a smooth, well-practiced tip of his wrist—tossed the rest of the amber liquid back.

Jim thought about the look he'd seen etched on Casey's face, how she'd glazed over like something else had taken over. She'd seemed simultaneously out of control but…

weirdly *completely* in control. A total dichotomy. And, Lord, the ranting, the spitting! Anger emanated from her very being, rolling off her in waves like heat spilling from an overtaxed oven. Jim had seen her eyes, wide but utterly dead with no light within them, no soul peering out.

He'd been trapped in his own office with something wholly *different* from the pretty but tired woman who walked in for their first session. And the worst part? He had a sense *she* could sniff out the fear wafting from him, suspected it outright *delighted* her! If the braying timer hadn't distracted her, he worried she might have pounced on him, desperate to channel her rage onto him and he held no illusions he would survive *that* encounter. He pictured her thrusting a gun at her husband's head, a smile of delight dancing across her face as she pulled the trigger, splattering the poor sap's brains everywhere.

Which reminded him—he better enter her information in the FOID database, the last thing a nutso like her needed was a gun.

Jim smoked his cigarette down to the filter and marveled at how much clearer his head felt. The clouds of apprehension and fear, blown away by a powerful wind called nicotine. A true wonder drug. Wrenching open his office window, he waved his arms to dissipate the smoke smell. The last thing he needed was for his wife to pop in for a surprise visit, nose wrinkling in disgust at the smoky smell, eyes filled with accusations.

Jim eyed his personal calendar. Only two more sessions with Casey. That was two more sessions than he was willing to spend with the psychopath. Couldn't they discharge her early so she could terrorize her poor husband for a change? Jim considered: maybe he could surprise the wife with a week of vacation. He did have some uncashed PTO time. She'd been begging for years for a road trip up to the Northeast to watch the leaves change. He could win some real husband brownie points, maybe even score a blow job! Best of all, he could dodge Casey's last sessions and let some other poor sap try to heal her mind. Good luck to them!

As the sun streaked across the sky, Jim's memory grew fuzzy regarding Casey and his last session, but a survival instinct—a holdover from cave dweller days—warned him, *stay far, far away*. So, Jim requested a week's worth of vacation which was summarily granted. A week to be states away from Casey's nauseating smile. And those cruel eyes.

Jim waggled the mouse of his old trusty desktop, and—with a sputtering groan—the screen changed from black to his preferred background: his wife grinning broadly on a beach with beautiful white sands, pina colada in hand. It'd been years since the two had done something like that. She was gonna beam ear to ear once he surprised her with this impromptu trip and the best thing about vacation? Vacation sex! His mouse cursor hovered over the link that would direct him to the FOID website, but dreams of his wife scantily clad, gesturing him towards her with an eager finger, won out. With a contented sigh, he pulled up Google instead and searched bed and breakfasts. He could worry about Casey later. They wouldn't release her from the rehab floor to purchase a gun to blow her husband away today. He had plenty of time to worry about *her* later.

Preparations for his glorious vacation wiped away any apprehensions he had regarding Casey and her—ahem—*tenuous* emotional state and by the end of the day, he'd completely forgotten about entering Casey's information into the FOID website. Had she so wished, she could walk into any establishment and purchase a handgun or even an automatic. AK-47s *were* the latest accessory and completely necessary according to any Republican.

But Jim needn't worry—it wouldn't have mattered had he entered Casey's information, prohibiting her from buying a firearm.

Casey had no need for a gun.

Thousands of miles and several state lines separated Jim and Casey the day she was released from the hospital—earlier than expected. Casey walked out of the hospital doors while Jim shared a flaky, hot buttered lobster roll with his wife after a rousing day of driving along back roads jam-packed with other tourists, each jockeying for position to take pictures of the changing leaves—photos no one would ever glance at again.

Jim would never have to worry about Casey again… until he read the news reports, that was.

35

My Type-A personality certainly aided in my recovery. Dr. Yang and my physical therapists agreed I'd recovered wonderfully and could continue the rest of my rehab journey in the comfort of my own home, with the support of my loving family. At least Eleanor might cheer me on. I'd have to attend cardiac rehab at the local gym five times a week, hoofing it side by side with people recovering from triple bypasses, heart attacks, and the like. Like a celebrity, I was one of the rarities: a former LVAD patient. A veritable unicorn. I had a packed dance card, filled with upcoming doctor's appointments. I really ought to get frequent flier miles or some sort of punch card—nine doctors' visits and the tenth was free!

As the hospital's double doors snapped shut behind me, cool fall air stung my face. Above, gray clouds swirled, their bottoms a darker shade that threatened precipitation of some sort.

I was going home.

And as befitted my life, my welcome home was anything *but* sweet.

The task of couriering me home fell on Jack. He

143

brought the van, rightfully forgoing the Camaro. I always had to hunch down to cram myself in the sports car's bucket seats, and I was *not* a tall person by any stretch of the imagination. Not that I *disliked* the muscle car—it just wasn't appropriate for a post-op cardiac patient. The van served as another hideous reminder I'd spectacularly lost control of my life. What kind of person *wanted* to drive such a gas guzzling monstrosity? The damn thing advertised to all who glimpsed it, "HEY LOOK HERE, ANOTHER PERSON WHO FUCKS WITHOUT BIRTH CONTROL!" That would look great on a bumper sticker though, it'd be *much* better than the stick people Jack wanted to plaster on the van's back window. Sure, it might be trendy, but it made me think of a menu for child molesters to select their prey. Not that I opposed the idea of some kiddie snatcher taking Owen. They'd bring him back though, and that was sure to be disappointing.

My stomach roiled as I sat in the front seat of the van, white knuckle-clutching the red pillow I'd found propped on my hospital bed after my transplant surgery; a consolation prize for having a shitty heart. *Sorry your heart is a piece of shit, but here is this adorable pillow!* Each patient undergoing cardiac surgery received said heart pillow and, tragically, it was *not* a prize they bestowed on those who catastrophically died during the procedure. I doubted they gifted the pillow to the next of kin either. Cheap bastards.

Our ride home was silent, broken only by the rumbling of the engine and occasional clicking of turn signals. The quiet unnerved me and I coaxed the radio to life, settling on an oldies station, now playing songs that were popular during my high school days. The idea of *NSYNC being classified as oldies made me chuckle aloud.

Jack glanced over, taking his eyes away from the road, right eyebrow craned upwards. "What's so funny?" I *used* to find his cocked eyebrow expression endearing. Now, it made my blood boil since he only did it when annoyed.

"They're playing *NSYNC on the oldies station. Why not put them in rotation with Patsy Cline? If *NSYNC is oldies, maybe it wasn't surprising my heart went kapoot. I was living on borrowed time if boy bands are old fogies," I answered, trying to infuse some lightheartedness into the dismal drive home, even though I desperately wanted to slap the dumb expression off Jack's face.

"Sorry, I don't see why that's funny, *hon*." Jack sighed, flicking on the wipers as fat raindrops erupted from dreary clouds above. Thick *plonks* rattled the van as the rain picked up in intensity, reminding me of waiting in an automatic carwash.

I rolled my eyes. Leave it to Jack to be a total buzzkill. "Oh, I apologize. I didn't know they removed your sense of humor around the same time they gave me my new heart. Maybe I need to write to Jim Beam and ask them to print jokes on their labels, sort of like Laffy Taffy does? So, you can have a steady stream of funnies, *dear*?"

Jack's eyes narrowed at the barb; his face gloomy but he said nothing in return, taking the infuriating high road called *shutting the fuck up*. I sighed. My pussy husband was too beat down to even argue with his wife. Maybe he was still reeling from when I'd screamed at him about Owen's cake.

Part of me had been excited to go home but now that it was happening, I was filled with dread at the prospect of being around Jack and Owen. Eleanor was the only one I'd missed. Cardiac surgery wasn't exactly a vacation, but the nurses fluffed my pillows, pumped me full of fun narcotics, and my family was mostly *not there*. Which sounded *exactly* like a vacation now that I thought about it.

Rain slowed to a trickle as we pulled up to the house. Every light in the house switched on—and why not? Jack's parents didn't pay the electricity bill! Thick carpets of unraked dead leaves littered the lawn, much to my disdain. My nervous energy faded and was replaced by a thin anger, a much more welcome emotion. Anger had become comfortable, like a well-worn pair of shoes.

Jack killed the engine and—without a word—got out of the van, slamming the driver's side door with more force than was necessary, making the van shake. The sharp clap of the door closing made me startle in my seat. Rather than coming to the passenger side and helping me out or grabbing my bags, Jack skulked up the sidewalk and disappeared through the front door, closing it with a stark slam audible even through the rain.

Maybe he'd gone to fetch me an umbrella? But no… minutes passed and still no Jack. My thin anger morphed into a fuming hate: a much more dangerous emotion. Hate unfurled like smoke throughout my body as I grabbed my bag, my precious heart pillow, and braved the walk to the front door. Was he seriously still pissed about Owen's cake or the Jim Beam joke?

The rain, unrelenting completely soaked me and my belongings within seconds.

Having only two hands to juggle all my possessions, I struggled. Dr. Yang foolishly neglected to implant a third arm during my surgery. With some difficulty, I threw the front door open and walked in. Water cascaded off my body, pooling on the floor beneath my feet. My hair had already transformed into a rat's nest at the base of my neck and the rest of my body broke out in goosebumps thanks to frigid air conditioning blowing directly on me. Jack's parents didn't give a shit about our air conditioning bill either. I glanced at the Nest thermostat mounted on the wall: 64 degrees. No wonder it felt positively Artic.

A sticky-faced Owen strolled by as I stood shivering in the entryway. A smattering of yellow crud dotted his face, and his fingers were coated in a brown substance that I only hoped wasn't from shit. Unfortunately, it was not a possibility I could completely rule out since just last year, Owen shit the bed and finger-painted the walls of his bedroom with the resultant stool. I still remembered the horror walking in to wake him for school and seeing brown streaks everywhere the little asshole could reach. I'd seriously contemplated lighting the house on fire that day, but figured arson was a lot of work for a lady with an LVAD who couldn't walk over ten feet without getting winded.

Owen shot me a cursory look and raked his face with his fingers, leaving brown streaks on his cheeks that looked absurdly like war paint, and flitted off into the other room. *Please, please, please don't let that be poop*, I prayed. With a grimace, I set my bag down in the ever-expanding puddle at my feet.

From the kitchen, I heard Jack's parents—his mother's reedy voice and his father's deep baritone—followed by a shrill baby shriek. Even though a headache was starting up, hearing Eleanor still made me smile, even if she was loud. I let out a sigh; I wasn't exactly thrilled at having to see everyone else. Leaving my stuff in the foyer, I trudged along the hallway to the kitchen, wincing at the dull throb at the base of my skull. The pain pulsated with each loud noise and involuntarily, I gritted my teeth.

Everyone other than Owen was seated around the kitchen table. Debris littered the tabletop: unopened bills, uncapped markers, and smiling goldfish crackers, some smashed into fine orange dust. Owen was elsewhere, working on his shit Picasso masterpiece, just lying in wait for his mother's inevitable meltdown when I discovered it. Jack —by the looks of it—had sprinted inside and prepared himself a bowl of cereal. He sullenly spooned Cheerios into his mouth, pointedly avoiding eye contact with me.

Jack's parents greeted me with a nod and a hello—a somewhat formal welcome for them. They both remained seated, not standing, and embracing me as was their custom previously. They'd taken up a policy of handling me like I might be a bomb ready to explode at the barest movement, understandable when I had an enormous machine snaked into my chest, but now? C'mon. I'd give them the benefit of the doubt this time—I *was* completely soaked through with rainwater, and I imagined Jack's mom catching a cold and the resultant stones she'd cast at me. "I just knew I shouldn't have hugged you! What if this turns into pneumonia and I die? Pneumonia at my age is no joke, you know!" I plastered a smile on my face, certain it looked as fake as a new pair of tits on one of those *Real Housewives* that Jack's mom fawned over.

Baby Eleanor offered up a much better greeting than her brother, favoring me with a wide toothless smile, although there were barest hints of teeth coming in on top. Man, did they grow fast! Eleanor's smile twitched and her mouth gaped open, releasing an ear-splitting squeal. My skull smarted at the clangor but still, I enjoyed the happy reception. Eleanor danced in her highchair, wriggling her arms and legs about, as if celebrating my triumphant return. Jack and I agreed on keeping the kids home after the initial post-surgery visit. Eleanor was far too young to understand what was happening and Owen... well... he gave no fucks about his mom being laid up at the hospital and was more likely to wander off and unplug some vegetable's ventilator. Eleanor held her chubby arms thick with baby-fat rolls out to me just as an alarming *URK* noise originated deep in her body.

Oh no... I intimately recognized *that* noise. Before I could react, the *URK* took shape, morphing into a geyser that covered my already soaking wet shirt with brown vomit. She'd upchucked whole green peas and I watched as three rolled off the bottom of my shirt and underneath the table. Jack paused, halting the spoon just shy of his open mouth, watched the Old Faithful-Puke Rendition for a few beats, and returned to his cereal bowl with a look of significant concentration.

Apparently, the vomit didn't harm Jack's appetite any. He always made himself scarce at any mention of bodily fluids, disappearing into thin air when someone had a dirty diaper or shitty pants. He'd scrunch his face up in a poor imitation of suffering, clutch his stomach, citing a horrible gag reflex and intolerance for nasty chores whenever I enlisted his help. He maintained such burdens fell solely into the realm of *women's work*, a nice catch-all term that encompassed such things as changing blow-out shitty diapers or scrubbing fetid vomit laden with kernels of corn from the tile grout.

Jack's parents erupted in laughter seeing me dripping with both rainwater and brown spew, as if *it* were *the* height of hilarity. Sides heaved violently under the force of their laughter; a wonderful joke just for them, made by their darling granddaughter! I gritted my teeth, my jaw aching. They wiped tears from their eyes and without further ceremony, hurriedly climbed into their coats, Jack's mother crying out, "We better give everyone some family time!" They moved with the speed of Olympic sprinters towards the front door—no starting gun or racing spikes needed— calling out a quick, "Goodbye!" No need for other chit chat or pleasantries. The frame of the house shook with the door slamming and more vomit dribbled onto the floor, landing with wet *smacks*.

Eleanor howled with indignant rage, cheeks beet-red, and thrust her hands in the steaming pile of puke, grabbing a handful and plopping it directly in her hair like a glob of mousse. Jack dumped his bowl in the sink, neglecting to either wash it out or—God forbid—place it in the dishwasher, and exited the kitchen, stage left, without a word. The puddle of water at my feet took on a dingy brownish cast and several peas swirled lazily within. My body thrummed with resentment and my jaw clenched so tightly that my molars squeaked. Every molecule blazed hot except for my chest which as always since the surgery, was cold and hollow.

This was what I'd fought so hard for? A life filled with vomiting children, shit finger-painting sociopaths, and deadbeat husbands? I'd been home for less than five minutes, yet here I was, on hands and knees, a heaping bucket of suds beside me. I attacked the floor with the scrub brush, applying pressure that made my palms weep, working like hell to scrub the vomit from the grout before it stained. The puckered scar tissue of my chest throbbed with each movement. A familiar creeping red haze worked its way across my vision. Steaming puke puddle appeared as if I were viewing it through a red viewfinder with a smudged eyepiece. Vision doubled, then tripled, two spews, three spews looming in front of me. Salty tears dripped down my face, joining the soapy water I'd sloshed onto the tile. I wasn't sad though, not by a long shot. Glossy tears fell from my eyes in a steady stream of bone-crushing ire. A blistering nugget of fury rested just behind my eyes, held at bay for the moment, but bid its time with insidious patience.

With enough provocation, it could and *would* spark an inferno of pain.

36

Life took on a different rhythm after my triumphant return. Even the most mundane of things changed. In my younger years, I never had issues falling asleep. When my head hit the pillow, mind dimmed, and I was out like a light. Like any teenager, I could have used a crowbar to aid in my getting out of bed and 8 a.m. classes in college were sparsely attended thanks to my snooze button. Even after Owen was born—who, for the first year of life played the part of the ideal baby and slept through the night almost immediately—I got enough rest, especially considering that new mothers were essentially walking zombies covered in assorted bodily fluids. Obviously, the LVAD put a crimp in restful sleep, what with the constant noise and hard edges. I'd expected to resume normal sleeping patterns once I was no longer a cyborg.

Wrong again!

Most days—the sun nowhere near the horizon—my eyelids snapped open in darkness. The east was an inky void, not yet tinted with any hint of the customary pink that heralded the coming sunrise. I imagined my eyelids producing a *clack clack* noise, like old-timey blinds rolling up in one of the *Looney Tunes* cartoons when Wile E. Coyote chain-smoked and chugged pots of coffee while waiting for the Road Runner. Even birds remained hunkered in their nests, instead of unleashing their cacophonies of screeches as was their custom—sounding far too cheery. My eyes burned, feeling as if The Sandman filled them with regular sand instead of magical, restful sleeping powder.

Typically, I fell into something resembling a thin doze with dreams only half-remembered on waking, gasping, fingers curled into talons clawing at my chest—horribly reminiscent to the sensation of my lungs insidiously filling with fluid. The resulting racing heart, heaving diaphragm, and cold sweats did *wonders* for my anxiety. Organ rejection was my first thought, followed by a horrifying conviction that I hadn't received a heart after all—that I was suffering from some delirium born from sedative medications mainlined into my veins while I languished in an ICU somewhere, tethered to even more machines. Only my clammy fingers running along my chest, over the puckered scar tissue—sans mechanical bullshit—brought the truth racing back: someone, somewhere had died. And their death was essentially my Golden Ticket, figuratively handing me the keys to the factory. Their misfortune was my gain.

I started suffering from recurring nightmares, thin fragments flashing like cut scenes from a blockbuster Hollywood thriller: running, endorphins roaring, sensation of pursuit. My role within the nightmares was more difficult to discern. Details disappeared the instant I jolted back to consciousness, leaving me with feelings of supreme pleasure and animalistic need. But I didn't think *I* was being chased.

I was chasing. Or *something* like me.

37

Days bled together.

Awake by 4 a.m. day after day. No restful REM sleep where my brain recovered and recharged. I wandered through the daily tasks of caring for my family, my temper thin and fraying with each lost hour of sleep. Feeding Eleanor became infinitely more difficult, far more complex than heating a bottle of formula. At one of my many appointments—this one at Eleanor's pediatrician's office—I thumbed through a parenting magazine, tired of scrolling through Facebook. I'd skipped past the breastfeeding section, glanced at the toy recommendations to build intelligence, filing The Busy Cube away (and it was bilingual! ¡Que bien!), and on the next page—

The article's title caught my attention right away.

Want to develop your baby's emotional health?

Most definitely.

I wanted my daughter to be grow up well-adjusted. *Not like Owen.* And the article was written by someone with a multitude of initials behind their name—one of them being MD, lending credibility. According to the article, puréeing your own baby food, filled with vitamins, minerals, and antioxidants, was the best way to increase your kid's chances of success.

It was also a complete pain in the ass.

Buying fresh ingredients, steaming vegetables, puréeing, sanitizing, labeling. Rinse. Repeat times infinity. But I did it because Eleanor deserved the best in life. I had to admit, I missed simply unscrewing an apple sauce pouch lid and handing it over to Owen. Easy peasy. At the time, it had never occurred to me to check expiration dates… and there was *that* tendency for them to grow mold—a fact I learned later and stressed over. While I doubted toxic mold was the *sole* cause of Owen's problem… it probably hadn't *helped*. And interspersed between the organic homemade baby food saga from hell, were other obligations.

Packing Owen's school bag and lunch. Cutting his sandwiches into fun shapes—not that he gave a tin shit; and fixing breakfast for Jack, who proved incapable of cooking without alerting the local fire department. Jack sometimes met clients over lunch, running through boring figures and spreadsheets all while billing the firm, but if he planned to eat at his desk—I dutifully packed his lunch, sometimes even cutting his ham and cheese sandwiches into fun shapes if I felt like it, like Owen's. If I were in a particularly good mood, having grabbed more than two hours of sleep, I might slip in a note. Nothing too wild, just a simple "I love you." Even if the words were a fucking bald-faced lie.

Sometimes—to pass the time while slapping meat on white bread—I fantasized about sprinkling poison in between the ham and cheese. Something fun like arsenic or cyanide but I didn't know where one might procure such things. The dark web probably. Not that I would ever do such things, but… it was a nice daydream to tuck into. Cozy like a comfortable pair of slippers.

With all my morning tasks concluded, other obligations

reared their heads: doctor's appointments, cardiac rehab, and unfortunately, lunch with Amber, Amanda, and Jenny.

"What's it like having someone else's heart inside of you? OMG," Amber asked.

"Yeah, does it feel weird?" Jenny chimed in as she frantically calculated macros.

Wistfully staring at the cocktail menu—*still* unable to order a margarita thanks to all the damn medications—I considered. "It's okay, I guess." Truthfully, I was elated. Someone met an unfortunate end and rather than vultures, transplant surgeons descended. Instead of tearing talons and beaks—scalpels. The dead sap's loss was my gain.

Amanda, true to form, already drained her mojito. "Were any of your doctors hot?" She'd always had a white coat fetish and famously hung around the bar near the medical school during college, hoping to land herself a future surgeon. She got somewhat close, marrying a paramedic.

"I mean… Dr. Yang is attractive if you're into women holding knives," I replied.

Amber rolled her eyes at Amanda and asked, "How are Jack and the kids adjusting?"

Adjusting? Jack hadn't changed a bit, still working hard to develop cirrhosis before the ripe old age of forty. And the kids? They seemed fine, relatively unaffected by recent events. "Fine," I answered, although… was it?

No, it wasn't. I feared for Eleanor, making it a rule to always know Owen's whereabouts, keeping him at an arm's length from his sister. But I couldn't be everywhere, all the time—a fact that curdled my gut. Eleanor had to nap, I had to do housework, and Owen—when properly motivated— could move with the slithering grace of a snake encircling a bird's clutch of eggs.

Twice Eleanor had let out shrill shrieks that made my blood run cold.

With a hammering heart and roaring in my ears, I ran to my daughter's crib, finding her purple-faced and wailing. Both times after inspecting Eleanor—delicately undressing her, scouring her body—I discovered nasty red welts roughly the size of Owen's fingers, hidden beneath layers of clothing and diaper. They'd bruised already in the centers and as I studied the wounds, I noticed areas of broken blood vessels dotting Eleanor's pale skin. Petechiae, they were called. I learned all about those during my pregnancy, when suffering from low platelets. After retching fits, my face resembled a red-spotted Dalmatian from the force of my vomiting.

Amber and Jenny, both had a knowing look on their faces. They knew my "fine" was total bullshit. Owen, after a lengthy expulsion, just returned to school and I doubted he was on his best behavior. Sure, there had been no phone calls from his teacher or Mr. Wilson, but that didn't mean much. It just meant Owen was getting sneakier... more proficient at being evil away from prying eyes.

"And... how is Owen doing back at school?" Amber asked, striving for an innocent expression that fell well short of the mark.

"Great!" I replied, voice far too high.

"At Field Day last week, I saw him with Eleanor... he was being such a great older brother!" Amanda added, flagging down the waiter for another drink.

My hackles went up. "Yup, he sure is." More bullshit. Publicly, Owen had never done anything outright mean to his sister, even feigning a sort of starstruck older brother role for everyone. Again, I was reminded of a prodigy child actor, like Macaulay Culkin's character in *The Good Son*. During Field Day, he laid it on thick. Grabbing his sister's hand and kissing it, proclaiming, "I love my little sister!" earning a chorus of "Awwww's!" from all within earshot.

"There's nothing quite as special as siblings that love each other," Jenny said.

A rictus grin spread across my face. "Definitely." Love? Was it *love* when Owen's face darkened gazing at his sister from across the dinner table. His eyes filled with an eerie expression that reminded me of a predator calmly watching. A *hungry* predator. Waiting.

That night, I readied for bed. Washed face, brushed teeth, and gulped down handfuls of pills. I'd foolishly thought shedding the LVAD would result in less medications, not more. Organ rejection would be a real bummer though, so dutifully, I tossed them back. Filling a plastic cup from the bathroom tap, I nestled into my side of the bed. Not that I had to worry much about *my* side and *his* side. Jack had taken to staying up most of the night and crashing out on the couch or the guest bedroom. Not that I was complaining. It meant I didn't have to feign sleep when he came in, ever mindful that my dear hubby wasn't above acting without consent, keeping me on my toes. And it gave me time to pursue my extracurricular activities.

During recuperation from the transplant, besides coming home to Eleanor and my cozy bed (sans Jack), I couldn't wait to dive into my to-be-read books piling up on my nightstand. My standard cheesy fare: shirtless hunks with flowing locks decorating the covers, cringeworthy sex scenes, and predictable love triangles. My first night back—after deep-cleaning the kitchen for hours, thanks to Eleanor's pukefest—I plucked the top book from the pile, eager to lose myself in tawdry trash. Only a chapter in, I put in down, suffering from second-hand embarrassment and shook my head.

One trip to the bookstore later, I'd made more eliminations. Picked up an autobiography of John F Kennedy and tossed that aside. It reminded me too much of middle school history which was a snooze fest at the best of times. Sci-fi was interesting but I couldn't suspend belief long enough to lose myself in the plot.

Then, I found something I thoroughly enjoyed. All I needed was something with more octane and grit. I started out with Stephen King and devoured *Carrie*, *Rose Madder*, and *Dolores Claiborne*, all featuring vengeful women. But they didn't quite scratch the itch—didn't satiate me. Sure, they were frightening and creepy, but… they weren't real. Fiction.

Back to the bookstore. Picking my way through the aisles, eschewing romance (pre-transplant me would have been horrified), mystery (it was always the butler), I found exactly what I never knew I needed.

True crime.

Helter Skelter came first, all 700+ pages of it. Every few pages, I flipped to the photo inserts, and gazed at Charles Manson. Even through a camera lens and the passage of time, his eyes conveyed unsaid ideas and machinations.

Onwards I went, through the pasts of BTK, Ted Bundy, and Aileen Wuornos. Death and carefully controlled mayhem captivated me. And since my sleep was thin at best, I knew I could while away the early morning hours reading.

Currently, I was on Ann Rule's *The Stranger Beside Me*, all about Ted Bundy and how they worked at the same suicide hotline, once upon a time. I could have used their phone number during my girls' lunch today, especially once Amber and Jenny started discussing ovulation and the state of their cervical mucus. I turned to page 142 and started reading.

Before long, words blurred, and my eyelids grew heavy. Off went the light, and my head hit the pillow.

Falling asleep wasn't really the issue for me.

Staying asleep and what happened during those supposedly restful hours was.

39

Darkness.

Then—

Something darted through my consciousness, like a lightning strike—gone just as quickly. I felt as if I stood removed from myself, watching from afar, like a movie-goer with eyes on the local cinema's big screen. The electric flashes were meaningless by themselves, but more came, filling the darkness. They became a rolling thunderstorm, a shifting kaleidoscope of black and red, the same rusty color of spilled blood congealing. And like an afternoon storm lighting up the black sky, I was left with impressions I remembered on waking. Initially, the details were fuzzy, like surroundings hidden by a dense fog, but cleared as the miasma burned off.

Each nightmare was different. But also, the same.

Locale changed each time. While I watched from afar, I also was starring within the nightmares. Sometimes I found myself moving stealthily through woods thick with trees, an indifferent moon sending down beams through the canopy, while other times my footfalls were crisp and loud against hardwood floors. A deserted parking lot cast in shadows, its only illumination from an ailing overhead light. Bars, gleaming liquor bottles rattling while a flunky band played in the corner.

No matter where I was, a singular purpose filled me. *Want.* Of the most desperate sort. *Need.* A predatory instinct consumed me. Moving with a languid ease, I stalked my target, who often came to me, like a bottom dweller drawn to a bright beacon, completely unaware they marched to their death, which came in the form of an anglerfish's razor-sharp teeth and primitive cunning. Rarely, the lure failed, or my prey had a sixth sense for danger, taking off at the first hint of sour intentions. So sometimes, my surroundings blurred around me as I gave chase. Pursued. Both inside my body—feeling my heart roaring in my ears, large muscles burning as I churned my legs, and outside—watching a feature film playing out in my own personal theater of horror.

I watch as they fled.

Women.

Not one the same.

I chased *them* when they fled, an odd thrill coursing through my veins. I coolly observed their flight from the sidelines. Like God, I was everywhere all at once.

With a hammering heart, I saw the furtive looks they tossed behind them—bulging eyes brimming with tears, red spots of color splashed across their cheeks, visible even within the murky darkness. Some of the women sent a flash of recognition through me, striking me with a familiarity that bordered on déjà vu. Where had I seen them? Passed them in the grocery store while searching out ingredients for dinner or on TV, a quick blip about a missing person, before the evening news? Who knew? They seemed intimately familiar yet alien. Some were brunette, others had porcelain skin courtesy of Nordic ancestors, and a few had olive tones that spoke of Mediterranean roots. There were blondes with locks that might be natural or more likely, came from a box of hair dye. One auburn haired beauty—apparently a favorite since she made several separate nightmare appearances—with startling green eyes sent an electric jolt down my spine, into my nether regions each time I gazed upon them.

Like an eager bloodhound, I followed my hapless prey, sniffing the air with murderous intent. Desire swelled within me, making my body run hot—apart from my heart, which always tended towards frigidness. A small part of me fought against these hideous impulses, within my mind I yelled, "Casey, stop! What you're doing is wrong!" But even at full volume, the voice was meek, unsure, just like I used to be. Probably because—

I didn't *want* to stop.

Why would I stop? I moved powerfully, heart pounding steadily and reliably, sending richly oxygenated blood to every part of me. Hours and hours I ran, without tiring. A certain disembodied sensation within me reigned. My body didn't exactly *feel* like mine but... ever since my heart betrayed me, it *hadn't*. I'd been trapped within a prison of flesh, slapped with a terminal life sentence, and had expected to wither away. To rot. To die.

But after my new heart, *everything* changed. I'd *changed*. Energy crackled through each muscle and each movement was easy, me in complete control of my body. It was *glorious*. With utter power, I chased the women, and they ran, or at least, tried to.

I eventually caught up with them. At first, I hadn't known what the outcome would be.

I quickly found out.

My hands clawed outwards, reached, and grabbed. Hooked fingers twisted themselves within their hair—brunette, blonde, auburn—grabbing thick handfuls that ripped out in clumps, jerking their heads backwards with a violence that was both terrifying and exhilarating. They'd teeter precariously. Most lost their balance—only one ever recovered and ran on—falling woodenly amidst thick carpets of leaves that cushioned their flailing bodies or struck gleaming hardwood floors that offered nothing in the way of comfort.

And I *seized* my prize. It felt so *primal*. I felt… alive.

My hands—strong and filled with evil intent—clamped around their necks, steadily squeezing, and a part of me relished the popping sounds as bones snapped and tissues tore like wet rags. I couldn't tear my eyes away from their faces. Their identical looks of terror, facial expressions of fear twisting their features. Something twisted and sexual filled me, reminding me of watching someone reach an orgasm at my hand but…

Oh, *this* was *even* better. Waves of delight swam through me as their eyes bulged, from fear and lack of oxygen—their mouths twisting in wordless screams. I savored the way the tiny blood vessels in their faces burst, dotting their skin with pinprick hemorrhages. How the whites of their eyes filled with blood, leaving their irises bathed in red-tinted pools. The look on their faces was always the same: a mix of pleading and incredulous surprise.

My desire escalated to a fever pitch, feeding off their agonies.

Boy… was I hungry.

40

I jerked awake, startling myself.

Sweat dotted my brow and my chest heaved.

Disequilibrium struck me.

What… was I doing?

Instead of the comfortable confines of my bed, I stood shrouded in darkness. Blinking, adjusting to the dim, I took in my surroundings.

A doorway.

Had I been sleepwalking? I hadn't done that since I was a girl, terrified of Pennywise coming out of the bathroom drain to murder me after my parents foolishly allowed me to watch the *IT* series.

I was looking into Owen's room. His back moved, slowly with the deep breathing of a sound sleep, ribs flaring outward. He faced away from me, so I couldn't see his eyes but there was no doubt within my mind he was out. The only times he was tolerable was when unconscious. A spark of anger flared within me, upset that while I paced the house, apparently unconscious, yet restless, Owen slept without a care in the world. Eyes narrowed, focusing in on my son, and my fists clenched. I let out a yelp as my right palm cramped, my fingers stony and creaky. Hands twitched and something clattered to the hardwood floor, startling me further. Jumping back, I nearly tangled within my own feet and only by a miracle, retained my balance.

"What the fuck?" I whispered. Shot a quick look at the bed. Owen hadn't moved. Thankfully. But what had I dropped? My eyes hadn't adjusted fully, so like Velma from *Scooby-Doo*, I crawled around on my hands and knees, searching. Palms brushed against hardwood, the thin runner, and... something cold. Cautiously, I ran my fingers across the object, but a sharp pain rose from my palm. Involuntarily, I hissed, and drew my hand back.

A thin line of blood dripped from my palm. Cool air blew across the cut, and I grimaced. "Shit," I muttered, instinctively bringing my wounded skin to my lips. A copper taste filled my mouth and the salt in my saliva stung but was oddly soothing. With my hand pressed against my lips, using only my eyes, I continued foraging.

A glint of light caught my attention, and I crept forward.

My eyebrows knitted. "Shit," I repeated, carefully picking up the object and inspecting it.

A knife.

Its edge was stained with fresh crimson. My cut throbbed just looking at it. But... why? My mind racing, I made my way down the stairs and hurried into the kitchen. Bare feet slapped against the floor. My grip around the knife handle made my palm ache—how long had I been holding it? I pulled up short, my eyes seeing but unbelieving.

The combination lock was off the knife block and one slot was empty.

And only I knew the combination.

09-02-17.

"Fuck," I whispered, sitting down heavily in one of the kitchen chairs, where I remained until the sun rose on the horizon. Not that daybreak helped the dark thoughts swirling about.

41

I moved stealthily, footfalls light and a gentle breeze caressed my cheek, increasing my desire. Wanting. Needing. *Craving.*

Ahead, a thin cry and the rustling of brush and branches rattling against one another. The voice was hoarse, filled with gravel—equal parts exhaustion and terror. I'd heard it before, many times, and knew she wouldn't last much longer. Pure fear and adrenaline only took them so far, filling them with feverish energy, giving them superhuman strength. Each kick and frantic punch—when they connected—acted as starters, whetting my appetite. The line between pain and pleasure was thin, far thinner than most knew.

A heavy thump and another sharp yelp. An errant root or her own clumsy feet? Either way, she crumpled to the ground, and even from my vantage point yards away, I heard the air whoosh from her lungs.

Then, I was on her. My hands flashed, one shoved her to the ground, while the other clutched a knife I hadn't even realized I held. It felt so *natural*, like an extension of myself rather than a mere instrument. With practiced ease, I plunged the blade into supple flesh, opening skin, releasing precious lifeblood. So warm and *alive*.

Her delicate tissues and mouth screamed. And I added my voice to their chorus, howling with animalist delight.

Again, and again, steel flashed, quickly growing tacky. Pulsatile arcs of blood appeared each time the blade sliced through a vital artery. Dark blood spilled from other holes, more languid than the arterial blood, but damning all the same. Pink, coiled intestines herniated from ragged abdominal wounds, releasing body temperature steam into the cool night air.

But, before the woman's last breath escaped her lips, burbling with ichor and unsaid pleas, I wrenched the blade from her chest and brought the sharpened tip to her face. A brief pause, I admired my unadorned canvas. Then, delicately, like a child taking painstaking care to stay within the lines of a coloring book, I carved into the fragile flesh of her face, ignoring her strangled pleas for mercy.

X.

X.

Matching wounds on each cheek, a sanguine letter. X marked the spot.

The ritual, having been completed, ignited another firestorm of need within me. A pulsing heat in my nether regions erupted, a desire so overpowering that it overtook me completely. My fingers fumbled with a belt buckle, fingernails scrabbling against metal, and I hurriedly yanked my zipper down, along with my jeans.

I jolted upright, sweat dripping from my temples, gasping for air.

Instead of a dark forest, I was in my bed. Sheets tangled around my feet, ripped up from the mattress, and the covers were damp, as if I'd run a great distance. Part of me remembered the doctor in *Pet Sematary*, waking up in bed with dirt caked on his feet and I reached down, expecting soil and leaves to rasp against my fingers. Just sweaty feet. A cloying pine scent filled my nostrils, as if insisting *yes, Casey, you were there*, and instead of the nightmare receding into my subconscious, the images lingered.

I examined the nightmare, the dream, turning it over in my mind as an archeologist might with a newly excavated treasure, looking at it from every angle. Part of me felt unsettled and dirty. But a far greater portion of me was filled with exhilaration. A sense of ultimate power and as much as the dream disturbed me—

I loved it.

Bloody X's, knives, overpowering another—a woman, no less. As time wore on, I started recalling more and more details, enabling me to analyze my nighttime forays. Knowing that sleep was out of the question, I took to Google.

Knife. Enter. I read the interpretation and rolled my eyes. Knives symbolized violence. Shocker. Yet, some academic probably spent years of their life coming to that conclusion. What did stabbing someone mean? A hidden penchant for murder? Sociopathic tendencies? Maybe I had more in common with Owen than I thought. I typed in *stabbing* and searched. Apparently dream stabbing symbolized the need to take back control over a past wrong, to rid oneself of guilt and regret. Even that hack Jim could draw that conclusion. "Preach," I muttered aloud to the room, not that anyone heard me. Jack's side of the bed was empty, the sheets unmarred compared to the damp jungle I'd cultivated on my side.

Setting my phone down, I closed my eyes, and tried to recall every detail of that night's dream. They came almost nightly now, snatching away my sleep, and certain features blurred together. Similar yet different. Each time, it started with a chase, each step stoking my desire ever higher. I was reminded of a delicate amuse-bouche, preparing me for the main course. Frankly… it reminded me of my childhood cat, Muffin, when she caught a poor mouse and instead of killing it in one fail swoop, she batted it around. Played with it.

I thought about when I caught the woman, putting an end to the foreplay. Replayed it within my mind and a detail struck me, creasing my brow. Odd. My eyes studied their contorted faces—dread marked in every wrinkle—my passion inching ever closer to release. Hands filled with eerie strength reached out but instead of seeing my own slender fingers wrapping around her windpipe…

I saw something else.

Having resided in my body for decades, I *knew* how my fingers looked (like the back of my hand, as they said), whether they were slim and dainty or puffy from retained fluid.

Those fingers weren't *mine*.

Fine tufts of black hair dotted the backs of the hands, meaty, broad, and strong—those of a strapping man in his prime. No shitty little diamond on my left ring finger marking me as Jack's woman, a traditional convention I'd come to despise. A sudden realization struck me, and I shivered. Nights ago, the details spilled from my head the moment I bolted awake. There, then gone. Poof. But like someone recovering from amnesia, it came back to me in a flash.

I'd pursued my prey, bloodlust rampaging within me, and once I caught the slight brunette, I shoved her face deep in a rainwater puddle. Frantic bubbles rose to the surface as she sucked in brackish water, and I savored each spume like a drink of rich wine hitting my palate. Watched the froth slow, like a fishing line that suddenly slackened after a whopper broke away. The woman's body grew lax.

And stopped—the ripples smoothing out as if I'd taken an iron to the surface.

I'd caught a glimpse of my face—no, not my face, *a face*: alien, but handsome, staring out from a puddle's reflection, backlit by jaundiced moonlight. A burning grin made my cheeks ache. Emotions flooded me: happiness, contentment. *Satisfaction.*

I'd stood and peered once more into the puddle.

A chiseled face peered back at me.

Rugged jaw was dappled with a five o'clock shadow. Fine cheekbones highlighted eyes blazing with an unholy intensity, like a furnace jampacked with coal. A predatory grin stretched the features—filled with straight white teeth with slightly pointed canines. An expression of extreme gratification on the handsome face matched the serenity that filled me. Then… the image rippled away, my presumed-dead prey's frantic gestures churning the puddle into a roiling mess, and I commenced onward with my nasty business. At the time, I hadn't registered surprise, had just accepted it.

And once the woman was good and dead, I was compelled and signed once more—

X.

X.

Marking ownership, like a cattle rancher heating an iron shaped into their brand, and stamping it on a squalling calf's rump, fur singeing, filling the air with a burning stink.

Once the women were no longer in the land of the living, things became fuzzy. I wasn't an idiot, especially these days after consuming an obscene amount of true crime—I knew what came after their deaths, how I used their bodies for my grim purpose. Maybe I didn't *want* to remember, especially since it reminded me of that fateful night when

Jack came home and changed the entire trajectory of my being. Repulsed or not, each time I woke, a burning need for release filled me, as evidenced by the wetness between my thighs.

And truthfully… I liked that too.

42

Nights of minimal sleep wore on me. Even in my dreams, I couldn't be sure who or what I was. During my waking hours, I went about my daily routines on autopilot. Numbly preparing breakfast, packing lunches, making Eleanor's meals. My thoughts were detached, almost foreign. As time inched on, I harbored a growing feeling I wasn't *alone* in my body. Something skirted around the corners of my consciousness, flitting in and out like a dying lightbulb, a half-glimpsed entity creeping in the shadows. I didn't share my concerns with Pat, who I still saw on a semi-regular basis, although since my transplant, I hadn't felt the itching need to confide in her. Could you imagine? Me waltzing into my appointment, flopping on the couch, and proclaiming:

"Pat, I think I'm really losing it. I have recurring dreams of chasing beautiful women and when I catch them, I turn them into a human pincushion. Then I carve X's in their cheeks and take advantage of them. How does that make me feel? Well… I like it, I think. And while I'm awake, I feel as if something or someone else altogether is inside me. Yup, they're here now!"

I imagined Pat fighting to keep a neutral expression, murmuring the right things, while aggressively hitting a panic button, summoning nice, burly men who'd fit me for a straitjacket and toss me into a loony bin where they'd pump me full of nice anti-psychotics. And maybe I *needed* it. But if the CVICU and rehab floor sucked, I could only imagine how shitty a stay would be for a psychotic break. What was the mental hospital's version of Frau PT? Some psychiatrist who fancied themselves as The Second Coming of Sigmund Freud or some nut who wanted to lobotomize me? No thanks.

The notion of something else inside me was easy enough to dismiss, especially once the first rays of daylight streaked across the sky. Light had a way of banishing ludicrous thoughts. Morning sun somehow acted as an eraser for the bizarre which had seemed all too real in the menacing moonlight.

But, often, thoughts flitted through my head, utterly foreign and alien in nature. While at a postop appointment, sitting in one of those uncomfortable chairs, a sense of discomfort filled me. Was it the tight pants? Shooting a look around the room, I reached to adjust… what? My crotch? *Cock* flitted through my head, and bewilderment filled me. Wait… what *cock*? Memories popped into my mind of places I'd never visited and of people I'd never met.

Everything felt wrong.

But also… *right*. And maybe that's why I didn't tell Pat or Dr. Yang. If by some miracle I wasn't sent to the nut house, they'd probably prescribe potent medications that corrected my fucked-up brain chemistry. I wasn't ready for that. I felt better than I had in… years? Had I ever felt so good?

No.

And I wasn't ready to give it up.

43

Because I didn't mention anything to my medical professionals, nights continued in the same vein: undulating cycles of pursuit, blood pumping, endorphins coursing through me, followed by gruesome slaying that left me craving more. Waking with my heart fluttering in my chest like an overtaxed hummingbird's, drenched in sweat under twisted sheets, I spent my time staring up at the bumps patterning the ceiling until the first streaks of light colored the gray walls. With bleary and abused eyes that felt as though someone poured a cupful of sand in each, (not The Sandman, that *was* for sure)—every blink was gritty.

Despite feeling like dogshit warmed once over—as my father sometimes remarked, much to my mother's consternation—I *looked* better than ever. I hadn't thought much of the compliments offered up by acquaintances and friends. What were they supposed to say? "Oh hey, Casey, you got a new heart, but you look like the back end of a food-poisoned goose?" People were pretty much required to give me unearned praise.

"You look great!" said the check-out lady, Eileen, her silver hair dyed purple at the tips in honor of a dearly departed granddaughter who'd passed from some horrible cancer.

"Did you change your hair?" Stella, the next-door neighbor asked when I lugged my trashcans down to the curb. I'd noticed the way she refrained from staring at Jack's collection of empty beer cans that comprised 75% of the recycling bin. I made a mental note to drop her off a batch of cookies the next time I got the gumption to bake.

At one of the dreadful monthly meetups with the gals, Amanda casually said between massive gulps of wine, "Casey, you're just glowing! Are you sure you're not pregnant?"

My hands twisted into fists under the table and my jaw muscles clenched. Somehow, I kept my cool, injecting pure sugar into my voice despite the venom that coursed throughout me. "Oh Amanda! Don't be ridiculous!" Unballing a fist, I flapped my hand dismissively. It was *such* a shame that I accidentally bumped Amanda's just-refilled glass of Cabernet Sauvignon with the gesture, upending it into her lap. That deep ruby stain was gonna be a *bitch* to launder out of that vintage white Saint Laurent dress.

Departing lunch, with an empty promise of *send me the dry cleaning bill!* to Amanda, I studied myself in the van's rearview mirror. I'd never been accustomed to studying myself like other girls were, bemoaning my big pores or fretting over a pimple. In college, I favored a more au naturel appearance, occasionally dusting my cheeks with blush and applying globs of black mascara for dates or nights out, rare as they were. I wasn't exactly ugly, but I was never going to be stopped by Tyra Banks for the next season of *America's Next Top Model*. Once my health took a dive, I actively avoided looking at my reflection, not wanting to see cheeks puffy with water weight, and dark circles ringing my eyes.

Amanda was right though.

I looked less like tired, frazzled Casey and more like confident, strong Casey.

An attractive blush lit up sharp cheekbones and my lips had fullness about them, almost as if I'd invested in fillers. The fine crows-feet that had taken up residence in the corners of my eyes had receded, leaving smooth skin behind. Even my brown eyes sparkled, although, they were a bit pink-tinged from lack of sleep. I looked years younger, as if the heart transplant had an inadvertent Benjamin Button benefit. Maybe it had been in the fine print of one of the forms Dr. Yang had me sign before the procedure.

Whatever the case, I wasn't complaining.

44

Morning was a delightful time to lose one's shit, and I recalled the morning I lost mine with startling clarity. It was a school holiday of some sort (Festivus, Flag Day, or something equally as ridiculous), leaving me saddled with Owen all day rather than punting him off on his poor teacher—a woman in her twenties with an anxious disposition. Not that I could blame her, Owen made me nervous too.

I'd been scrolling on my phone, reading about a brutal double murder in a neighboring town, when I walked into the kitchen, intent on preparing lunch for the kids. Organic, obnoxious food for Eleanor and a PB&J for Owen with perhaps a sprinkle of melatonin dusted on the jelly, to facilitate a nice afternoon nap. Rather than my immaculate white cabinets and sparkling countertops, I was greeted with a horror scene.

Everything—and I mean everything—was splattered with black. The stark contrast of what I expected, and reality bowled me over. "What in the actual fuck?" I whispered to myself. Blinking rapidly—hoping it was nothing more than a hallucination brought on by shitty sleep—the kitchen came into focus. Details sharpened and it was then I noticed Owen sitting on the floor, forearm deep in a can of black paint. His eyes were slitted nearly shut, the tip of his pink tongue poked from his lips as it did when he concentrated, and the corners of his lips were drawn up in a smirk. Utter rhapsody and contentment—the only times I saw those expressions on my son's face, was when he was either maiming or burning something, or trying out new curse words. Where did the little shit even get a can of black paint? I racked on brain, coming up empty. Jack's Camaro was a cornflower blue, my van a sad tan color—the color of baby shit and depression—and not a single thing in the house was painted black, as I favored crisp white lines and modern furnishings.

My shock rooted my feet to the formerly white tile, and I stood there dumbly, mouth agape. Owen—completely unaware he now had an audience—removed his arm with a squelching noise that made me think of dinosaurs drowning in tar pits, laughed, and slammed his fist into the cupboard. *SPLAT!* An inky stain that looked absurdly like blood spatter from a depraved murder scene in a black and white movie materialized. My eyes were everywhere at once. Looking at the paint dripping down onto the tile floor—freshly mopped, naturally—more of it pooling in the light-colored grout.

A blinding film of rage settled over my vision, tinting the kitchen various shades of red, a color I had grown intimately familiar with. Still ignorant to his mother's presence, Owen's countenance was that of the cat who ate the canary: fat and happy, a lazy sort of grin spread across his face while eyes danced with delight. As my anger grew, his handprints and smudges were no longer obsidian, having taken on a hematic appearance most often seen in crime scene photos.

Fitting since the kitchen was about to become one.

My senses overloaded, taking in the disaster, and I shot across the kitchen. My left shoe tracked through a paint puddle, and—without conscious thought, totally contrary to my beliefs of outlawing corporal punishment—I wrenched Owen's right arm behind his back.

"Ouch! FUCK!" he yelled. A sickening crunch radiated up my palm as I forced his arm into the unnatural position, and instead of feeling shame, I felt... *elation. I* was in charge now, *not* him. He let out a whimper and I momentarily relaxed my grip.

Big mistake.

With his unpinned arm, he administered a roundhouse punch to my temple, rocking me on my heels. A thunderclap of pain shot through my skull, but instead of letting go, I clamped on tighter, my fingers digging into his thin limb. Thanks to the precarious position I'd maneuvered him into, I couldn't see his face, but I suspected I'd wiped off the maddening smirk. Small yips escaped his lips. Each sniveling cry, instead of making me feel merciful, enraged me further. I thought of the red welts he'd created on Eleanor's chubby legs, blooming painfully, fading slowly to bruises; the disembodied animals I'd discovered in poorly concealed hiding places; and the joy that danced in his eyes with his every evil action.

And I thought about what he *might* do. No, *would* do. My lips pressed themselves into a thin line with each grunt he made, sounding like a baby bear caught in a trap, probably producing the very same noises animals had under his cruel hands. Innocent creatures, my innocent daughter, and who knew who or what else. Even with his arm pinned behind him, Owen struggled, wriggling violently under my iron grip. My free hand itched, begging to be used. Before I even realized it, my hand flashed through the air, on a collision course with my sociopathic son.

SMACK!

The kitchen echoed; the *SMACK* resonated off cabinets that had once been perfectly white. The force of the blow spun Owen towards me, and I hated to admit it but: I delighted in his hurt expression! My palm stung and already my skin was turning an alarming shade of scarlet, but I relished the burn. If it hurt *me* to slap *him* with such ferocity, *imagine* how badly he ached! A cherry-red, hand-shaped welt instantly bloomed on Owen's cheek, and his face contorted into a mask—one of immense pain. Tears swam thickly in his eyes, which shone bright with animalistic fear—as if he hadn't inflicted similar tortures on countless small creatures. Owen sure didn't enjoy the taste of his own medicine and I almost lost myself then, thinking of Eleanor and my son's outstretched hands reaching through the crib slats, grabbing a fingerful of skin and *twisting*, an evil grin stretching across his face.

"Listen here, you little shit," I hissed, images unfurling in my mind. Eleanor's poor abused body, Timmy's ragged bite wound (another pricy expense since we'd covered the hospital cost, hoping to stave off a civil suit), the bird *incident…* the list went on and on.

Do it harder, came an unbidden voice in the back recesses of my consciousness. *Really give it to him. He fucking deserves it.* I really thought about it, wanting to give in to my dark desire. If I forced his limb *just* a hair more, his shoulder would either dislocate or one of the sturdy long bones—humerus if I had to guess—would snap like a dry tree branch.

My hand balled up in a fist, quivering with anticipation. Time slowed.

Owen's chest shuddered and mucus streamed from his nose. Puffy eyes trained upwards; pupils dilated… all the better to see me with. Instead of the budding monster I expected to see, I saw a scared little boy, cringing under his mother's immense fury.

Who cares? Do it anyway.

No. No. I couldn't. I was his mother for God's sake! Like a balloon with a minute pinprick, some of the rage ebbed away and with colossal effort, I stopped myself, although I longed to give the little shit a taste of his own medicine. My fist and jaw unclenched. Fingers quivered. Chest heaved as I sucked in deep breaths. Each of my tissues thrummed as if my red blood cells were loaded with fury rather than oxygen, skin burned, boiling the surrounding air.

Even holding back as I was—

I felt *alive*.

An earsplitting wail broke through my intoxicated reverie, and I startled. What in the world was I doing? A budding horror took root within me, and I released Owen's arm. Immediately, he brought both of his hands up to this face—favoring the right arm—and burst into tears. Sobbed.

How could I let myself lose control like that? And even more concerning... why had I downright *enjoyed* it? Shit. Time for damage control. I leaned down. "Mommy's sorry, Owen. She didn't *mean* to hurt you! But you know better than to make messes like this. Mommy will make it up to you." My words came out high-pitched in almost baby talk, stopping just short. Gazed into his eyes as I spoke, striving for an apologetic tone, although, truthfully, I felt nothing of the sort. Sure... I felt a bit bad that I'd lost it like I had but... he *deserved* it.

Tears tumbled down Owen's cheeks, one tear cutting a jagged path through a black smudge near his nose. His normally olive toned skin—souvenir from some Mediterranean ancestor—appeared washed out, as if he were a victim of bloodletting by a vampire or suffered from some hideous consumptive disease. A snot bubble bulged from one of his nostrils, shrinking and growing with each gusty sniffle. Gross. Revulsion filled me. Look at him, playing the victim... really putting on a show. Oscar-worthy.

After plopping Owen in the tub—rinsing paint off until

the clear bathwater was rendered coal-black, then washing the tub with bleach—I banished Owen to his room where he could rip action figures' arms off to his heart's content. He could include today's slights in his manifesto.

The rest of my day was spent with rag and bristled brush in hand, furiously scrubbing paint from the cabinets. Under my labors, the kitchen reverted to its sparkling, former glory. No black streaks of paint, no ugly fingerprints. Clean. Luckily, Owen remained mum—as if fearful of stoking his mother's anger further—so Jack was none the wiser on his return home that evening. A cloud of cheap whisky followed him inside like Pig-Pen traipsing through a *Peanuts* comic strip. He offered up a grunt and blinked owlishly under the bright kitchen lights, squinting, his gaze lingering on the newly immaculate cabinets. Jack's eyes narrowed to slivers as if he sensed something was awry. He grunted again, made an abrupt about face, and stalked out to the garage. Wow… he must have taken a Rosetta Stone course on speaking caveman at some point—so varied and nuanced were those grunts! That last one clearly meant, "Hon, I'm going to tinker with my old shitty car and quaff a few more cans of Pabst, maybe jerk off to Tara, IDK" as if he were *so clever*, hiding lukewarm cans of pissy booze amongst his well-worn tools. Jack wasn't exactly an evil mastermind.

Jack didn't need to know what transpired today anyway.

45

After the exertions of the day—what with buffing the kitchen to a sheen and administering justice to Owen—I settled on the couch with my tablet and a bowl of popcorn. I tossed a fistful in my mouth. Chewed. Wondered. Grabbed my phone, looking for new articles on the latest true crime case. At first, the details were sparse, but what was known? Not good. A psychopath the media dubbed The X-Killer—given his penchant for kidnapping woman, raping them, etching an X into both cheeks—was running amok. With quite the super villain name too. Slashing women to pieces while wearing a cape with a red X on the back.

Scrolling through my feed, I located an article and read. I frowned. A sense of déjà vu seized me. That otherworldly sensation that I'd *seen* this, lived this in another life, or at least, another day. What? What was it? Drudged the file cabinets of my memory and came up empty. Damn. *Something* about it seemed oddly familiar. X marks the spot? *The X Factor* TV show?

I heaved out a sigh, tossing more popcorn in my maw.

The answer wouldn't come, and I allowed it to retreat from the forefront of my mind. Continuing the article, I thumbed past an advertisement for a penis-enhancing pill. When I finished the article, I felt let down. I hadn't really learned any new information.

The X-Killer enjoyed dumping his mutilated victims' bodies on minimally trafficked roadsides. If he wanted to fly under the radar, he would have conducted his nasty business in the wilderness, never to be discovered again by man. I didn't need some journalist who probably used to write for BuzzFeed to explain the psychology to me. This guy *wanted* his work to be admired. He fancied himself a master of his craft, not unlike Leonardo DaVinci with his Vitruvian Man or The Mona Lisa. Signing artwork with his signature: **X. X.** His body count estimated somewhere in the teens—for the time being. Police expected the number to increase if he eluded capture. People were hopeful though. The X-Killer hadn't hunted for a time if one went by the re-appearance of his only surviving victim, Brittany Snell. Not that she was just showing up on the scene, she'd been around for months. Police kept her identity secret but finally, the case's final girl broke her silence, ready to speak her piece. Her interview was riveting. I watched it on the news, totally enraptured, and again on YouTube, where only hours after being posted, it had nearly one million views.

Brittany gave off major Laurie Strode or Sidney Prescott vibes. Shoulders squared and back, with a firm voice, Brittany spoke into numerous microphones bearing news station logos. Hordes of people gathered, hanging on each word.

"We matched on Tinder. Cam Smith, *short for Camden,* he told me." Brittany's eyes looked wistful. "He was *so* nice. Respectful. Flirty without crossing the line. Smart." A rueful laugh. "Played the part of the perfect gentleman. After a week or so of texting, we met up at a bar. Cam greeted me with a hug—hands above the waist. Ever chivalrous, he bought me a drink."

My heart sank at that, did every time. Every woman knew what that meant: Brittany got date raped. An unsettled feeling entered me, like it did anytime I heard or read about sexual assault, worse now, obviously. *What a fucking creep*, I thought.

She cast her eyes down. "At first, I figured it was because I hadn't had much to eat that day. Alcohol went straight to my head." Shook her head. "No. He slipped me something. And I didn't realize it until it was too late. My body felt heavy, and I couldn't raise my head, let alone cry out for help. Cam carried me out and at some point, I passed out." Her finger rose to her cheek and traced a pinkish scar. She cleared her throat. "When I came to, he was on top of me, a knife in his hand. I still remember looking up, seeing the knife tip stained with blood. My face—" Brittany's façade cracked then, just a little. A tear rolled down her cheek, illuminated under the brilliant lights. Her voice hitched. "At least he only got one cheek." Ragged scar rippled. "I acted on instinct and caught him by surprise. Kneed him in the groin and took off. It was raining. I heard his breathing intensify until it was practically on my neck, then he screamed."

Mud. The X-Killer slipped in mud. Either he'd given up the chase or she outran him. Only sported the one X rather than the matching set. Through a mouthful of popcorn I said, "Damn, she got lucky." Not too many people encounter a serial killer and live to tell the tale.

After Brittany's interview, public interest surged. Then waned. Natural disasters across the world and some perv exposing himself to kids in Chuck E. Cheese beat out X-Killer coverage, since no bodies were materializing.

Not that I forgot about him. I kept an eye out. Something about those damn X's itched my brain and I couldn't, for the life of me, shake it.

46

I n other news, my sex life continued to be non-existent. Not that I wanted to fuck Jack, no way. But a woman had needs.

Also, not to say my sex life before my life went spectacularly to shit had been exactly booming. Like at the beginning of any relationship, we screwed like rabbits. Before Eleanor's sordid conception, we had "sex" at least once a month. Not that I would qualify it as sex—more like Jack using my body to masturbate. Once he came, he either passed out or rolled off. I approached sex like a wifely duty (crazy that I used to enjoy fucking him), enduring it, then faking an orgasm so Jack got the hell off me. Never trust a man to do a woman's job. If I wanted to get off, I did it my damn self. Like any disillusioned housewife, I had a host of fantasies starring none other than Paul Walker or Jason Momoa and those did the trick just fine.

After the traumatizing night of Eleanor's conception, I waved off all romantic overtures. "Not tonight, dear" or "I have a horrible headache" or "didn't you hear? I have pre-eclampsia, no sex for me, thanks." And how much could Jack really protest? He did of course, feeling entitled to sex since he was *married*, but by that time, I'd stopped really giving a shit.

One of the unexpected benefits of my LVAD—other than getting me out of social functions—was that Jack was terrified of it, repulsed, or both. Despite his love of those Arnold Schwarzenegger movies, he didn't want to bang a robot.

Jack didn't try the first week after I came home after the transplant—probably still pissed off about my Jim Beam crack—but occasionally he made a move. Not because he loved me or couldn't live without me. Nah, he wanted to get his rocks off and who better than the woman who coincidently lived in his house? One could only jerk off so much in a chilly garage to Tara's photograph or fuck barflies with God knew what diseases. Like any married man, Jack eventually crawled back to the ol' ball and chain, dick in hand, wearing a sheepish grin.

Imagine my surprise when Jack invited me on a date. Had I been pre-LVAD when he asked, I would have keeled over from shock. Dead on arrival. An honest to God date! I'm not sure where he found the gumption and despite not wanting to be alone with him for more than a few minutes, I was intrigued enough to agree. Plus, I never turned down free food. Jack asked his parents to watch the kids and whisked me away; to a romantic dinner at the local Italian place, Pastasciutta. The restaurant was widely regarded as *fancy*, mostly owing cloth napkins the servers personally deposited in the laps of all female patrons, and they boasted a tiramisu purported to be *better than sex*, which obviously had my attention.

Jack wore his best suit—one of only two he owned, the other strictly reserved for funerals—and insisted I wear my favorite dress. Despite my trepidation of being out in public with my husband, I was excited to get gussied up, out of my standard uniform: sweatpants and ratty shirts. I opted against my favorite dress though, for two reasons. One: Its plunging neckline placed my sternum's lovely waxy pink scar on display, and I *hated* feeling stranger's pitying and/or gawking eyes crawling over me. Two: I didn't like Jack telling me what to do. I'd had more than enough of that.

Playing the part of the absolute gentleman, Jack escorted me to our table, strutting like a proud peacock, and went to pull my chair out in a moment of inspired chivalry. The old Casey would have fallen over herself at this, *oh how charming!* But the new Casey? Fat chance. I shook my head and wrenched the chair from his grip, seating my own damn self. I drank in Jack's crestfallen expression at the slight and inwardly chuckled. Served him right. Seated, I admired our table littered with red rose petals, colors already bleeding onto startling white tablecloth. Jack must have called ahead, telling the manager, *"Hey, I need to get laid so make this shit romantic!"* Scattered candles—tastefully lit—were randomly placed amongst the flowers. At my place setting, sat a heart-shaped box of chocolates—which I hoped wasn't from the grocery store bargain bin since Valentine's Day was nowhere in sight.

Dinner was equal parts laughable and cringeworthy. Straight from a shitty rom-com, complete with a flabby leading man. And I'm by no means a snob. I find Seth Rogen wildly attractive. Unable to help himself, Jack ordered an Old Fashioned. Shirley Temple for me. Reaching into the breadbasket, I had a distinct sensation of being watched. Roll in hand, I looked up, recoiling at Jack's creepy gazing into my eyes. "Jesus Christ, Jack! What? Am I bleeding?" I frantically dabbed beneath my nose. Dry. His expression didn't change. "Jack, okay, what? You're creeping me out." Spread butter on my roll, happy to look away from Jack's absence seizure or whatever was going on.

Mid carb-swallow, Jack seized my hand and smothered it with repugnant kisses. I yanked it from his grip. "Ew, Jack stop it. We're in public." If he kept this up, my appetite would be ruined and that would be the real tragedy of the night. I picked at my cuticles and watched the other tables. Near the window, a young couple—at least twenty-one based on their filled wine glasses—dined, animatedly talking. Sneaking glances at each other, smiling broadly like goons. In love and having a good time. A sense of regret filled me and I turned my attention to the table next to us. Two elderly men shared a slice of tiramisu and my stomach growled. It *looked* better than sex.

With flourish, our waiter delivered our entrees—steak for Jack, tortellini for me. Gleefully, I picked my fork up and speared a piece of pasta. A greasy-haired Italian man appeared at my elbow, seemingly from nowhere, startling the shit out of me. "Christ!" I exclaimed, dropping my tortellini-laden fork on tablecloth, then, the floor. I started, "Um—"

Without preamble, the man cut me off mid WTF, and belted out a song, in very loud Italian. His voice reverberated off every glass in the room and all surrounding conversations hushed. Great… now in addition to Jack staring at me, everyone else was too! Rivers of sweat poured from the man's red face; he gestured broadly hitting a high note during what I thought might be the chorus. Instead of freshly-ground parmesan, pools of perspiration. Right on my untouched tortellini. "Great," I muttered, crossing my arms in front of me. Mercifully, the warbling ceased before my blood poured from my ears. Sweat-soaked tortellini really soured my mood—torpedoed it down the shitter. At least Jack looked slightly mortified at the display, not that it affected his appetite. He devoured his Delmonico steak, not even offering me a bite. When our tuxedoed server dropped by with a thin menu in hand—the coveted dessert menu—I rejoiced. Tiramisu was the only thing that would redeem this night. Jack fluttered his hand dismissively and before the waiter could retreat, I practically yelled, "TIRAMISU!"

The waiter nodded. "Right away, ma'am," turning on his heel. Jack leaned forward, face flushed and whispered, "Babe, I promise you an even better dessert later." Then tipped me a wink, conspiratorially, just in case I'd missed his innuendo the first time. S-E-X. Blech. The man had the flirting prowess of an adolescent boy. I rolled my eyes. Whatever Jack planned? It wouldn't come close to a slice of better-than-sex tiramisu. Eating a dog turd *had* to be better than sex with your alcoholic, dead-beat husband who raped you. Not to discredit the tiramisu. A kernel of irritation burned behind my sternum, blanching away the cold.

After paying, Jack told me to close my eyes. Instead of doing that, I fucked around on Facebook. Lost deep within the depths of Jenny's timeline, noting she'd taken down all pictures of her husband, I didn't even notice when the car stopped.

"We're here!" Jack proclaimed.

I looked up and saw towering office buildings rising into the darkening sky. Swiveling my head, I read the sign: HOTEL, in trendy-fluorescent pink block letters. Ah, he'd brought me downtown, incidentally the only downtown that Jack would visit tonight. Mine was off limits. Still, I reluctantly smiled. I loved hotels. Crisp luxurious linen, room service, lazing around watching TV. And at HOTEL (obviously ironically named), there were no crying infants or worries about Owen setting the place ablaze.

Okay, I'll let the night play out, I thought, stepping out of the Camaro's passenger seat, take-out bag slung over my arm. Glass doors whooshed open, spilling us into a modern lobby—all sleek lines and *interesting* artwork. Paintings adorned the walls and as Jack checked in, I observed patrons mentally masturbating over them, remarking over how *lovely they were,* like they knew the first thing about art. Not that I knew anything about it, for all I knew the art in the lobby was porn drawn by a ragingly drunk and/or high Picasso. I spied an inordinate number of tits scattered throughout the pieces.

Jack booked us the honeymoon suite which came complete with its own hot tub and—apparently—unlimited porn on the TV, a fact I soon found out after limited channel surfing. I was unsure if porn was an included perk of honeymoon suites or if Jack specifically requested it. Either way, it was gross.

He shut the door, making a show of engaging the deadbolt and chain. Turning around, he shot me a huge, shit-eating grin. I knew that expression. At one time, it totally worked. It was Jack's soon-I'll-have-you-out-of-those-clothes-and-in-my-bed look. The chances of *that* were slim to none, unless Jack brought some chloroform, and it wasn't like my husband was above taking advantage of women.

My only wants and needs centered on the slice of tiramisu in the hotel mini-fridge next to overpriced almonds dusted with chili powder. Turning away from Jack. I inched towards my dessert—still clad in my second favorite dress.

Jack moved quickly behind me, and I felt something rest on the sensitive skin of the back of my neck, adjacent to my braid. Revulsion. Jack's… lips. Horridly chapped, yet nastily wet like a bloated slug. Had he never heard of Chapstick? I pictured a leech attaching to me with a wet, greedy mouth, bloating itself on my blood. Disgusting. I shuddered, unconsciously (or so I told myself) tossing my shoulder back as if to shake parasites loose. Too bad Jack's nose was in the way. Our bodies collided, producing a meaty *thwack*. There was the sensation of something giving way, wet papier mâché collapsing inward.

"FUCK!" Jack screamed; voice threaded with pain. He clutched his nose, failing miserably to contain the blood leaking out. Tears collected in the corners of his eyes, threatening to overspill and join the crimson. Already, faint bruises had budded underneath his eyes and come the next morning; he'd strongly resemble a pudgy raccoon who'd gone a few rounds with Mike Tyson. Thinking of him turning up to his boring accounting firm with fat shiners filled me with malicious joy. He'd invent some BS story, probably assigning blame to Owen. Having met his colleagues at many a Christmas party, I knew they'd give him shit. "Did you mouth off to Casey again? Har har har!" But it would all be in jest. The dunderheads wouldn't suspect cute, meek, little Casey to do *anything* of the sort! I was just *too* nice and sweet! With effort, I stifled a budding grin, opting for a sheepish look that I nearly pulled off.

Almost.

"What the fuck! God, you're such a fucking bitch!" Jack said. The words were nasally. I hoped his septum was deviated.

"Jesus, Jack, it's not like I *planned* on sucker punching you! You surprised me is all, coming up behind me like that. It was an accident!" I protested. I hadn't *meant* to hurt him… not really. Hadn't *meant* to fling my shoulder back, but—

I wasn't exactly heartbroken about it either.

"Whatever. Seemed like you enjoyed it quite a bit. I saw that shit-eating grin on your face. It's still there." Voice edged towards sulkiness, making him a petulant child of forty. Even called out, I couldn't erase my expression. It felt *too* good. Jack turned away, hocking back blood and tears, and rummaged in the wet bar while blood streamed from the clenched fist wrapped around his nose. My half-smirk transformed into a spiteful smile as I watched several droplets of blood dot the pale hotel carpet.

Drip.

Drip.

Drip.

The sight of his blood thrilled me. Casting my gaze

down, I saw the delicate skin of my chest had flushed—save for the waxen scar—and my stomach and nether regions fluttered, a not-at-all unpleasant feeling. Wow. Was I— maybe—*turned on* by this?

More blood dribbled to the floor as Jack struggled to twist open a liquor bottle, reminding me of a baby intent on prying off a medicine bottle's childproof cap. The carpet had begun to resemble one of those Rorschach tests they made crazy people interpret in the movies. Jack wouldn't be getting that incidentals deposit back. Briefly, I considered shoving my husband through the TV, watching sparks fly, screen shattering, drawing more blood. Flatscreens probably didn't have the same effect—not like the old box TVs did. I waved the idea away, not that I wasn't enjoying the spectacle unfolding in front of me. Blood staining the floor, my husband's bruised and broken flesh, his struggle with the liquor bottle as if basic first aid called for booze first, putting pressure on the wound second. Before I could stop myself, laughter burbled out of me, small at first, then building up steam as I got going.

Jack shot me a petulant look which only made me laugh harder. With a great effort, I stemmed the guffaws spilling from me, caught my breath, and wiped tears of glee from the corners of my eyes. "You're right. I'm having a fucking blast right now, watching you bleed all over everything. It's a real hoot." Let the asshole decide if I was being sarcastic or not. Fuck him and whatever he thought. I took several steps towards him. Not to comfort him, though. My coveted tiramisu was in the mini fridge behind him. Laughing had really worked up my appetite and I relished the look that flashed into his eyes as I inched closer to him. Hurt. Pain. *Fear. He* was afraid of *me*! HA! As I neared, Jack shrunk back —a dog terrified of his master's cruel fists. Five minutes ago, Jack wanted to cram his cock in me, but those thoughts quickly went the way of the dodo once shit went down. Pain wasn't the aphrodisiac to Jack that it was to me apparently.

Jack finally wrestled the cap off the whisky bottle, and he drained it with one gulp. Straightened up. Bolstered with liquid courage, he spoke again, injecting his voice with venom, "Don't you fucking touch me! You cold fish bitch." I stared at him. After several seconds, he dropped his eyes. Jack's new-found bravado was short lived. Typical. Still clutching his nose, he turned and shuffled off.

Match point awarded to the vindictive, abused wife. "Cold fish bitch! That's a good one! I'll have to file that one away. Ten points for creativity, asshole!" I shouted at Jack's retreating back. His shoulders slumped forward like the beleaguered dog he was, and he slouched off to the bathroom.

SLAM!

The pictures on the wall shook with the force of the bathroom door slamming, Jack's last feeble protest. "Whatever," I muttered to myself. Let him sulk. He could drink the contents of the liquor cabinet up if he wanted. What did I give a shit?

Truth be told, I couldn't have asked for a better night. The massive king bed was all mine and after changing into my comfy PJs, I sprawled lazily within high thread count sheets and fluffy comforter, fork in hand, and attacked my tiramisu with gusto. The first forkful convinced me of the dessert's merits: it *was* better than sex!

Even better, I scored four hours of uninterrupted sleep, a record for me as of late!

Except, the dreams still came.

I'd come to enjoy them though.

47

This time, it was a chase through the woods, rain spilling from the sky. Thick branches overhead caught most of the moonlight, leaving the ground below a minefield of obstacles: exposed tree roots, errant rocks, fallen tree limbs. With a keen hunter's sense, I hurdled over the impediments, chasing my prey with avid hunger filling me. A long-bladed knife glinted in my fist, catching scant moonbeams. I heard the woman's gusty exhalations and sniveling. I drew almost even with her. My free hand reached to grab a fistful of streaming hair, ready to yank my prize backwards, and—

I slipped.

My head slammed down into a mud puddle and mucky water covered my face. Gasping, I sucked gritty water down my throat and gagged. My diaphragm spasmed and I wrenched myself upwards, retching. Brown water and vomit tumbled out, a horrible taste scorching my taste buds. Ever mindful of the chase, I rubbed mud out of my eyes. Sputtered and choked some more. My prey's figure grew smaller as she put distance between us. A flash of rage filled me, and I let loose a bellow, voice deep and ragged, completely unlike my own. The moment wavered and blackness creeped over my vision.

A flash of yellow, an engine flared to life, then—

Pain. Searing pain lancing through my head.

Pink goo fell to the asphalt, looking like chewed bubblegum mixed with blood. No. Not bubblegum. Brain. *My* brain.

Wait. WHAT?

I gasped, bolting straight up. Unfamiliar surroundings, shadows in darkness. Where was I?! My heart raced, hammering quickly against my ribs, and I clutched my head in my hands, fingers exploring my skull. No step-offs, no holes, everything was fine other than a faint headache.

You're in the hotel, Casey. You're okay. Everything's fine.

It had seemed so *real*. The agony, the blood, pink brain matter leaking from me, spilling to the road slick with rain. I shook my head, wincing. The movement made my head hurt.

Sympathy pains, I figured.

48

Jack resigned himself to the couch of their honeymoon suite, a bag of melting ice perched precariously on his rapidly swelling nose. Despite the amount of cash he'd shelled out for the room ($500 plus the $250 incidentals deposit he wasn't getting back based on all the blood) the cushions were lumpy. A hard pole lodged in the small of his back, no matter which way he shifted. He thought about complaining to the hotel staff, but then they'd know he struck out and that his wife had banished him to the couch. His pride couldn't handle complete strangers knowing that.

He flicked on the TV. Cheesy porn music tinkled in the background, punctuated by "yes, yes, yes" and forced cries of passion. An avid porn watcher from his teen years when he first typed in "boobs" on Ask Jeeves, he understood that most women tended to orgasm 5.3 seconds after insertion of a girthy, veiny penis—further proof that his wife was an unfeeling, cold fish bitch. He remembered their college days, when getting Casey off was easy, not as easy as it had been with Tara but… easy enough. Giving her orgasms had since grown into a chore. The last time they'd been intimate was… when they'd gotten pregnant with Eleanor, as far as he remembered. Jack didn't recall much of their roll in the hay, but he remembered waking next to Casey, limp dick streaked with blood. Panicked, he ran to the bathroom, closely examining his dick, terrified he'd hurt himself but found no wounds. With no clue where the blood had come from, Jack figured that Casey started her rag while they did it.

The muddled memory faded, and Jack contemplated his lot in life as he gazed at all the fallen soldier liquor bottles littering the floor.

God… how he missed life *before* Casey sometimes.

Tara—

No.

It was better for him not to think of her.

Yet… he did.

49

I nursed my coffee and munched. A Bloody Mary (virgin unfortunately), thickly buttered toast with raspberry preserves, poached eggs, and a small carafe—plus a hefty surcharge on Jack's credit card. This must be how Kevin McCallister felt when he got stranded in New York with Trump and Tim Curry. Room service rocked. The honeymoon suite was also amazing. A separate sitting quarters that included its own bath, divided by the master bedroom door. Or as they used to say on *MTV Cribs*: "Where the magic happens." Not in this case. Ears on alert, I listened for signs of life beyond the shut door. I wasn't exactly in the mood to watch Jack slink around, battered, and hungover, shooting me wounded looks.

All clear. Other than my chewing, silence.

Good. I still had time to sit in peace. Reaching for the coffee—an Italian blend of some sort but truthfully, I never could tell the difference after adding copious amounts of sugar and creamer—my wedding ring caught the sunlight streaming in, right into my eye. "Ouch!" Hands over my eyes, I fought momentary blindness. "Fucking ring," I said. Oh, how things changed! The ring used to give me such a thrill and now, I'd come to despise it. When Jack popped the question—taking me on a surprise, romantic hike, hiding the ring box under a carefully curated picnic lunch—I hesitated for the barest second, pushing aside Grammy's voice in the back of my mind. *Casey, think about it.*

I *did* think about it… I just came to the wrong decision.

At first, the ring felt oddly heavy on my finger. Not that it was huge or anything. It was a dainty, modest solitaire. Because I'm a nosy bitch, I looked up the very same ring online and saw Jack spent upwards of $750 on it. To a college student with a part-time job—it seemed exorbitant. While studying for my MCAT, sometimes the diamond distracted me, reminding me that *someone* loved me. Who cared if Jack wasn't perfect? No one was. But like a car driven off the lot, Jack's value depreciated significantly after the "I Do's."

Still… I'd never have thought we'd end up like this. Sleeping in separate rooms in a honeymoon suite. Instead of a healthy glow from a vigorous fuck session, Jack sported a matching set of shiners. I *really* hadn't meant to hurt him, at least, that's what I told myself—even though I knew *that* was a lie too. As far as I was concerned, he'd earned it.

When our honeymoon stage wore thin and real life started back up, things changed. For starters, I was a married college student—automatically in a different category compared to my classmates who, for the most part, were all single and ready to mingle. Other than taking a week and a half off for the Maui honeymoon, I was still deep in the throes of MCAT prep *and* working a part-time job, while Jack joined a local accounting firm. The formerly exciting, can't-get-enough-of-each-other, morphed into a sort of despondency. Like any woman with no real close friends of her own, I turned to *Cosmo* and tuned in to articles on how to improve one's sex life. Place an ice cube in my mouth Place an ice cube in my mouth and give him a blowjob? Tried it. He went limp in my mouth. Lingerie. Did it, but only once. The lace gave me a rash that required a prescription for Prednisone.

The way things were going now—Jack throwing himself at me, who much rather would go down on tiramisu than her husband—it was like someone tossed an UNO reverse card on our marriage. Rather than admiring my ring like the Casey of old, I was wondering how much I might get if I hocked it, cleared out Jack and my accounts, and ran away in the night with Eleanor.

As expected, when Jack roused—sulk city. I was on my last bite of toast when Jack's fist rattled the locked door in its frame, scaring the shit out of me. Half-masticated toast went down like a brick, scraping my esophagus. "What do you want?" I choked out.

"I need my clothes." Jack said, sounding stuffed up. Except, instead of a sinus infection—broken nose.

Rolling my eyes, I rolled off the bed and opened the door for him. A cloud of body odor, unbrushed teeth, and Jack Daniels lingered about him like a poltergeist. Looked bad too. Rocky Balboa after a few rounds with Apollo Creed. Without another word or sparing me a glance, Jack walked in and started riffling through the duffle bag he'd packed us. I hadn't even given it a second thought, using the provided toiletries, and sleeping in my undies. I cringed when he moved a pair of pink fuzzy handcuffs into view. It would be naïve to think he hadn't used them with someone else. He'd come home one too many times reeking of cheap perfume. Putting two and two together wasn't exactly difficult. Disgust. Look at him. My husband. The human red flag. And I ignored it. Made excuses.

So, what if Jack liked to drink? Me too! We were college students. It was expected. Except when Jack drank—it was to complete and utter excess. A Dr. Jekyll and Mr. Hyde situation. Kind, attentive Jack became cruel, flinging compliments barbed with insults—mostly at me. I shrugged it off. He's just drunk, I reasoned. A new job right before tax season would make anyone batty. Unwinding with some drinks with co-workers a few nights a week? How could I really begrudge him that? I rewarded myself with a glass of wine after rigorous study sessions.

Drinks a few days a week escalated. Every other day. Daily. All the fucking time.

And now look at us.

After date night, Jack moved into the guest bedroom. Permanently.

I didn't mind.

50

Freshly showered and sufficiently pilled, I crawled into bed. My thighs ached, thanks to new exercises at cardiac rehab. Exhaustion was a great sleep aide and boy could I use quality shut eye. The kids dropped off early—a blessing. Eleanor's bottom lip pouted outwards 75% of the day with tears on a hair trigger. Teething probably. She was that age. Owen contented himself with video games and judging by the amount of gunfire and laughing I'd heard through the walls; he'd had a great night. Whatever. At least he was occupied and accounted for. Jack was wherever Jack was—and with glee, seeing the clock was 8:36 p.m.—I was happy to turn in early.

Head nestled into my pillow. Eyelids fluttered and my breath deepened.

I was out.

———

RAIN, a trickle at first, then an outright downpour. Everything in the forest rattled with the deluge. Plinks on large maple leaves, dull smacks on rock and wood alike. A mixture of sweat and precipitation matted my shirt to my chest. Eyes trained to the ground, I followed a trail not unlike Hansel and Gretel's, except instead of bits of bread—blood spatter. Not much. A few dark beads on stones, splashes on bark. Easy to see, once you know what to look for.

Through the bushes ahead, I saw a streak of pale skin. She stepped into a clearing and turned. Eyes locked with mine.

One cheek lay in tatters, the inflicted wounds—courtesy of a knife I held, a faint blush of red at its tip—making an X. Her other cheek was unblemished, save for tears, smeared blood, and snot. An electric flash crawled up my spine. Heartrate increased. So close. All I had to do was catch her.

I lunged forward. Speed was my strong suit. If it came down to a footrace, I'd win every time. Wet dirt gave way to a slick, snotty puddle and gravity yanked my body down, eyes to the stormy sky, and a mixture of mud and bog water enveloped me. The impact forced air from my lungs and involuntarily, I gasped, sucking in brackish water. Everything blackened and a sharp JOLT shook my body. My dental fillings rattled in my jaw.

Rain still, but now pounding on pavement. Heavier. Nature's metronome, lonely but it filled the world at the same time. *Tick. Tick. TICK.*

A flash of yellow and—

CRUNCH. A scream—mine?

I shot upward, gnashing my jaw. A vice-grip gripped my temples. Between my ears felt like a soda shaken within an inch of its life. Ready to blow.

"WAAAAAAAAAAAAAAAAAA!" came an earth-shattering cry, blasting from both the baby monitor on my bedside table and down the hall. Eleanor's nursery. The noise intensified my headache into a roar. I thumbed the monitor

off. Why have it on now? Our neighbors had to have already heard Eleanor's screams and might as well preserve the battery life. Standing up, I swayed, fighting a sense of vertigo. Room wavered. Closed my eyes and everything settled. "Hold your fucking horses, I'm coming," I muttered, thrusting my feet into slippers. Out my bedroom door, I treaded down the hallway. Carefully. No sense in waking Owen up—sometimes he slept like the dead and I'd learned that a sleep-deprived Owen wasn't exactly a treat. Not that he ever is.

The guest bedroom door was shut. Muffled snoring seeped through the cracks of the door; Jack, sleeping off his latest garage bender. Even Eleanor's tempest of sound did nothing to penetrate his cocoon. "Sure, sure, I'll just do everything like I always do, *hon*." I said walking past the shut door, my tone conversational despite the empty hallway. Slippers whispered along the hardwood, quieting when I reached Eleanor's nursery and stood, taking in the room. Moonlight streamed in from the full yellow orb hanging in the sky, illuminating dust motes hanging in the air like dancers twirling in a spotlight. A small teddy bear night-light plugged in near The Diaper Genie provided a weak glow, coloring the gender-neutral paint a ruddy orange.

"*WAAAAAAAAAAAAAAA!*" Eleanor screamed. Her fists bunched, balled up in fury. She kicked her legs out, alternating as if swimming, baby fat jiggling with each movement.

"It's okay. I'm here," I said, striving for a soothing tone. Leaned forward, plucking the irate bundle from her crib and cradled her to my chest. Rather than the hoped calming effect, Eleanor redoubled her efforts, flailing. One foot— pointed like a blade—struck me in my still tender, waxy scar tissue.

"Oooooof! Fuck!" The blow reverberated, sending lancing needles straight through my back. Air burst from my lungs—not unlike in my dream, just minutes before. Déjà vu. And like in the forest, chasing women, anger squeezed me in its comforting grip. Fury—a frightening but *powerful* emotion filled me. Still clutching Eleanor tightly, a sudden, *murderous* urge seized me. To hurt her. Like she hurt me. Even as I argued with myself, yelling internally, *CASEY! What are you doing?!?*, my gaze was drawn to the window. Second story. A picture flashed in my mind: shards of glass exploding out into the dark night, littering the air around my daughter.

"Nooooo," I moaned, shaking my head. I fought back a sob, choking it down at the last second. Eleanor quieted, sniveling back tears. The infant's body heat felt like a warm coal against my chest. Tears prickled my eyes and a wave of shame cascaded throughout my body. Why would I even have such a thought?!? *It's the lack of sleep, Casey. That's it.*

Was it?

Well... it wasn't like you acted on it, right? Everyone had intrusive thoughts, right? Driving down the Interstate and that little voice whispered, *what would happen if you yanked the wheel really hard to the left?* You don't actually *want* to die, but the idea possessed a certain attractive quality. As the French say: The call of the void.

No, I would *never* hurt Eleanor.

Would I?

I took a ragged, painful breath in, stifling a sob. Inhaled air stung as if laced with acrid poison, and my diaphragm shuddered. Another deep breath in, less caustic than before. Fresh oxygen cleared my head. Chased away repugnant ideas, whispered by that voice—driving them off like a night watchman clearing a group of mischievous teenagers from a graveyard on Halloween night. Not to say they wouldn't return. They might.

What if Eleanor wasn't safe *because* of *me*?

Eleanor stirred and I tried to push away my guilt. She

wailed. Bathed in moonbeams that slowly receded as the night bled on, I tried soothing her. "Tut, tut, there, there, baby," I said, low-pitched. Rocked back and forth. I snuck glances at the window, trying (and failing miserably) to drive the image of shattered glass from my mind.

51

L ike clockwork, every fifteen minutes Eleanor screamed. Volume sailed from 10 to an 11, like that stupid *Spinal Tap* movie Jack loved quoting. Eleanor's lungs made a tornado siren jealous—all undulating noise demanding strict attention. With each outburst, I rose like a zombie from bed, weary, each knotted muscle aching, and shambled down the long hallway to Eleanor's room. The distance felt like it increased each time. My head still ached, slightly dulled by two Tylenol I dry-gulped earlier.

Brilliant oranges and yellows flecked the horizon— herald of the coming dawn. Treetops shivered under a light breeze, bobbing slowly in and out of view of the nursery window. I jerked my gaze from the glass, dropping my eyes but still—shards exploded outwards in my mind's eye. Unease clutched me in its grip, and I sighed.

Eleanor had been at this for *hours*. Hours and *hours* of ear-piercing screeching. As awful as it sounded, I understood why parents snapped, exhaustion and bone-weariness overwhelming rational thought. Hands reaching into the crib, doing *anything* to make the goddam noise stop. Worse? I had no clue what her problem was. Teething? Maybe—she did have two budding nubs poking through irritated gums. A teething ring fresh from the freezer and a dose of Motrin did nothing to assuage her irritability. *What did she want?* Eleanor eschewed any offered bottles. The thermometer continually read 98.2: no fever, although she protested mightily each time I checked—understandable, I too regarded the rectum as an exit only orifice, but rectal temperatures *were* most accurate. Plenty of piss and poo in her diapers, although I couldn't completely rule out GI upset. Some of the organic spinach I'd used yesterday looked a little bit off, but I wasn't about to head back to the store for more.

WHAT DID SHE WANT? Was she colicky? Was she testing my sanity? WHAT?

Each time, I calmed my baby, I marveled at how her skin assumed the same shade as a prize-winning tomato. The thin rope holding my patience in check steadily frayed with each passing minute. It was holding—at least, for the moment. A flame named Eleanor, burned the remaining threads with exquisite slowness and surgical precision. *Don't lose it, Casey. Hold it together.* With each blink, grit collected in my eyes, and crushing fatigue tugged my shoulders forward. Each time Eleanor started crying, I wasn't sure whether I'd laugh or cry. Or both. After the pitiful crying jags, I laid her down, hopeful she'd finally cried herself out. Tears streaked her chubby cheeks but… no new waterworks. I thought, *that was it. She'll drop off right away.* Her breathing slowed, and the promise of sleep hung thickly in the air. I tiptoed back down the hall, hoping against hope that I might snatch a few zzz's. Just a few minutes of sleep; was that so much to ask?

And when my eyelids fluttered shut—for the briefest of moments, a hair longer than a blink—like clockwork, the screaming ramped back up. Forget Chinese water torture or pulling a person's fingernails out, the CIA (or whoever tortured in the name of the United States of America these days) ought to make their prisoners care for pissed off infants on minimal sleep. Anyone's spirit would break.

Fifteen minutes went by before she quieted. I put her down with the delicacy one used to handle a grenade and pulled her door shut behind me. Jaw cracked as I let out an immense yawn that made my toes twitch in my slippers. Giving my eyes a good rub with the heel of my hand, I blinked and saw that Eleanor's cries had stirred another.

Jack.

He'd exited the guest bedroom (or as I liked to think of it, *his* new bedroom), *hours* before he normally woke to get ready for work. Shocking. Dim morning light showcased red spindles threading the white of his eyes. Skin hung from his cheeks, giving the barest hint of jowls. Head jutted forward, perched precariously on his neck, he shambled like a man of eighty. It was like looking into the future, seeing how Jack would look when elderly. *Assuming* he lasted that long. Alcoholics were notorious for totaling cars. Assuming an accident didn't claim him, he was sure to develop cirrhosis, a rather nasty disease.

Another shriek blasted from the nursery. Jack thrust his hands up over his ears. "Jesus, can't you shut that kid up?" He bore an absurd resemblance to one of those monkeys: see no evil, hear no evil, speak no evil. Uncanny.

I shot him a glare. "What do you suggest I do, Jack? Tie her up and shove balled up socks in her mouth so you can get your precious sleep? Drug her until she stops breathing? Drop her off at the fire station? Hmmm? I'm all ears."

He dropped his gaze. "I don't know," he mumbled.

"Well… how about you shut the fuck up then?"

A look of surprise crossed his face and his mouth dropped open. I waited, wondering what bullshit would come out. Reconsidering, he snapped his jaw shut, and without another word, slammed the door, prompting another chorus of screams. Faintly, I thought I heard "bitch" on the other side of the door but with all the noise, who could really tell?

"Fuckin' asshole," I said, in a louder voice than necessary. I hoped Jack heard me. Help wasn't coming from Jack, useless prick. Not that I wanted him around. But it was *his* kid bawling and the fact of the matter was, he conceived her through his own thoughtlessness. The cavalry wasn't coming, although in a pinch, I could call my mom for help. Although, calling in the early morning hours—not a great idea. Dad recently had an abnormal stress test and was waiting for his cardiac cath to be approved by insurance.

A phone call before 6 a.m. universally meant bad news, and there was no sense in overtaxing his heart with undue excitement. A resigned sigh escaped my lips; no more sleep for me. Not even a doze. Might as well give up trying. Eleanor's jag of screaming prompted by Jack's slammed door dealt with, I was dead standing. Dying for a pick-me-up. Might as well take advantage of the calm, however brief it was. Coffee. Caffeine soothed all wounds. Well, except maybe for caffeine poisoning. I glanced at Eleanor. Sleeping. Or dozing. Not crying. Please God stay quiet.

I tiptoed downstairs and moving with as much stealth as I could muster, poured coffee beans into the grinder. Dreamt of a steaming cup of java and sitting down with a book. A stack of books from the local library's True Crime section was awaiting me.

Freshly ground coffee beans tickled my nose, making me almost feel human despite the lost hours of sleep.

Almost.

WAHHHHHHHHHHHHHHHHHH.

God, it never ended, did it?

52

On reaching Eleanor's room, I frowned.

Something was off.

I knew I'd shut the door, remembering the *click* it made on latching. But… the door was ajar, allowing a small sliver of weak sunlight into the hallway, illuminating my slippers. I glanced down the hallway. Jack's door remained firmly shut.

Owen's, also normally closed—

Hung open.

Shit.

Rushing into Eleanor's room, even on entering, I felt it —different. *Wrong.* Something dark and oppressive. An iron scent hung in the air, not overpowering but there. Tossing Eleanor's blanket off her, I recoiled, clapping my hand to my mouth to keep from shrieking. Breath warmed my palm and stomach rolled with nausea.

Blood. *So much blood.*

Eleanor's mint green onesie, rather than being uniform in color, had streaks of crimson throughout, reminding me of a tiger's stripes. Fat tears rolled off Eleanor's cheeks and she let out pitiful mews as I hurriedly undressed her. I took in the horror Owen inflicted upon his little sister. Oh, there was no doubt in my mind who was the culprit—only one person in this house was capable of such depravity. As I inspected my daughter's wounded body, my rage grew, Owen's actions fanning the flames of my ire. My breath quickened.

Everything came down to this moment, as I knew it would one day. The day that Owen crossed the line, and I was forced to act. Thin red lines crisscrossed Eleanor's body. Head, arms, and legs were spared her big brother's assault but her torso—mostly her chubby stomach and flanks—were irrevocably marked and would surely scar. Beads of blood dripped from several of the larger cuts, the longest of which was about the length of my thumb and was located directly over Eleanor's belly button. It wasn't terribly deep, nowhere near any vital vessels and Eleanor wasn't in danger of bleeding out but… just a little more pressure and Owen would have sliced into her abdomen, maybe nicking the small intestine or God forbid, puncturing her aorta. Small white bubbles of fat protruded from the big wound, curdling my stomach. The smaller ones had already begun to clot and were well on their way to forming scabs. I picked my squalling daughter up and pressed her to my chest. "There, there baby, it's okay. It's alright, Momma's here." Instantly, Eleanor calmed, taking in a gusty inhale and sniffling back tears. Warmth bloomed against my chest, followed by a sticky wetness: Eleanor's blood, staining my shirt. Briefly, I thought about taking her with me to my bedroom and changing my shirt but…

There was no point. I had some unfinished business, and it would likely prove messy.

I had to put a stop to this. It had already gone on for far too long.

Eleanor quieted and slackened in my arms. Her soft exhalations puffed on my shoulder. Thankfully, she'd dropped off quickly, exhausted from her tribulations.

Gingerly, I pulled her away from my body and set her down in the crib, examining the cuts as I laid her down. Counted nine. They followed no obvious pattern, no cryptic pentagrams, or swastikas. I imagined Owen's gleeful expression as he inflicted pain upon his defenseless sister, randomly selecting squares of skin to disfigure. Had his grin widened while watching blood well up? Did he feel an electric tingle in the pit of his stomach, a feeling that would mutate, becoming far more powerful after hitting puberty?

And what had Owen used—what tool had he selected for his nefarious deed?

Given my child's predilections for violence, I'd long hidden away all sharp implements. Tucked them away in places he wouldn't think of looking or removed them from the house altogether. There was the knife block in the kitchen… but only I knew the combination. It couldn't be that. I wouldn't put it past Owen to fashion a shank from some common household item, carving a bar of soap into a weapon.

My eyes swept over the gashes, examining them closely.

Squinted.

They reminded me of something…

No, none of these formed an X, not even if I unfocused my eyes a bit. I thought of blood running down my leg into the shower drain, a faint hiss escaping my lips after I nicked my ankle with the razor. Closer, but no.

Jim. Jim and his stupid office, that was it! I remembered the puke-worthy inspirational posters that made me want to set the place on fire and the uncomfortable chair that sagged in the middle just outside his office, perfect for waiting—not. Five minutes late, Jim, not me. I had no other place to go other than physical therapy hell and was *always* on time. Again, that Type-A personality at work. I remember being bored out of my mind, twiddling my thumbs. Then his door opened, and a young woman came out. Her face was blotchy, eyes puffy from crying, and her sweatshirt sleeves were pushed up over her elbows, revealing innumerable thin scars—some red, some a silverish white—over pale forearms. A cutter, one of those poor souls who inflicted pain upon their body to feel *something* or in turn, created wounds to relieve emotional pain. I'd seen the *Afterschool Specials*. Feeling my eyes lingering on her scarred skin, she hurriedly pushed her sleeves down, casting her eyes downward as she hurried past me. *That* was *exactly* what these wounds looked like, although the woman's wounds were old, and Eleanor's were—unfortunately—quite fresh and not self-inflicted. Such crisp, precise lines, almost surgical, as if they'd come from a scalpel wielded by an expert physician. Steel flashed in my mind's eye, and I gasped, the answer coming to me.

Jack. Of course.

Last year, he decided he wanted to grow out his facial hair, hoping to cultivate a beard like Jason Momoa in *Game of Thrones*. Not that he told me that, but I didn't have to be Sherlock to figure out his motivation. He'd developed quite the jealous streak over Khal Drogo, his eyes narrowing and lips pursing when I went into raptures each time he graced the screen. Jack had been so proud, crowing over the subscription box when it was delivered. One of those kits they advertised on TV and podcasts, and within a week, a conglomeration of unnecessary shit overtook the bathroom counter: beard oil, beard balm, shampoo and conditioner, a brush, and scissors and—

An old-fashioned straight razor kit—fiendishly sharp and utterly unnecessary. Only an old timey barber-surgeon had any business wielding such an implement. Jack's beard cultivation went about as well as my pregnancy with Eleanor. Rather than a thick, luscious beard, his facial hair grew in patchy like a dog afflicted with mange. He persisted for a time, hoping the patches would fill in, but all for naught. One morning he came down, clean-shaven (leaving a disgusting amount of hair in the bathroom for me to clean up) and all the beard-care supplies mysteriously disappeared. I figured Jack gave them to one of his friends with prodigious facial hair and promptly forgot about it. But clearly, my son had gotten his nasty little hands on the straight razor kit, squirreling it away for a rainy day. For a special occasion like today.

It was obvious what had happened: Eleanor's cries woke the sleeping monster and he'd exacted his revenge on his sister for interrupting his coveted slumber. Again, my eyes crawled over Eleanor's marred torso. We'd gotten lucky Owen elected to inflict superficial wounds, barely breaking through the delicate skin but… what would happen next time?

A voice whispered, reminding me, *there will be no next time, will there?*

I shook my head. No, there would be no next time.

Owen's behavior would only escalate, it was practically forecast in the stars. If I allowed a next time, Owen might stab his sister, leaving Eleanor to bleed out. Or maybe, desiring a more hands-on approach, he'd wrap his hands around his little sister's throat and choke her until the life ebbed away from her?

No. I wouldn't allow it, wouldn't allow my son—a demon masquerading as a human—to hurt *anyone* else, *especially* not my daughter.

Something within me broke, a levee gave way, and a murderous urge filled me as I pictured Owen tiptoeing down the hallway, watched him pull the small stepstool away from the changing table, climbing up to look in at his sister, taking the straight razor from the pocket of his pajama pants and—

Eleanor's cries broke through my thoughts and my ears rang. The headache I'd woken with worsened, and with each wail, Eleanor tightened the vice-grip around my temples. Another quarter turn with each fresh cry. *Squeezing.* My vision blurred, from lack of sleep and from the headache well on its way to a migraine, the type that incapacitated its sufferer, leaving them retching, until they brought up only acidic bile.

Rage boiling my blood, I re-snapped the blood-stained onesie and laid Eleanor down, giving her a soft kiss on her forehead. Eleanor quieted again. Labeling the feeling rolling through me as anger was far too simple; it grew exponentially, taking root in my mind and spread like a germ throughout my body, pumped to all my tissues by my trusty new heart. Infecting me. My fists clenched.

The nursery took on a dreamy cast, fuzzy around the edges. Yellow walls pulsed and breathed, wavering. Dawn had given way, sun bright outside the window. The barest hint of wind ruffled the treetops. Spring would soon bloom out there, a time of rebirth and renewal.

For some. And maybe… for me. And Eleanor.

Life stretched out in front of me, images streaking through my mind: a previously happy marriage, now loveless; separate bedrooms; Owen—malicious, and unrepentant; my precarious health, teetering on a tightrope, maintained by only good luck—which was often in short supply—and a truckload of medications. The only thing that brought me any measure of joy was my daughter. And she was in danger. Owen revealed what brutality he was capable of and *that* would only escalate.

And I feared what I might be capable of too… the sudden fury that seized me, completely unlike me, when I thought of tossing Eleanor out the window. Shards ripping through Eleanor's tender flesh, a blood-curdling cry as she sailed towards the ground…

No. I would protect Eleanor from harm.

Even if that meant protecting Eleanor from myself.

The voice whispered then, speaking in low, reserved tones. I listened intently to words that suggested—*no*—instructed. Forehead wrinkles smoothed, worry lines receded. My lips curved into the hints of a smile.

My mind stilled. Calmed. A tranquility washed over me.

Take control, the voice said.

I wrapped Eleanor in a fluffy blanket—a gift from Jack's boss and wife—swaddling her. Grinning giraffes marched along the blanket's edges. She let out a contented sigh and closed her eyes, drifting off. "I love you baby, don't forget that," I whispered, kissing my daughter for one of the last times.

I retraced my steps, closing the nursery door.

The time had come to reclaim what was left of my life.

53

I crept down the hallway. Framed photos stared down from either side. Owen's serious toddler face, just before his diagnosis—his *issues*. Oppositional Defiant Disorder: a bullshit, flowery name for child psychopath. With each outburst, each refusal of affection—giving and receiving— my love for him diminished until it snuffed out completely, like a candle extinguished at the coming dawn. Not that I could admit that to anyone. How to admit that my feelings towards my son veered wildly between frank dislike and downright hate? Mothers don't say such things, at least, not out loud.

Glancing to the right, I saw the picture of me and Jack on our wedding day. I was dressed in the requisite white, playing the part of a deceptively virginal, blushing bride and Jack beamed, our arms intertwined. The mere sight of Jack clenched my stomach with disgust, and I fought against a rising gorge of vomit and swallowed sour spit, relocating puke to my stomach—barely.

The last picture right before the stairs—one of the entire family, taken a few months after Eleanor's birth. I wore a sweater that tried to camouflage my LVAD, but my torso still looked bulky, and my face was puffy—full of water weight. The Stay Puft Marshmallow Man from *Ghostbusters* had nothing on me then. Owen stood away from the rest of us, seated on a fallen tree, his face horribly blank. Everyone else, even baby Eleanor, gazed into the camera lens, wearing grins. Jack's smile was radiant as he held Eleanor in his arms, eyes crinkled up at the corners. My gaze lingered on my face. My eyes—lifeless and dead. Smile plastic, fake. A snapshot in time that told a lie, showing a "happy" family that was anything but. Instead of feeling the expected infusion of warm love on seeing my family, an icy chill burned in my chest while the rest of me radiated a sickly heat, borne not of love but of a complete and utter rage.

Without thought, I cocked my right hand back, fingers clenched in a fist and punched the picture, splintering glass and cracking the wooden frame. Knuckles came away crisscrossed with cuts—reminding me of Eleanor's chubby belly. Blood dripped to the floor, leaving red dots that looked absurdly like button candies on the rich hardwood. Abused knuckles went into my mouth and I savored their coppery flavor. Nostrils flared, feasting on the scent and my mouth filled with saliva, as if I were about to dine on a gourmet meal. Between my legs grew wet and buzzed with anticipatory heat.

Leaving the shattered glass in a heap near the stairs, carefully picking a path that avoided errant shards, I made my way downstairs. My body moved easily, my legs mostly bare, partially covered by a well-worn pair of Jack's boxer shorts. As much as I disliked him, I had to admit, his clothing was rather comfortable. With each step, shadows of muscles danced beneath my skin, more toned than they'd been in years, thanks to cardiac rehab.

The kitchen.

Soft light splashed across the cabinets—not a splotch of ugly black paint in sight—from a small night-light plugged in by the sink; a cartoon shark held a bulb clenched in jaws drawn up in a grin. Owen's doing. He picked it out during a shopping trip, and I'd reluctantly purchased it after he pitched an absolute shitfit after I told him no. The elderly woman in line in front of us shot me a dagger-edged look through tortoise-shell glasses perched on her nose and the bag boy glowered at me as if I were the devil incarnate. Sheepishly, I'd tossed the nightlight on the belt, all the while thinking of how *lovely* it would feel to paddle Owen's ass to a red pulp. Fuck that stupid light! Gritting my teeth, remembering their disapproving stares, I smashed the nightlight, shattering the bulb. Cartoon shark cracked in half. A fresh bloom of cuts appeared, joining the others. The kitchen's newfound darkness clung to me like a funeral shroud, inviting and comfortable. I'd always loved the shadows.

The voice whispered to me again, and I tilted my head, listening to its rough words, inviting the stranger into roost. *To stay*. Standing in the kitchen's gloom, I savored the silence, thinking.

Once what I considered nightmares became treasured dreams, and while their memories evoked a sick pleasure within me, another part craved something *much* more violent. *Bloodier.*

A dark part of me had been slumbering—resting fitfully —had awakened, spurred on by Owen's actions, its broad nose sniffing about eagerly, delighting at how I'd spilled my own blood in the upstairs hallway and now here, in the kitchen. Some ancient evil within me woke at the first taste of blood on my lips and cried out for more, desiring an even more sanguinary climax. It wished to feast on others' pain, fattening itself on the ichor of suffering, growing corpulent. Rejoicing in its newfound resurgence; it would live again as it had within the hearts and souls of others throughout history. Despots. Tyrants. Others like Hitler, innumerable kings and queens, human monsters, and crowd favorites like Ted Bundy... even The X-Killer, all would have nodded along in grim understanding. They too heeded the call of the beast; the siren call that drove one to kill, kill, kill until satisfied and spent. I embraced the monstrosity with open arms and listened intently to its grim desires.

54

Hunger rose within me, a physical need for sustenance. I was ravenous. Eating on its own wouldn't ameliorate the anger dominating me—it needed something else. It would stop my hollow stomach's grumbling at least. A woman should always take care of her appetite before embarking on other business. I made a sandwich, tossing two pieces of wheat bread in the toaster, smothering each side with peanut butter and honey. Meal was demolished within seconds. Using a blood-stained finger, I scraped up the last traces of peanut butter on my plate, bringing them to my mouth. The nutty taste paired quite nicely with dried blood.

Hunger satiated; I contemplated.

The sinister whisper demanded *blood*, and I hated to disappoint. Standing with my empty plate at the counter, my eyes alighted on the padlocked knife block—a wedding gift from a friend. Every knife snugly in place—more damning evidence that Owen used the straight razor as I suspected. Oh, how my mother had objected to my acceptance of such a gift, demanding I return it to the store and give the gift giver a piece of my mind! She'd been so damn upset about it, exclaiming with a shrill voice clouded with worry, "Knives are bad luck! Don't these people know they signify a relationship that's broken or will become broken? Everyone knows that! Don't invite such luck into your new marriage!"

Her superstitions seemed childish then and I laughed them off, but I had to admit... she might have been on to something. The revelation made me giggle.

09-02-17 and now, knives were free for the taking.

I selected the longest. Its wooden handle felt reassuring in my grip, like it *belonged* there, and the 10-inch blade cheerfully winked in the sunlight. Grabbing the honing steel knife sharpener from the block, I spent several minutes readying it. No sense in embarking on my dark business with a dull knife, after all. Once sharpened to my heart's content, I drew the knife across my right palm—testing its cutting ability—with barely an iota of pressure and relished the blood springing up beneath the newly honed blade. A thin bite of pain, but it wasn't a bad feeling, instead it reminded me of rough sex—where hair pulling and biting were a welcome painful pleasure.

The grandfather clock sounded from the living room: *GONG, GONG*, alerting all in range it was now 7 o'clock. Time to wake up, motherfuckers! Typically, I rousted Owen around this time, for his *special*—not to mention hideously expensive—school. This task fell solely to me since Jack couldn't bother himself with such things. Child-rearing tasks naturally fell to the woman, in Jack's opinion, as did most everything else. Well, I intended to keep on schedule. Owen would soon wake.

I took in a deep breath, fighting back excitement threatening to overwhelm me. Steeling my nerves, enjoying the waves of cascading elation washing over me on the precipice of my upcoming task, I made for the stairs again, darting up without sound.

I pushed Owen's bedroom door open and took in a

room filled to the brim with toys Owen regularly maimed. Near my left foot, a Care Bear head gazed up with dark, lifeless eyes. White cotton candy stuffing dangled from the base of its head. Body was strewn near the closet; based on the heart symbol emblazoned on the belly: Tenderheart. Quietly, I edged to Owen's bedside; greedy eyes drinking him in like a whisky connoisseur sampling a fine vintage. Had I not known he'd been lurking about and cutting the living shit out of his little sister; I might have thought him almost *innocent* looking.

But I knew better, didn't I?

Owen was either feigning sleep—and doing a fine job at it—or had fallen back to sleep, satiated by his cruel acts. Normally he slept on his stomach (like his dear ol' mom), this morning no exception. Ruffled hair well on the way to bed head tipped to the left, his bangs flapping with each noisy exhalation. Gusts of air came out as thin whistles, a consequence of a chronically stuffed-up nose. Owen was allergic to literally anything and everything that swirled in the air and throughout the year, he cycled through allergies to trees, grasses, ragweed. Naturally, he resisted taking his daily Claritin since it was his life's mission to be an obstinate cunt about *everything*. Before having children, I never realized how maddening they could be about such things. Well, he wouldn't have to worry about taking a pill again.

Scooby-Doo and the gang flounced about on his fleece pajamas—tops and bottoms. Owen's head rested atop his pillow and cautiously, I probed underneath. Cold metal touched my fingertips, and I carefully grasped and pulled it out.

As I suspected, the straight razor—the smoking gun, so to speak.

A thin streak of tacky blood clung to the fiendishly sharp blade; proof Owen had been up to no good. No need to call the crime lab to verify it was Eleanor's blood. The proof was in the pudding, as they said. I gazed at the blade. Pictured it dipping down, cutting Eleanor's fragile skin, blood welling up from wounds. With anger in my heart, I tossed the razor behind me, heard it land softly, cushioned by either carpet or maimed stuffed animals.

Nestled under the covers next to Owen was the *only* stuffed animal he hadn't torn apart: a narwhal with a long white horn. Disquiet filled me. Owen really loved that thing, assuming he were capable of such a complex emotion as love. I highly doubted that but—

Still, feeling slightly ridiculous, I grabbed the narwhal and turned it to face the wall. Something about the stuffed animal having a front row seat gave me a case of the creeps and goosebumps bloomed on my forearms, prickling fine arm hair. Not that the goosebumps were only from *that*… no… a distinct delight filled me—a lustful quality that had nothing to do with sex in any shape or form. It was *intoxicating* and I understood how someone might crave it, like a craving for salt and vinegar chips.

Owen's violence wouldn't end with superficial cuts, foolish thinking it would. And while I might have been ignorant in my prior life—what, with marrying an idiot like Jack and all—I wasn't a *fool*. No, I was much smarter than anyone gave me credit for, straight A's notwithstanding. Owen was the type of monster that escalated, committing more and more heinous atrocities, until it involved the loss of life.

And who was his easiest, most accessible target?

Eleanor.

I bared my teeth, imagining I looked equal parts protective mother panther sheltering her cub and deranged. Eyeing my son, I saw the man he would grow into, supported by a system that rewarded white male mediocrity, consistently overlooked because he just wasn't *that* interesting. What horrible dastardly deeds would he commit, flying under the radar?

He would pass as charming (he already had experience in that realm, playing the part of the adorable big brother to everyone else) and persuasive when needed—downright manipulative with a deft hand when required. Not drop dead gorgeous but not ugly either. He had Jack's nose—a bit too large for his face and had inherited his other features from my side of the family. Owen would draw women in, like a murderous spider luring unsuspecting flies to its web. Good-looking enough to be exciting, but not devastatingly handsome in a way that was intimidating to the opposite sex.

Women would think it was *their* idea to approach *him*, foolishly assuming they were in control of the situation, thus initiating their fatal chase at Owen's hand. The lucky ones might get a few bruises and broken bones, frequent visits to the local ER in the middle of the night, always with a BS story about falling down the stairs or running into a pesky doorknob. I shuddered to think what he might do to the unlucky ones. Torture? A slow, drawn-out death? The visions of the nightmares that haunted me each evening?

I paused. The moral part of me protested. *Owen is your son! Your flesh and blood. What kind of mother would you be if you went about this dark business? Stop. You can still stop. It's not too late.*

Then the other voice whispered to me, and I grimly nodded along with its silken words. It was right… I was a *great* mother. Protecting my daughter, the one true innocent in all this disaster, plus, I was doing a favor to humanity.

Bending over, I clutched the long knife in my right hand, keeping it hidden behind my back. I roughly shook Owen awake, drawing immense pleasure at his stunned cry. I doubted he had been pretending to sleep—he'd fallen asleep the second his head hit the pillow (razor underneath, like a macabre tooth awaiting a pink-garbed Murder Fairy). Had Owen been the slightest bit awake, I imagined he would have replayed the previous events of the night, thinking how lovely it felt raking the razor across his sister's chubby stomach, watching beads of blood bloom like drops of condensation on the windows.

As if sensing my poisonous thoughts, Owen thrust his arm up. Even in his sleepy state, striking out at me. Hoping to inflict pain, suffering.

Not anymore.

I hissed, "Keep your hands off my daughter, you little shit." My words dripped with poisonous contempt and even as they spilled from me, they sounded nothing like the voice I had grown used to. Not that it mattered.

Quick as a viper, I grabbed Owen's wrist with my left hand and—in a well-practiced motion—wrenched his arm behind his back, just as I had the day that I slapped the living daylights out of him. The Paint on the Cabinets Day: A day that lived in infamy. As much as a mother couldn't… *shouldn't* admit things… I *enjoyed* slapping Owen. He'd grown into a cruel child—through no discernable fault of my own —and would become a brutal monster, given enough time. Remembering the sharp clap against his cheek, the sting in my palm, and watching his head reel from the force of it all… how it sent joy flowing through me! Under my palm, Owen's tendons and bones grinded together from his forced position.

The sense of control I exerted over my son—destined to inflict pain and suffering on any he came across—was pure euphoria. Endorphins poured into my bloodstream and made me powerful. The only time I even came close to such exhilaration? College. Jack smuggled pot brownies to the Florida beach during Spring Break, and we proceeded to get completely and utterly stoned. Someone handed out Molly and I'd swallowed an orange pill that looked like candy, stamped with cartoonish shapes on either side. An hour later—minus clothes—we floated in the bathwater warm Atlantic, all limbs intertwined. A deep, serene peace took hold. Pleasure invaded every nerve ending. The half-moon illuminated our night, its moonbeams scattering across the scant waves, giving the moment a certain mystical quality. The sounds of the night: water breaking as creatures dove in and out, the far away sounds of a DJ at a local trendy hotel spinning trance tunes, and the sounds of my friends' and future husband's laughter.

That had felt like *heaven*, and I wasn't certain I'd ever feel such nirvana again.

This was even better.

Owen cried out, struggling to free himself. Sucked in a deep breath. I saw what he was aiming to do. Filling his lungs with air so he could shriek and, with any luck, bring my dead-to-the-world husband running—assuming the noise penetrated his hangover haze. Couldn't let *that* happen. Even armed with a knife, I would have a hell of a time fighting off an alcoholic lard-ass with plenty of weight and adrenaline behind him. And he alone could stop me from protecting Eleanor—not to mention countless others.

Moving with a speed that startled me, I drew the knife from behind my back and time slowed. Each second stretched into minutes, each moment warm and pleasant like the tepid Florida beach, when I rolled under the influence of Molly, skinny-dipping, with a nice Indica body high.

I took everything in, taking immense pleasure in all that followed.

Owen inhaled, one of his last breaths, as it came to be— readying himself for a primal tribal cry—

And… his breath faltered. Owen's eyes widened, pupils dilating as they crawled over the glistening knife, now in full view. Expressions of defeat, betrayal, and a sinister hatred flickered across his face, before settling on a contortion of facial features more consistent with utter terror.

It was the realization for Owen that *I* was in charge. *In control.*

Finally.

The knife moved, almost of its own accord, and I pressed the blade down to Owen's neck, his trachea shuddering with unspent cries. Not exerting the pressure needed to split the skin.

Yet.

Metal caught the sunlight and the knife shimmered. Bobbed up and down rhythmically, resting against Owen's pulsing carotid artery safely ensconced in layers of skin and tissue. Owen's heart rate quickened. Acrid fear filled the air.

Only a thin layer of skin denied the knife entry.

Owen's mouth gaped open soundlessly and lips quivered, threatening to unleash a bellow. I leaned down, applying pressure ever-so-slightly to the blade and—with a flourish—swept my hand to the right.

An explosion of color spurted from Owen's carotid in a thick spray.

The sudden eruption of blood made me think of videos I'd seen of Old Faithful erupting in Yellowstone Park or churning volcanos in the Hawaiian Islands, reminding me of a building orgasm, deliciously close to completion. To the point of no return.

My other senses heightened. Nostrils flared at the coppery, penny scent of Owen's blood and my tongue darted from my mouth, lapping up a spot of blood, bathing my taste buds with it, triggering flavors of umami and fine, dark red vintages. The taste captivated me. Enchanted me. I was a sommelier of torment, able to identify each extract and flavor. There were oaky undertones of unadulterated fear rolling off Owen, leaving a delightful stink. Fear had its own smell: a perfume more addictive than anything else in the world; far worse than nicotine or heroin.

My eyes indulged on a feast of their own. Pulsatile arcs of blood, initially spurting in cascades like a sanguinary geyser quickly lost steam, sputtering as Owen's strong, powerful heart pumped the entirety of his blood volume dutifully onto the walls and floor. I surveyed Owen's skin— once a nice rosy pink—taking on a pallor usually only seen after horrible traumas… or in the morgue after someone bled out.

I was putting a stop to his reign of terror before it truly started.

Only one's death could satiate his awful cravings and I wouldn't let that happen.

And now, for The Grand Finale: Owen's eyes. His pupils were black and absurdly dilated, swimming with abject dread, firmly focused on my face. Overtones of incredulity and blame radiated outwards. What might Owen say, if given the chance? No doubt a curse word or some derogatory comment about my patronage… as if Owen wasn't descended from my loins and shared my ancestors. If only it weren't so. I wished we didn't share an ounce of DNA. Twisting helices rose in my mind, lighting flashing as enzymes knitted code together, following an ancient template of nucleotides, A, T, G, and C. Years of biology classes made the task easy to imagine. And it hammered home the point that we shared sections of DNA. The sheer thought disgusted me.

Another thought occurred to me. *Are you any better than Owen?* Here I stood, taking away life but for far different reasons.

No. We were not the same. I *had* to do it. *Had to.*

I would break this cycle, of men dominating, women submitting, and society allowing it to happen.

Eleanor's face flashed through my mind, two white nubs

poking down from her gums, a delightful squeal rolling from her mouth as she thrust her arms up, wanting a hug from her mother.

Love.

Then streaming tears, red-faced, snot running down, bloody lacerations stamped lewdly against my daughter's soft skin. A motherly instinct rose, my daughter's needs superseding that of my own tainted blood.

Hate.

I plunged the knife deeper, slicing cleanly through the thick rings of Owen's trachea. Air escaped his body and his back shuddered uncontrollably. Each movement flapped the thick cartilage of his trachea about, the strong tissue split by the superior blade.

More blood.

Owen's eyes widened further, thick lashes framing stark white conjunctiva, giving him an almost angelic look, if one ignored the slowing but still steady, stream of blood flowing from his neck. Arms and legs twitched; his muscles crying out sorely for oxygen that never came. I watched his brain dim, neurons trying and failing to make connections to sustain further life. Like houselights in the night, the nerves switched off, one by one. Owen's body stilled, the blood from his neck slowing to a fine trickle. At the onset, with the wicked flashing of the knife, the flow had been a proud river, and now, a dying tributary. Owen's eyelids drooped, appearing weighted down. Eyes unfocused, and I imagined a curtain descending over his vision.

What was he thinking? Were his last images of life replaying, increasing in speed, taking on a freakish sped-up quality? I imagined what he might see: his mother splattered with blood—*his blood*. The sweet smile spreading across my face, serene as if I'd discovered the meaning of life. But I knew that my smile was cold. And *hungry*.

I remembered cradling him after coming home from the

hospital. How I'd loved him then! When he'd been achingly sweet, filled with love. Each night, I sang to him, lulling him to sleep. I cradled him again, my little boy, evil as he was.

"Hush little baby don't say a word, Mama's gonna buy you a mockingbird," the words spilled from out and even though I knew I'd done the right thing, a tear slipped from my eye.

My son died with a shudder and gasp. Body slackened.

A warm draft gusted through my body, filling me with searing heat that blotted away any sense of cold, heating my core. Was I feeling Owen's soul—his earthly form nothing more than a bloody husk—dissipating into the great miasma of beyond?

Maybe. Just as quickly, the sensation ebbed.

My tears dried.

It was done.

I absentmindedly licked Owen's blood clean from the knife, just as I sucked peanut butter off while making my sandwich. Something primal within me had awakened, and it released a heaving sigh of relief. I rested a moment, but the voice had already whispered to me…

It wanted more.

55

While Owen's soul departed the mortal coil, Jack slept fitfully, ignorant to the events taking place within his own home—his son nearly murdering his daughter. His wife murdering his son. As of late, his sleeping hours were restless but for a far different reason than his wife's. It reminded him of the insomnia he suffered after The Breakup. One *Dear Jack* letter and his world crumbled. Back then, alcohol acted as a dual sleep-aid and painkiller: numbing in both respects.

But it didn't stop *everything*—not in the beginning and certainly not now.

Jack's subconscious delighted in torturing him with thoughts of: *What might have been?* Not to say that he didn't think about such things while awake, because he did. He thought about what might have been *all the time*. While reviewing client accounts; sitting in the lunchroom and eating the ham-and-cheese sandwiches Casey packed, each bite tasteless with the texture of sawdust; during the drive from work to the bar; hell, even while sleeping! Morning, evening, night, it didn't matter.

But Jack's best periods of introspection and personal torture came perched on a barstool. While the seat wasn't as comfy as a La-Z-Boy (after about 45 minutes, his ass felt like a mouth deadened by Novocain) there was something pleasant about the bar setting. Or maybe it was the buzz that swarmed around his head—taking the edge off.

Occasionally, he made small talk with fellow patrons—especially those bearing two X chromosomes who had an air of desperation—but mostly, he stared into his glass at the amber elixir. Starting with whisky was best, he preferred the clean, crisp intoxication it offered: warm and light.

It truly was the best part of his day: the initial slip into oblivion.

———

Hours earlier, before Owen set The Day's events in motion, Jack swirled his glass. A thin delight spread through him, hearing the ice sphere tinkling against glass. It had an almost lulling quality, reminding him of a stage hypnotist swinging a watch on a chain. Each clink drew him deeper into a melancholy reverie.

Jack lost himself in the past. In possible futures that were easy to imagine but were never to be. He slugged back whisky, the liquid sparking and igniting, bathing his esophagus in a pleasurable heat.

And he *remembered*.

Remembered balmy summer nights when each inhalation felt furred and thick, like breathing in a dense cloud. Sweat dripped down the small of his back.

Nights were better then.

Because he had Tara.

A large portion of their time was spent in a local park's forgotten corner, long fallen into disarray, thanks to helicopter parents that demanded all playground equipment be removed after a child broke their neck. Teens claimed the spot as their own. It was the perfect place for making out or smoking pot. It was also a prime spot for budding young love.

Jack procured a bottle from a buddy—cheap bottom dollar stuff, but it did the job. Tara and he passed the bottle back and forth, Jack's skin tingling each time their fingertips touched. Forbidden nips of whisky and stolen kisses. Perfection.

He remembered the naked ecstasy shared, shielded from the moon's indifferent eyes by a blanket he filched from the basement. Sipping his drink, he thought of Tara's sweat-slicked skin and the hungry look in her eyes before she pounced on him, tracing her tongue around his lips, and grasping—tugging, *hard*—his hair, making every nerve ending in his scalp burst into flame. Jack's fingers tightened around his perspiring glass. Instead of the coolness of his snifter, he imagined their interlaced fingers and the desperate dance of their tongues exploring each other's mouths; his soul marinating itself in panting gusts that grew in intensity as their frenzied bodies melded together. Then, sheer bliss: a nuclear explosion of pleasure and connection —two wayward souls finally united. A coupling that transcended all earthly limits. Afterwards, they laid on their backs, the thin blanket pulled under their chins, each staring through the trees at the blinking stars above. A sleepy sort of contentment always overtook Jack at this stage: the comedown. Lazily scanning the stars, fixing their position in his mind, he thought about how those same stars would follow them through life together. He'd felt certain of this, in the way only a high schooler deep in the throes of first love could.

Blind certainty was for the young. And for fools.

He'd been both.

———

College came.

Jack departed for the state school with a jam-packed car while Tara elected to travel abroad, bunking in hostels with kindred souls desperate to see the world beyond, tortured artists searching for inspiration in each remote corner, and—

Jean-Paul.

That fucking French prick.

Jack didn't know the specifics regarding this unholy union, but after his "Dear Jack" letter, postmarked from Jean-Paul's hometown of Toulouse—a fact he learned much later—he'd had *plenty* of time to ruminate, structuring a crude timeline of Tara's betrayal.

Initially, she called at every opportunity, bubbling over with stories of her travels: this dish, that drink, this historical landmark, and Jack intently listened, loving her soft twang of pleasure rolling off her words.

The calls came less frequently. Once a week, then biweekly, monthly.

He slept with his fingers curled around the phone, volume cranked, anxious he might miss her *one* call, terrified he'd spend another month imaging what she might be up to.

And with whom.

The answer to that question came when Jack perused pictures Tara posted on Facebook and green tendrils of jealousy wrapped around his lovesick heart. *Poisoning him.* Tara's smiling face, eyes dusted with silver makeup, hair tied back, revealing a studded row of earrings, and a thin whisper of a tattoo behind her right ear. A tattoo—he found out much later—composed of a thin black snake intertwined with the letters "JP."

Jean-Paul.

She wore peach hued denim shorts, a thin tank top that

did nothing to hide mocha-colored nipples having forgone a bra that night, and tattered black Converse—a 18th birthday gift from Jack. Raver jewelry adorned her wrists. In the background, sat a DJ booth awash in a rainbow of lights. Music throbbed with a bass muted by the camera, that went unheard by a stunned Jack, who clicked through the photos with mounting dread.

Tara, firmly ensconced within the crowd of blissed-out people packed together writhing to a secret beat—some sipping drinks from pineapples while others held red Solo cups. A baseball-capped DJ stood on the booth, hands raised as if praying to a God of Sound who held court only in Ibiza; and—

Jack's tender, poisoned heart dropped.

The last photo: Tara wearing a broad grin, cheek to cheek with another man.

Jean-Paul.

His hand was wrapped around Tara's waist, long, lithe fingers draped downwards, fingertips brushing the tops of her skanky shorts. So casual and secure in the knowledge that his face would be buried in her cunt later, his tongue coaxing moans of pleasure from her lips. Anger rose as Jack pictured Tara bucking against JP's eager mouth, her orgasm throttling her body with euphoria. He thought of Tara, dripping wet, two high spots of red coloring her sharp cheekbones, climbing on top of that froggy fuck, straddling him, surrendering herself to him. She probably didn't make *Jean-Paul* slip on a rubber before fucking *him.*

A hot inferno engulfed him, toes curled and cramped, and his jaw tightened until his back molars squeaked. A roiling nausea brought up sour bile that scorched the back of his throat. Fingers flashed over the keyboard with voracity, keys clacking violently as if being tortured.

Tara, who the FUCK is this?

Her flippant reply came hours later:

A friend ☺

The *friend*—as he came to find out after the "Dear Jack" letter—was *considerably* more than that. And the letter? Pitiful. Three hastily scrawled sentences. The Cliff Notes summary essentially amounted to: Get lost.

So—he did.

Like anyone suffering from heartbreak would, he distracted himself by guzzling sugary overpriced drinks at local clubs, fucking women that meant nothing to him after he came. During sex, Jack closed his eyes and pictured Tara under him. Late at night—after last call, if he struck out— he walked home with hunched shoulders and, unable to help himself, logged onto Facebook, scrolling through pictures of Tara and Jean-Paul's disgusting new life. They grinned in selfies with backpacks slung over their shoulders, imposing white peaks in the distance; dined at fancy restaurants with Michelin Star chefs plating six courses; and… Tara thrusted a diamond-encrusted ring finger at the camera, the photo captioned "Jean-Paul asked, and I said yes! I'm engaged!"

After *that* knife to the heart, Jack deserved a *real* bender. He skipped class and popped open his first beer at 10 a.m., pounding tallboys until happy hour. Then shots, mixed drinks, glasses filled with whisky until his vision blurred and wavered, giving the world a relaxed lens he could finally look through without wanting to rip the skin off his bones. On Day 6 of the bender—at a dingy bar where a whip-thin man with furry sideburns and a mullet crooned off-tune ballads, backed by a black guitarist who bore a grim expression as he strummed—Jack met Casey.

Safe Casey. Often, boring Casey, but most importantly: *safe.*

She'd tried—unsuccessfully—to flag down the bartender. Her frantic waving caught his attention at the other end of the bar. Cute, he thought, in a generic, All-American kind of way. The girl next door. Nothing to write home about.

"Need help?!" he'd yelled, cupping his hands together so she'd hear him over Kid Rock-lite's rendition of *Strawberry Wine*.

"What?!" She cupped her hand around her ear. "What did you say?"

"I said, 'Need help'?!" He leaned in, smelling the perfume she wore—Clinique Happy. A flicker shot through him, something just under the surface of his consciousness.

Want?

Desire?

What?

Casey laughed; the pleasing notes barely audible over the wailing music. "My God, YES! I thought for a second there that I'd died and was a ghost trying to order drinks. I didn't think anyone saw me!"

Not true. *He saw her.* Jack dipped his head, his lips nearly touching her ear. "What do you want to drink?"

A Long Island iced tea, as it turned out—a potent drink that had Casey slurring her words after drinking only a third of the cocktail. She'd gazed at him through half-hooded pupils. "You'rre cute, you know. Maybe a little sssad, though. But it makes you broody and… *interesting*." Clearly, she wasn't accustomed to the nightlife of college, confiding in him that she was only out that night because her organic chemistry partner begged her to come. They chatted, retreating to a quiet corner outside in the beer garden. Ignoring the snatches of *How Do I Live?* being completely slaughtered by the drunk redneck. Trisha Yearwood would have been horrified. Casey watched Jack, her pupils not once drifting from his face as he spoke, giving him her 100%

attention, as if no one else in the room or world existed. Only Jack.

They shared, at first the superficial: Favorite movie? Favorite book? Where are you from? Then they delved into deeper topics, emboldened by the liquid courage flowing through them: Do you believe in soulmates? Do you want to get married? What do you want from life?

Truth was, he did believe in soulmates.

Tara.

Always Tara.

But if anyone could make the sting lessen… it was Casey. At least… he hoped.

Theirs was an easy relationship. No big fights but… no massive upswings either. It was *safe*.

Casey was pure sugarcane, pleasing to the tongue but nothing exotic. Tara was like a spoonful of smack, and he'd become hopelessly addicted to her, mainlining her into the fat veins in the crooks of his arms. But Casey? No hurt. No pain. No euphoria. But it was secure, steady, and easy. The sex was good, nothing like it was with Tara but comparing the two was like comparing crap from a high school art show to a painting hanging in The Louvre. No contest.

Their relationship was marked by comfy sweatpants, takeout, and lazy Sunday morning fucking, sharing Bloody Marys at brunch, the smell of Casey still lingering on his skin. He never worried about Casey talking to another guy because… she didn't talk to *anybody* outside her school groups. And she was smart, anxious to apply to medical school after college. Sometimes her intelligence made Jack feel insecure about his own, but he tried to push that aside and was mostly successful.

Casey was so safe and secure. It seemed like a no-brainer. So, Jack asked her to marry him.

And she said yes.

A low-key wedding, followed by a honeymoon in

Hawaii. The in-laws were generous and ponied up the cash for the trip. After sipping drinks from coconuts by the pool, they'd streak up to the room and furiously fuck on crisp white hotel sheets, something Casey couldn't get enough of. When returning from the honeymoon, they settled into a routine that reminded Jack of playing "house" in elementary school.

It was good—at first.

During his free time, Jack tinkered with his car, dreaming of restoring old muscle cars as a career, absently thinking of Tara. Jack had brought up his desire to be a mechanic to his folks during his senior year of high school and they'd laughed the idea off—their son... going to a *trade school?!* Absolutely not! No, their son would have a college degree, even if the subject matter bored him senseless. And it certainly did, further fueling his angst.

Spontaneous sex dropped off, especially since Casey was deeply absorbed in MCAT prep, hoping to apply to medical schools if she scored high enough.

Safety—as it so often did—became a rut.

Something needed to change.

And like plenty of people in flagging marriages, they both thought a baby was just the ticket, a band-aid to cover the widening wound. After discussing it, they felt that they might as well "get it over with" before life further encroached on their plans—before they got too settled in their ways. Plus, a baby *was* the next logical step in their relationship.

Casey scored high on her MCAT—unsurprising since she studied nearly every waking hour—but put her medical school aspirations on the back burner after the positive pregnancy test. "Applying to medical school could wait," Casey said, sharing concerns that she'd be too pregnant to handle the grueling workload of studying sixteen hours a day and thrice weekly anatomy labs. Jack definitively shelved his dreams of opening his own autobody shop (not that his parents would have ever approved) and worked hard as a CPA, even if he despised it.

He'd been certain things would get better.

Owen came into the world, squalling and red faced, filling the delivery room with a strong cry that filled Jack's heart with wonder and love. He had a son. Someone to carry on the Philips family name. Half of his DNA somehow unwound itself and joined with another's, creating life.

Try as he might, Jack couldn't help but wonder what it would be like if it had been Tara instead of Casey, even as he looked at his sweaty, exhausted wife in the delivery room. Jack cradled his son while Casey rested, staring at all the ridges and fine baby down that covered Owen's scalp. His lips were undeniably his mother's, a little rosebud, but the nose—all Jack. And when little Owen reached out and clutched Jack's index finger, massive compared to Owen's tiny hand, a starburst of love surged within his heart.

Casey stayed home, minding the little nugget while Jack looped a tie around his neck and lugged a briefcase around, filled with documents riddled with columns of numbers and credits/debits—providing for his family, just like a man was supposed to do. Casey brought up daycare, but it was an expense they couldn't afford. Jack rushed home each evening, eager to play "airplane" and loaded pureed peas onto a spoon, "landing" them in Owen's waiting mouth. Being a father was wonderful, all fun while Casey took care of the nasty business. Jack couldn't handle the diapers filled with nasty loads of shit that came in a rainbow of colors and smells and he never woke in the night when Owen let out his siren screams. Jack needed his beauty sleep after working all day. The idea that caring for an infant *was* full-time job never occurred to him.

Then Owen was crawling… walking… running. Owen's

personality shone through and for the first time, Jack felt the faintest stirrings of disquiet whispering in the back of his mind. Owen showed no interest in typical father-son activities. His son's eyes only lit up when hurling the ball at faces or testicles. Each day, when Jack came home, Casey told him stories of her day, filled with frustration and irritation. Her mood was stony, like a garden filled with misaligned rocks that tripped up any who tiptoed through, and their sex life petered into non-existence. He'd run a hand up her thigh, walking his fingertips upwards, and she'd turn away, expelling a violent huff of indignation that spoke volumes. No longer did they banter or hold each other's eyes at the dinner table while winding spaghetti around forks, an unseen spark heating the air around them, even if it wasn't the furnace of feelings that Tara invoked long ago.

Life grew cold.

Rather than coming straight home from work, Jack found himself sitting on barstools, gripping a sweating glass filled with elixirs that gave him hope—for a little while at least. It helped dull the sharp discomfort swirling within him. His mind turned from the shitshow of his life—cold-fish wife, worrisome son, shitty job—and he pondered other things, Tara, mostly. But… thinking of Tara brought on its own pain and regret, sending waves of disquiet through Jack.

Drinks were the balm to his trauma.

Despite the gold wedding band on his finger—or perhaps, *because* of it—he attracted attention during his solo outings. Women turned their eyes in his direction: harried businesswoman only in town for a conference looking for a quick fuck; giggling college girls sipping on colorful martinis that wanted to make it with an older man (Jack wondered when 30 became old?), or wives stuck in dead-end marriages like his—they all sat next to him, murmuring empty platitudes while placing a well-manicured hand high on his thigh. They took him back to hotel rooms—each uniform and sterile, interchangeable—where they raided the minibar and screwed with reckless abandon. And for the next hour or so, he'd lose himself, his brain swimming in an intoxicating combination of booze and oxytocin. Jack didn't think of Casey, of Owen, of his shitty job. He thought of Tara while seeking out his own pleasure and for the briefest of moments, usually right before and during orgasm, life seemed okay.

The truth was never too far from his mind: it wasn't.

He returned home, reeking of stale sweat and high-octane whisky, another woman's perfume clinging to his collar. When walking through his front door, he was reminded of the shit storm of his life, his mind clouding over until a supercell of pity and self-loathing dominated him.

Rinse and repeat.

His wife became a stranger—something entirely different inhabited Casey's body: a pod person.

There were blurry memories, one in particular: him coming home from the bar, well sauced. Crawling into bed for a bleary roll in the hay that he only half remembered.

Then—

Another baby on the way.

Jack's spirts lifted. A second chance at fatherhood! A new baby was a life preserver that would prevent him from drifting off to sea and could only bring him and Casey closer together.

Wrong again.

Pregnancy complications became post-partum issues, culminating in Casey's health spiraling like an airplane hurtling to the ground at breakneck speed. Jack didn't know what to say and didn't know how to comfort Casey, feeling hopelessly awkward anytime Casey's health was brought up… which was constantly.

The rut that became a canyon grew, becoming a massive maw that threatened to swallow him up, gobble him like an inconsequential insect.

Nothing a drink couldn't fix of course.

At least temporarily.

56

"A mother's work is never done" was the tagline on one of the mommy blogs I frequented in my previous life, when newly pregnant with Owen, when I still had the luxury of dreaming big. Would my unborn son be a firefighter or own his own business? Foolishly, I believed he could do anything, become whoever he wanted. The possibilities were endless! While stroking my swollen belly, I constructed elaborate fantasies: prom pictures in front of the fireplace; Christmas break from college; Owen introducing us to his beautiful girlfriend (or boyfriend, whatever made him happy); helping plan his wedding; babysitting my grandchildren.

Events that would never materialize—not that that was completely my doing. Owen could be anything he wanted. He chose to be a killer.

The blog was correct on one count though: A mother's work is never done.

But I was sure getting close to the end of my list of nasty chores. One more pesky item of business left. One last item to check off my list. A mental to-do list popped into my mind, like those I carried during grocery runs—when I had the strength required for performing such menial chores. I always came prepared with a red pen, dashing off a brisk checkmark while running through the list. Eggs, *check*, milk, *check*. My personal checklist showed a big, fat red checkmark next to "Deal with Owen."

Except this list was different, the red checkmarks weren't made with ink. They were made with *blood*.

One more to go.

I smiled and made my way to the guest bedroom.

To my lawfully wedded husband.

Grasping the guest room doorknob in my hand, I marveled at its coolness in my warm palm. I turned the knob slowly, praying it didn't stick in that telltale way that signaled my darling husband engaged the lock. If needed, I'd break down the door, splinter the damn thing around the lock, but why alert Jack unnecessarily? I preferred our business as drama free as possible. There was no sense in grappling with a fully grown man if I could avoid it.

My worries melted away as the knob turned easily and quietly. The door opened with a dull *click*. The guest bedroom was shrouded in darkness, its shades and curtains shut tightly against the bright morning light. Jack preferred isolation, escaping from reality, and the bright stabbing sunlight was sure to start his day—and hangover—off on the wrong foot. The furniture had a fuzzy quality in the thick gloom, but I traversed the room easily, navigating by a mix of instinct and touch. I mean, I was the one who cleaned the damn room, thus achieving an easy sort of familiarity a housewife gained in her house.

My *prison*—let's call a spade a spade. A prisoner knew how many steps it took to cover the entirety of their cell, didn't they? I sure did.

A cloud of stench rolled over me: malodor composed of the sharp smell of stale sweat and testosterone, along with a hint of cheap whiskey. My nose wrinkled in disgust. Oh, how far Jack had fallen! During our courtship, I'd loved his scent: a mix of cologne, soap, and his own unique, manly musk. Often, I buried my nose in the soft flesh of his neck, inhaling as I kissed the spot where his pulse thrummed. This smell was *nothing* like that. This acrid odor was something else entirely—another reminder of just how much things changed.

Jack was merely a shadow of the man I'd once loved.

I picked my way through the murky room, easily avoiding Jack's discarded jeans and rumpled clothes carelessly strewn about the floor. Another cruel reminder that he considered me "the help." How did he think his clothes ended up in the hamper? A helpful little cleaning fairy? No silly! His wife, who also doubled as a nice, warm hole to cram his cock into. And sometimes, I cooked too! My mouth twisted into a grimace. Jack was *such* an asshole. Thoughtless would be the nicest thing I could call him.

The room's only light source spilled in from the hallway, casting the entrance of the bedroom in a pale-yellow glow. Standing motionless at the side of the bed—like a sentry guarding their charge—I held the knife casually at my side.

Time passed, how long, I couldn't say.

I observed Jack's sleep, like I had in the beginning when we shared my small bed in the dorm. Each time we made love, I watched Jack fall asleep, mere minutes after his orgasm. The adoration that filled me then, watching his steady breathing and fluttering eyes deep in REM sleep! I stifled a rueful chuckle and a gust of air burst from my nose. Those old feelings of love were long gone, banished to the void. Loathing had stepped in love's place, infesting our marriage like a virulent pathogen. Now I watched Jack with the calculating air of a predator. His rancid breath polluted the air with each exhalation; a mix of rank morning breath threaded with undertones of liquor. Each breath added to the already pungent air quality of the room. It was enough to gag a maggot, but through the years, I had cultivated a strong stomach since it always fell to me to mop up the shit stains and the piles of vomit. Motherhood did have its advantages, and *this* was nothing compared to *those disgusting disasters.*

Jack's face was slack, his mouth hung open stupidly. A thread of drool stretched from lips to pillow. If I squinted and unfocused my eyes, I could *almost* see the man he once was. Handsome, sporting a chiseled jaw. Maybe he could have been a model if a talent scout discovered him but now, fat padded his facial bones, giving his face a doughy quality. A fresh cropping of stubble dotted his chin and jaw. He hadn't yet shaved, leaving hair scattered throughout the bathroom for me—his personal little maid/slave—to clean later.

The wheels of my mind turned. Aborting my deadly errand hadn't crossed my mind; of *that,* there was no room for reconsideration.

Oh no.

No, instead I watched Jack like a world class chess player examining the checkered board, waiting for their opponent's next move, extrapolating any further potential moves based off the first. Thinking, musing, re-adjusting my strategy.

I planned on enjoying this last checkmark on my list to the fullest. Wanting to *savor* it.

After careful deliberation, I decided and climbed onto the bed with my husband.

For the *last* time.

57

Tara, stood with her back facing him, gazing into the very woods where they'd lost their virginities together. Grass tickled his bare feet as he rushed to her, desperate to envelop her within his arms and never let go again. He stretched his arms out, aching to feel her creamy skin under his fingertips.

She crumpled into heaps of sand, losing form, becoming nothing more than a memory.

His dreams of Tara broke into tiny pieces and dissipated into the corners of his mind.

Nothing more than grains of sand lost in time.

He roused and sluggishly fought—in vain—to envelop himself once more into dreamland, where life was wonderful and perfect. But his desires lingered far beyond his reach, gone like smoke unfurling in the air from the tip of a lit cigarette. His head ached, pounding like someone with a sledgehammer tapped out a steady beat to Rage Against the Machine's *Bulls on Parade* from the inside of his skull. Every part of his body throbbed as if he had run a marathon, his mind sluggish; not firing on all cylinders. He needed energy. A big drink—maybe from the Bubba Keg that his coworkers gifted him since he often polished off an entire carafe of coffee himself—might do it: generously loaded with fresh coffee, a quaff or two of Bailey's tucked within. *That* would help him shake off the sludge. Jack struggled to hoist his leaden body into an upright position and found himself unable.

Sleep paralysis, his mind supplied, an idea he accepted readily, despite never having experienced it before. Opening his eyes, Jack winced at the rubbed, raw sandpaper sensation clinging to his eyeballs. Black dots raced across his vision, obscuring his view of the murky room. Sharp shards of pain pincered into his skull, aching like they did when Casey broke his nose. He longed to rub the heels of his hands into his wounded eyes, hoping to wipe the blurriness from them. His arms, though, remained stubbornly affixed to his sides. Blinking rapidly, his eyelids shuttered open and closed with slivers of irritation. The spots obscuring his vision wavered and disbanded, giving his eyes time to adjust to the darkness.

From the inky depths of the room, a face emerged—

His wife?

Casey straddled his body and a predatory, hungry look stamped itself across her features—clear even in the thick dim. It seemed animalistic. Sexual even.

He wondered, *was he dreaming? He* must *be dreaming. Why else would Casey be here?*

Surely, a dream within a dream. *Unless,* the thought occurred to him, *she'd finally come around?* It would explain *her* being on top of *him.* Here she was, waving the white flag, ready to move on and she knew make-up sex was a fantastic way to grab his attention! No wonder he'd struggled to move earlier—her inner thighs, warm and inviting, held his arms fast against his torso. Not that he was complaining, *definitely* not.

Jack gazed into Casey's eyes. She rewarded him with a smile—the first she'd given him in months. Teeth shone brilliantly white, and they beckoned to him, like a lighthouse guiding a boat previously lost at sea, finally found. Hope bloomed hot in his chest, desire erasing all feelings of exhaustion within him, and he grew hard at the delightful pressure of her body on his groin.

Maybe this could be the beginning of a healing period, he thought. The pain of continual rejection still stung, but he could push that aside and together, they'd mend wounds. A lump rose in his throat. Things could be different. Warm tears prickled his eyes and his vision wavered. He could forgive all the hurts she'd heaped upon him. Not that it would be easy.

A bloom of something foreign—happiness—budded to life within him and a smile spread across his face.

Things were looking up.

———

Sitting atop Jack's body, I perched like an eagle readying itself for a final frantic dive. Emotions flitted across Jack's face, playing out like a movie unfolding on a theater screen. My eyes had long adjusted to the muggy darkness, and I saw all, like a cat prowling in the dark. Contempt overtook me, and my upper lip curled into a sneer as I watched his eyes fill with hope, magnified by a thin sheen of tears. His dick was hard against my inner thigh and rage filled me, ratcheting my pissed-off-dial right up. His fucking cock was the reason I was in this mess to begin with! Jack had been more than happy to steal my health and independence, all for less than a minute of lackluster fucking. Only caring about his own pleasure, not mine. Not cherishing me, not holding me like our vows said. No. *Using* me.

Knife held in my right hand; I clenched both fists tightly. A thin bite of pain broadcasted from my palms, fingernails digging into tender flesh, leaving crescent gouges. Pain was good: it centered me, reminding me of the job at hand. I welcomed it and allowed it to envelop me in its cocoon. A deep inhale brought forth a calmness that settled my mind, steadying me. Funneling the rage taking residence inside of me, I transformed it into something useful, honing it like a tool—like a knife— really. I bent forward, dipping in closer to Jack. A look of pleasure shined radiantly from his upturned stupid face.

Disdain wedded itself to my rage, infusing me with strength.

―――

CASEY WAS GOING to kiss *him*!

Jack swooned, sure of this fact, and his cock became a piston: hot, hard, ready.

Her mouth hung open slightly, seductively, as she bent over his face, bypassing his lips completely—much to his disappointment—and she rested her mouth close to his ear. Small puffs of breath only increased his horniness, tickling exquisitely sensitive skin. Jack groaned softly and ground his pelvis against Casey, desperate for release. His erection edged towards painful, nearing dangerously into blue balls' territory if she didn't do something about it.

The words that left his wife's mouth weren't what he expected.

Hoping for an "I love you," or maybe "I want to fuck you"—they didn't come. Instead, Casey whispered the last words Jack would ever hear, and the words took him by such surprise, he wasn't completely sure he'd heard correctly. *That couldn't be right*, he thought. Confusion overwhelmed him and he had enough time to wonder if he was still enveloped within a dream, snugly tucked within the guest room bed... alone.

A blossom of pain interrupted those thoughts, and a symphony of agony overtook him.

Not a nightmare.

Reality. Shitty, stark reality.

———

THE WORDS that Casey whispered in her husband's ear?

"Till death do us part."

The inflection in her voice was like the "I love you more than anything," they exchanged after their first kiss as husband and wife, on the altar in front of their family and friends, but her words landed like sharpened daggers.

As she whispered the last words Jack heard during his mortal coil, Casey moved with freakish speed, sitting upright, and sliced across his throat with a quick flick of her wrist. The knife moved easily, cutting effortlessly. She imagined that the knife—like she—had developed a taste for human flesh, and it moved like a dream.

Like father, like son.

———

SCARLET SPRAYED from wounds on each side of Jack's neck, both carotid arteries and jugular veins expertly severed with one quick flick of my blade. Each contraction of the strong heart muscle sent up a fresh shower of blood.

I released his arms. There was no sense in keeping him pinned down now. Coolly, I observed as Jack tried to stymie the flow of blood erupting from his neck. He held his hands up to the mortal wounds; a fruitless gesture that painted his ignorant hands a vibrant red. The blood took on a frothy appearance as it poured through the cracks of his fingers uselessly pressed against his wounds. It reminded me of a mountain stream and how they often frothed, not from the water's turbulence as one might think, but because the stream contained decomposed animals and plants releasing their organic matter, forming a nature-made soap.

Jack's eyes were wide, unseeing, pupils so dilated that they obliterated the brilliant color of his irises. His mouth quivered wordlessly and when he mustered up some wind and trialed speech—instead of words, Jack coughed out a fresh speckle of blood straight onto my shirt, where it intermixed with Owen's drying blood. I hadn't completely cut through Jack's windpipe, as I had Owen, but instead, created a small nick within that communicated with the stale bedroom air. Each agonized inhalation funneled blood down the readymade hole into his lungs. Jack was bleeding out but at the same time, drowning on dry land, choking on cupsful of his own lifeblood.

Two different manners of death—both unpleasant.

What a shame.

I grinned.

———

JACK'S BODY shook like a leaf on a tree caught in a violent summer storm, in part from the adrenaline coursing through his veins, but mostly due to sheer, all-encompassing fear. The stress-induced chemicals his adrenal glands produced fruitlessly coaxed his body into continued function even as his circulatory system collapsed. Jack—rightly—discerned that these moments were the last of his time on earth, his clock winding down with a devilish speed, ticking slowly until everything ceased and his body's systems shut down, one by one.

Unfortunately, Jack's brain was still sharp and all-too comprehending of his plight.

Casey grinned at him through the murk of the room, only the white of her eyes and teeth visible since she was doused with a mixture of both her son and husband's blood. A deep sorrow threaded itself within Jack's mounting panic and fear. Memories flooded him, vivid and heartbreaking:

Riding his bike without training wheels; scoring the game-winning basket; senior prom with Tara on his arm, her face upturned and beaming; the agony of losing Tara forever. His wedding day surrounded by friends and family, leaves on the trees a jumble of warm reds, oranges, and yellows; Casey, absolutely stunning in her white dress and she gazed at him with an expression of utter delight. Even in that moment, supposedly the happiest day of his life, he'd thought *it should have been Tara.*

His heart slowed, deprived of precious oxygen, not unlike his wife's long ago. Hot tears prickled—the same temperature as the blood cascading over him.

It should have been Tara.

He thought of his children and the utter joy he'd experienced at their births, his jubilation growing after they were plucked from his wife's body and swaddled in a blanket for him to hold; Owen, the Owen of *before*; Jack sitting on the couch holding a snoozing Eleanor who was wrapped tightly in a blanket, and how each time she made a little snort during her sleep, his heart surged with pure unconditional love.

His consciousness shorted out; heart stopped.

Jack's soul left his body.

5 8

I beheld my husband's death with a ravenous interest and exhilarated in each deluge of blood pumping from his neck. Most of it spilled to the carpet, some coated walls ironically painted a crimson color. Watching Jack's ichor drip down the wall, I remembered what the worker behind the counter at Lowe's had said, conspiratorially dropping his voice, "It's a bright red color with a tinge of blue, often said to be the color of fresh blood."

How we laughed at that absurd piece of imparted knowledge, but—true to the man's word—it blended *perfectly* with the paint color, and I giggled. Some of Jack's blood sprayed onto my face and I beamed, intoxicated with each bead of the precious liquid coursing down my skin, luxuriating in the fresh, warm blood droplets. My ears delighted in the sweet music of my husband's dying, each sputter and groan a symphony of suffering that was more enthralling than any piece of music composed in history.

What sent my pleasure into overdrive, though, was the expression of terror carved into each line of his face. A film of sweat beaded his brow, his skin waxen in the room's gloom; I saw all, my vision heightened to near perfect levels.

Something powerful—maybe all the pain and suffering—strengthened all my senses, making me a better version of myself. Jack's mouth flopped open, wordless but occasionally burbling thick, wet sounds emerged from its depths. Glorious noises of death.

Jack's eyes, oh they were beautiful! Once I'd gazed into them with only love in my heart, but now, their distress enchanted me. I drank up the expression, lapping it up greedily like a kitten with a warm saucer of milk, and felt satiated, my thirst for blood, and revenge now quenched… for the moment.

It crested a zenith.

Then—*rapture*.

My body reacted, overwhelmed by the bombardment of each sense with complete ecstasy. Nostrils flared wide, taking in the sublime scents of torment that were heavy and cloying, mixed with metallic blood. My tongue tasted a wondrous conglomeration of umami, a flavor that five-star chefs strived their entire lives to create. Someone ought to tell the poor saps that they just need to develop a taste for human suffering and the flavors would come! Pores soaked up the pearls of blood, leaving my skin refreshed, as if I completed the world's most renowned spa treatment.

Jack's body thrummed with dying energy underneath me, and while his erection had long since deflated, I'd never been more aroused. Every nerve ending was raw and exposed, each texture and sensation magnified. My tender clit ached and pulsed with a pleasure that begged for release. Tension built deliciously inside, the promise of deliverance edging ever closer. Waves of pleasure crested and broke as Jack's body slackened beneath me; the culminating pleasure of gifting my husband a sweet death. The ultimate goodnight—or good morning, in our case—kiss.

He was *gone*.

Something cool rushed past my shoulder: Jack's soul departing his earthly shell.

And *I'd* made it happen. The power of it all.

Lightning rushes of climax overtook me then, my body arching like a cat, each muscle endowed with electricity. My brain released every feel-good hormone within its arsenal, leaving me beguiled by the dopamine and oxytocin flooding me. The ultimate high, far better than any hit of premium White China coursing through the most accomplished dope addict's veins. I experienced what few do, although any adept serial killer might say that *this* very moment was why they lost control repeatedly; why they had all-encompassing addictions that begged for them to kill and kill, over and over. I understood now, I truly did. The power was intoxicating, the rush unequaled.

My orgasm gripped me for nearly a minute, reducing me to a quivering mess. I gulped up delicious air fragrant with extermination, throat raw and ragged, each exhalation a shuddering gasp of pleasure. A sense of peace settled over me. Enlightenment: just like Buddhist monks always preached. The pure tranquility highlighted the fact that *I* was alive, more than I'd ever been.

Alive!

My heart beat strong and for once, I didn't feel the cold that normally clutched my heart in its vice grip.

Everything within me was aflame and joyous. I was complete.

59

The subject of Jack ceased existence in Casey's mind, other than when relieving the orgy of blood and pain she'd rained down upon him. While Casey thought little about Jack, someone else noticed his absence.

Jack's boss, John, watched the clock, unease growing with each minute. The clock ticked past 8:05 and still no Jack bursting through the door, freshly showered with an apology about traffic or kids holding him up. It wasn't like him to be late without a call or text. While his boozing wasn't exactly a secret, he almost never missed a day and called if something came up. John paced his office, face drawn in a frown, pointedly ignoring the papers strewn about his desk. He thumbed through his cellphone, brought up Jack's number and pressed the green call decal. Endless ringing, followed by a click. A cheerful mechanical woman said, "I'm sorry, but the person you have called has a voicemail box has not been set up yet. Goodbye."

The *wrongness* intensified, the air in John's office heavy and pregnant with the promise of bad news. Scenarios whirled through his mind. Jack was involved in a car accident, and he plowed into a light pole; Jack's sweetheart of a wife wasn't doing well; or the house slowly filled with odorless carbon monoxide while everyone was in their beds, completely unaware? The last image of them snugly cocooned in warm sheets—drifting off to a pleasant death, each lungful of tainted air bringing in more poison— decided John. He pulled his phone out again, this time dialing 9-1-1.

"9-1-1, what's your emergency?" The dispatcher said.

"Hi, uh, yeah, I would like the police to perform a welfare check on one of my employees. He hasn't come to work, and that's not like him," John said.

"What's the address, sir?"

Address? John frantically rifled through employee files and after discovering "Philips" in the "F" folder, gave her the address. He made a mental note to buy his secretary a subscription to Hooked on Phonics for her birthday this year. Fhilips? C'mon.

"Someone will get back to you soon, sir, after police check out the residence. Thank you." A *click* opened the line.

John sat at his desk, pulled a sheet of paper to him, and stared, not seeing the jumble of words and figures on the page.

And waited for the other shoe to drop.

———

"Officer Willard, come in," came a tinny voice from the radio.

"Officer Willard here."

"Welfare check at 218 Mockingbird Lane. A Jack Philips didn't show up to work at Bookkeeping by the Hour."

Bookkeeping by the Hour? The dumb name rang a bell —the accounting firm in the ugly beige building across town, across the street from his favorite coffee shop. He couldn't blame the guy for not showing up. Math was never his strong suit. Even now, he struggled with the metric system all the drug dealers used. "Copy, heading there now." Well, maybe not right then. His cruiser was next in line at the Dunkin' Donuts drive-thru. Jack Philips could wait. Willard ordered his coffee, briefly considering one of their signature donuts—pink frosting with sprinkles—but decided against it. Why satisfy a stereotype? Plus, he'd noticed his gut sloping over his tactical belt, making it harder to grab his cuffs. Coffee in hand, he turned to his newly assigned task: making sure the accountant wasn't dead. While welfare checks weren't exactly glamorous and often wound up turning into a shit storm, he was pleased to break up the monotony of his day—scut work or not. Normally, he patrolled a small area composed of strip malls and gas stations; a rather snooze inducing task. Podcasts about conspiracy theories only amused him so much. The most exciting events of the day involved old ladies committing unwitting hit and runs or teenagers shoplifting cheap makeup.

Officer Willard typed in 218 Mockingbird LN on his mounted computer. He sipped his coffee and his mustache twitched. More cream than coffee *again*, but what should he expect? The cashier's eyes were bloodshot, and a distinct skunky smell filled his cruiser when he'd paid. But… caffeine was caffeine, and as much as he bitched, he'd be back. Maybe he'd get that donut too.

Driving to the Philips' residence, he took in the scenery: a nice *Truman Show*-esque neighborhood. White picket fences, immaculate landscaping with every blade of brilliantly green grass a uniform height. The HOA fees had to be a real bitch. He pulled up to 218 Mockingbird Ln. Parked and left his rig running. Peered around, nothing amiss. Knuckles rapped against the door. "HELLO! It's the Police, just doing a welfare check!" Willard shouted and paused, ears primed, expecting to hear pattering steps.

Nothing.

Intensifying his knocking yielded the same results. Doorbell next—one, two, three times—triggering receding *DING-DONGs*.

Zilch.

Looking up at the house, Willard shuddered. Skin painfully tightened, hair prickled at the nape of his neck, and involuntarily, his hand stole to his hip and stroked his holstered gun. The cool metal soothed him, like a toddler's security blanket. Something felt *wrong. It's the horror movies you watch at night*, he told himself. *Got you freaked out.*

Except, what was it they said at the Academy: What do you call a cop that doesn't trust his instincts? Dead.

Willard searched the front stoop examining rocks for "hidden" key compartments that fooled no thief. He'd scold them later, assuming he found a key. He'd rather waltz in easily. Folks got irritated when police kicked down perfectly good doors. Officer Willard picked up a hideous lawn ornament—two frogs wearing matching overalls dancing a jig—and hit pay dirt. Grabbing the key, he hurried back to the front door. The key slid in true, and he turned, telltale *click* of the lock disengaging. Pushing the door open, Willard hollered, "Hello! Police! I used your key. No one was answering! Just checking in to make sure everything's alright!" The last thing he needed was a gun-nut unloading lead into him or finding the missus buck-naked. He let himself into the entryway, pulling door shut behind him; it was poor form if a pet or—God forbid—a toddler, ran into traffic. Pictures hung in the entryway, and he looked them over: a smiling couple hugging tightly; a grouchy-looking boy sat on a tree stump; and one of those newborn baby pictures the hospital took.

Hush descended. Air still and cool. *Like a crypt*, his mind supplied. Stifled a nervous giggle, the gibberings of a lunatic. *Just spooked yourself.* Still, his hand rested on his firearm again—just in case. He ambled from room-to-room downstairs, finding nothing amiss.

Until the kitchen.

Shattered glass littered the countertop, the light's corpse still plugged into outlet. He made out a cartoon eye whose pupil stared up at nothing. Sweeping the kitchen with his eyes, he noted a knife block on the counter, one slot empty. And—

A padlock? For a *knife block*? Not good. Who had to keep kitchen knives locked away in their own home?

Officer Willard unsnapped his gun from the holster, ensuring he could draw his weapon quickly if required.

Something was *very wrong* here, a certainty that grew with each passing moment.

Completing his search of the downstairs, finding nothing, he circled back to the entryway. Started up the stairs, cautiously placing his weight on each step; the last thing he needed was an errant creak giving away his position. At the top, was another heap of shattered glass, scattered atop a photo. Dried blood hid the family's faces. Glass shards stained bloody littered the floor. Sweat blossomed in Willard's armpits, and his skin crawled.

Time to load the boat before it sunk. Officer Willard spoke into his radio, pitching his voice low, "Dispatch, I need backup. There are signs a struggle ensued here, 218 Mockingbird Ln."

A murmured affirmative came, promises of backup in several minutes, units inbound.

Hackles up, he removed his gun. Training took hold, and he clutched it in a defensive position, thumbing the safety off. He ought to wait until more officers arrived, but —there might be kids here. Kids, blood, and shattered glass were a *bad* combo. Had to make sure they were okay. Officer Willard's testicles retreated into his abdomen, belly rolling with acid. Sweat popped out from every pore and rolled down his back, even in the house's relative cool. He feared what he might discover but he was a cop, dammit, and he'd be dammed if he slunk away with his tail between his legs when the chips were down. With leaden legs, feet moving as if encased in concrete blocks in his trepidation, he stepped carefully over the glass, feeling like he was moving through a thick soup.

To a closed door. To images that would follow him to his grave.

60

---

 un at the ready, Officer Willard quickly opened the door, and swept the room. The walls were painted a canary yellow. A rocking chair sat in the corner—thankfully still. Had it moved, bullets would fly. A changing table and a crib were pushed up against the back wall. Orderly rows of diapers, wipes, and tubes of various creams. Willard walked towards the crib—breathing deeply, inhaling baby lotion and wet pennies, a smell that instantly curdled his stomach. He knew what it meant.

The crib—

Willard peered into the crib and his breath caught in his throat.

Dots and splashes of dried blood littered the crib sheets. Not a lot, but *any* was too much.

Unoccupied. Really not good. Willard sent up a silent prayer that the baby was okay. It was a Schrödinger's cat situation: the baby was simultaneously completely fine and gruesomely murdered.

"Shit." He closed the nursery door and continued down the hall. A bathroom. Willard stepped inside. An open tube of bubblegum-flavored toothpaste sat on the counter; pink glob curling from its nozzle. His stomach clenched; bubblegum always reminded him of the dentist's office as a child. Those terrifying gloved hands forcing a mask over his nostrils and mouth, flooded with that disgusting artificial, slightly medicinal scent. Just what he needed to add to this situation: a fear of bubblegum toothpaste courtesy of Dr. Woodruff, his childhood dentist. A shower curtain patterned with tractors wrapped around a clawfoot tub. The scene from *Psycho*: dark, syrupy blood swirling the drain, complete with a sinister shadow lurking on the other side of the curtain. Trembling fingers clutched the curtain and gathering his courage, Willard shoved it back, using far more force than necessary.

Something crouched at the end of the tub, grinning sickly with sharp pointed teeth and Willard's gun came up, finger curling around the trigger, applying *almost* enough pressure to fire.

He blinked, and the figure vanished, replaced by a yellow rubber ducky wearing sunglasses. Feeling sheepish, Willard lowered the gun. He'd sweat clean through his cotton undershirt. "Get ahold of yourself, man," he admonished himself, with little conviction, and closed the bathroom door. Nothing in there but an overactive imagination of one of Appleton's Finest.

Next room, door shut. Door one and two scared the shit out of him already, and in this macabre *The Price is Right*, he feared what lurked beyond. Grasped the doorknob, turning slowly, minimizing the noise. Then, a low *click*. Door opened. Staring down his muzzle, the reek choked him first. Slaughterhouse, pools of blood.

"No." Willard moaned, slacked jawed, eyes bulging. Blinked. *Just another trick of the mind, just chill.* Opened his eyes. Still there. Sour spit squirted into his mouth. An alarming amount of blood, still dripping in some places. Faint *ploinking* noises. The last time he'd heard noise like that was a trip to

Carlsbad Caverns and like in the cave, a metallic stench filled his mouth and nose. He gagged, hearing the trickle of fluid that was *not* water, not even close. A fricking miracle he didn't toss his cookies. But when he caught sight of the crumpled figured in the bed—

He lost the battle.

Wiping his sour mouth, cringing at the lingering burn, he stared at a stuffed whale with a horn. Facing the wall, almost *posed*. A comforter was tucked around the body, something that struck Willard as odd. It implied someone had cared for the victim—however miniscule the feeling was —and didn't want to leave them uncovered. An almost loving act, in a brutal way.

Willard gulped. *No way* the boy was alive. No way, but still—he had to check. Thank God he'd called for backup; this was turning into a right shitshow, as welfare checks often did. This though, was more awful than anything he'd seen in fifteen years on the job. Plodding forward, his legs were gelatin instead of muscle. Each quivering step took him closer to the hump on the bed. The *body*. Willard struggled to pull on gloves, hands jittering as he thrusted them inside. The task made infinitely more difficult by the sweat pouring from his palms.

"Shit, shit, shit," he said, heart racing. What he found—

Was not going to be good.

He tugged the comforter downward. Shaggy brown hair popped into view, followed by a pallid face. Wide eyes stared into his own, sightless but pleading. Grayish tongue protruded from the mouth, looking like a macabre "Q" in an alphabet book of horror. Splashes of blood decorated the boy's tattered cheeks. Pulling the comforter down further, Officer Willard forced trembling hands to comply with his brain's demands.

The boy's neck

A low moan escaped Willard's lips.

Sizeable slashes mangled both sides. Despair filled him: *no way* the kid survived this, absolutely no way. Still, he *had* to be sure. With crawling skin that felt far too tight for his big frame, he pressed fingers to the boy's neck, where his carotid ought to be—although with this hack job, who knew? Delicate tissues blurred into one another—raw gore. Cool skin greeted Willard's fingertips.

No pulse. Dead.

The Dunkin' coffee curdled in his gut. Nothing worse than a dead kid. What a fuckin' mess.

Shaking his head, he thumbed on his radio. "Dispatch, I have a child here, bearing wounds on his neck and cheeks, likely from a knife. Unfortunately, deceased."

"Copy that, Officer Willard."

A sudden frigidness seized him, shivers rolled down his spine, and only gritting his jaw stopped his teeth from chattering. Averting his gaze from the body—looking anywhere but at *it*—he again saw the stuffed animal, pointedly facing the wall. *A narwhale*, he realized. His niece loved them, called them unicorns of the sea. Someone had turned the little boy's toy around, not wanting it to witness the bloodshed—another softhearted display, totally incongruent with the murder scene staring him straight in the face.

Where the fuck was his backup?!

61

S irens cut through the calm outside, polluting air with their ear-splitting shrieks. Back up, *finally*! The cavalry had arrived. Relief flooded Willard. Hearing the front door open, Officer Willard bellowed, "UP HERE!" He'd stayed with the little boy's body—facing away from it, much like the boy's narwhale—unable to muster up any gumption for investigating the rest of the house. Something told him it would be an exercise in futility anyway. Plus, this was now an active crime scene, and it fell to him to secure this room before others traipsed through, fucking up precious evidence.

Two medics burst through the doorway, armed with a backboard, and bags packed with medical necessities. The younger of the two dawdled, lingering in the doorway, until the other medic admonished, "What the fuck are you doing? You gonna go pick some flowers? Get in here, NOW!" The dilly-dallier looked as if he wished to mosey all day—or even all century—but he bolted forward like an obedient puppy desperate to obey its master's commands. An unhealthy pallor stretched across his face, and he swayed on his feet. The senior medic, elbow deep in a bag of medical odds and ends, spared a look at Officer Willard and chuckled. "Amateurs, amiright?"

Officer Willard offered up a weak nod. Poor kid looked like he felt.

The senior paramedic motioned for Willard to step back, tugged on gloves, and repeated Willard's prior motions, pressing fingers to the boy's neck. Or… where it *used* to be. Shaking his head, he announced the painfully obvious, "Kid's dead. Has been for a bit."

Willard fought a childish urge to say, "Yeah, no shit Sherlock." One look at the grayish blue hue of the boy's skin was enough to tell that tale—a shade only seen in death. The way the kid's tongue poked out reminded Willard of a white strawberry salad he'd eaten at a fancy wedding. Prominent, protuberant taste buds dried in the air-conditioned room, never to taste again.

The senior medic pointed, mostly for his partner's benefit. "See this? Lividity. Blood pools in the dependent areas, which explains the color on the backs of the arms and legs. A sure-fire sign of death." His young partner's eyes resembled tea saucers peering at the body—had to be the poor sap's first murder scene, maybe even his first real-life dead body. He clutched an unopened bag of meds to his chest, as if it were a talisman to ward off evil. *Too late*, Willard thought. Evil was already in the building. His gut cramped and cold sweat dripped down his butt crack. Diarrhea was in his future, no doubt about that.

A heavy *THUMP* from the corner took Officer Willard's mind off his impending Hershey squirts, and he whipped his head towards the noise. The traumatized medic was now in a horizontal position, fainted dead away. Fortuitously, his head was cushioned by a clump of stuffed animals, all in various stages of decapitation or amputation, Willard noted with alarm. What the fuck was with that?

"Goddam young pups!" The senior medic cried out,

hurrying to his unconscious partner who was already coming to, slowly sitting up with an expression of sheepish embarrassment.

"I don't think I can do this," the younger medic announced matter-of-factly to the room.

"No shit," the senior medic muttered under his breath. Willard couldn't blame the kid, he wasn't quite sure *he* could handle it, truth be told.

Officers poured into 218 Mockingbird Ln., heads on a constant swivel, as if expecting criminals to crawl out of the walls. If someone was willing to kill a kid, they certainly wouldn't think twice about killing anyone, even a cop. Willard met the officers at the foot of the stairs and debriefed them, pointing out the broken picture frame with blood-stained glass in the hallway and the shattered nightlight in the kitchen. Not to mention the dead kid upstairs.

Sergeant Taylor had twenty-plus years under his belt with an eye on retirement, making him King Shit of Turd Mountain: the most senior officer on scene. Taking control of the situation, he divided officers into groups to investigate the rest of the house more thoroughly. He and two officers canvassed the upstairs, keeping their guns drawn and at the ready. The first room searched was the master, containing nothing of interest other than a rumpled bed and covers strewn on the floor. Taylor lifted the covers up, feeling sheepish since, quite clearly, no one was underneath. But one dotted their i's and crossed their t's. Missing a dead body on a first sweep was a *real* faux pas.

Master bathroom: nothing of note.

The next room?

Not so much.

Its door stood slightly ajar. Sergeant Taylor cautiously opened it the rest of the way, only exposing his arm and groped blindly for a light switch. The air was too still yet heavy, like the weather before a corker of a thunderstorm that produced monster twisters. Fine arm hairs prickled, and his spit dried in his mouth. Locating the switch, he flicked it up. Light bathed the dark room, quickly unveiling the horror scene on the bed. His mouth opened to call out for the paramedics, but the words died. *That* would be an exercise in futility. They needed a coroner because the man on the bed was most *definitely* expired.

The walls were already painted a noxious blood red—a color that ought to be outlawed in Taylor's humble opinion, he'd seen far too much of it in his career—and *that* hideous base color was splattered with drying blood that almost matched the underlying paint perfectly. Bedsheets were stiff with blood. No amount of bleach would fix that. He stared at the corpse. The eyes bore a startled appearance as if supremely surprised by their death, which Taylor supposed *was* the case. Lips were parted—there was *something* in the man's mouth, but with his head cocked off to the side in an awkward angle, it was difficult to tell. Sergeant Taylor inched closer to the bed, eyes seeing but disbelieving.

Taylor's groin reflexively tightened. Clenched between the man's teeth was—

A penis.

And if Taylor were a betting man, a quick lift of the sheet covering the guy's crotch would reveal a missing member that found itself a new home. The base of the limp penis had been inserted first, leaving the head to greet the world. Drying whorls of blood were smeared across the man's face, but underneath the muck on either cheek: a crudely etched X. The two crossed lines were deep on the right cheek, leaving a flap of skin hanging, but the left cheek's X was pristine and crisp.

"Alright guys, this is a crime scene. Let's clear out and wait for detectives and forensics," Sergeant Taylor boomed. He made to shut the door but paused, turning to look at the man again, eyes drawn to the X's. Remarkably, the X's caught his interest more than the severed penis. *Something* tickled the back of Taylor's mind, the answer at the tip of his tongue. What was it? Groping, he came up empty. Sighing, he knew the answer would come days later while sitting on the john or driving to work. He shut the door and —at the bidding of one of the other officers—went to the other bedroom that contained yet another body. Officer Willard stood vigil at the bedside, giving him a curt nod.

"Damn, your welfare check turned into a disaster," Taylor commented, taking in the grisly scene.

"You ain't kidding," Willard answered. His face was drawn and pale. "I've never seen anything this awful," the officer said, shaking his head. Taylor wished he could say the same. The boy's bedroom and body were also a bloody mess, reminding him of the prom scene in *Carrie* after she got doused with the bucket of pig's blood and went ape shit. Someone tossed their cookies in the corner—not surprising. He'd barfed at his first murder scene too. The boy sported matching X's on his cheeks, mirroring his (presumed) father, although his were more polished. More precise and if Taylor had to guess, were probably etched in *after* his father's, after the assailant got a little more practice under his belt.

The only upside to the situation, if there *was* an upside, was the baby was nowhere to be found. Dead babies were a real buzzkill. Of course, the baby's absence didn't equate to safety—quite the contrary. Taylor examined the stained crib sheets and while the blood was minimal (especially compared to the other victims' rooms), it signaled *something* bad had happened.

"We gotta find the baby and the mother," Sergeant Taylor muttered to himself.

The lady of the house was conspicuously absent. Officers found an envelope on the counter addressed to Jack and Casey Philips. The perp abducted her for his own nefarious pleasures. He wondered if she'd begged for her son and husband's lives, offering her own up in exchange to the monster (not that he'd taken her up on that deal, as evidenced by the dead family members). The psycho responsible for all this carnage, not satisfied with just murder, likely kidnapped Casey Philips, planning to toy with her before finishing the job. Maybe he made her watch. Maybe keeping the baby alive was the only way to keep her obedient.

Heaped under the envelope bearing both Philips' names were several bills: an oil change for the van parked in the garage while the other was for a new clutch for a vintage 1970 Camaro. The Camaro was ostensibly absent, of course. Why wouldn't it be? The van could have been located with one call to OnStar, location pinged within minutes. A vintage 1970 Camaro? Not a chance. That car was old school, and the most advanced technology it boasted was *maybe* a CD player. Luckily, the Camaro should be recognizable. Muscle cars turned heads, inviting admiration, but the damn thing was completely off the grid.

Stationing an officer outside each bedroom, Taylor ensured no one entered before forensics showed. He didn't want to be accused of "Bouldering it" like those idiots in the JonBenét Ramsey case, letting hordes of folks traipse all over clues. Not happening on his watch. While waiting for their arrival, Taylor's mind kept circling back to those vulgar X's. Where had he seen them before? Or heard about them?

For the life of him, he couldn't remember. They reminded him of *something* he couldn't quite put his finger on. Maybe the swastika carving Charles Manson sported on his forehead, but that wasn't it. Obviously, it was a calling card of sorts for the murderer, like an artist scrawling their signature at the corner of a painting. Damn why couldn't he remember? Maybe it had to do with the rapidly expanding sea of gray hairs on his scalp. Age had a nasty way of creeping up on you, something he could attest to. At his age, he was up twice nightly, struggling to piss thanks to an enlarged prostate. There was a *sense* of what he was groping for, almost as if he were staring at an object wrapped in a blanket, its true nature hidden from view. The answer would come to him later—it always did, maybe even weeks or months later, but it would come. He hoped for this family's sake that it came sooner rather than later.

Forensics finally turned up, strolling self-importantly onto the scene. Soon they were plucking minute hairs from here and there, sealing them in marked plastic bags, bagging stuffed animals including a blood-dotted narwhal. While they mentally masturbated over the blood splatter, the police issued an APB for the 1970 Camaro, plates reading: BLUCMRO. A ridiculous vanity plate, but not unwelcome. Folks remembered stupid vanity plates.

They'd find Casey Philips.

And the sicko responsible for this carnage.

6 2

"**N**urse to front!"

Val sighed and stood up from her seat at the charge nurse desk. She'd just hung up the phone after getting reamed by a surgeon with a God complex for not having the foresight to tell all patients with surgical emergencies to wait until *after* his golf game concluded. *What now?* Val wondered. Getting called to the front usually meant someone was about to keel over, had keeled over or— more and more often now that everyone was a gun-nut— there'd been a homie drop-off. Mentally preparing herself for a great deal of vomit and/or blood, she hustled out to the triage area.

Patients stared up expectantly as she walked by. A man with a bloody towel pressed against his nose, an exhausted mother holding two snotty babies (twins if Val had to guess), and a middle-aged woman clutching her flank, doing the kidney stone dance—all with hope in their eyes that died when she passed them by. They'd get a room when one became available, even if they weren't happy about it. In an Emergency Room, waiting meant you weren't actively dying and that was always a blessing. Val turned the corner by the registration desk and instead of the expected ashen-faced, sweaty obese man clutching his chest, she saw—

A baby?

Fat crocodile tears stood out in the baby's eyes and below that, a quivering lip threatened to unleash a corker of a wail. Regina, the registration clerk, had removed the baby from its car seat and held it with the ease of a professional babysitter or a long-time mother. Val looked closer at the baby and saw sharp lines of rust-colored blood dried on the child's onesie. "Regina, what happened? Where are the parents?" Val asked, carefully plucking the baby out of Regina's arms. While waiting for her answer, Val walked to the adjacent triage room and began undressing the infant, assessing for any signs of trauma. They dried blood implied *something* had happened.

Regina shrugged. "I was just going over some old charts when a woman ran in with the car seat. She plopped the baby down, said she needed help, and then took off. Oh!" Her eyebrows shot up. "I almost forgot. She handed me this too." Extracting a folded piece of paper from her pocket, she opened it, smoothed the edges, and handed it to Val. Val put the paper into a front scrub pocket, next to her favorite pen, and finished her assessment of the baby (a girl, based on the private parts under her diaper), noting multiple superficial lacerations on the little girl's torso. None were actively bleeding.

After checking vital signs (stone cold normal across the board) and wrapping the baby in a blanket from the warmer, she reached for the paper, cringing at its warm, moist texture. If felt as if someone profoundly sweaty held it in a drippy palm. At least it wasn't blood-soaked. Val peered closely at the edges, noting faint watermarks peppering the page. A message was jotted in black ink, several words blurred or smeared beyond recognition. Whoever wrote the note had either been crying or sweating. She skimmed the note:

This is Eleanor Philips. No medical problems. No meds. No known drug allergies. Up to date on immunizations.

A series of digits—too smeared to make out—followed. A birthdate?

Please call Eleanor's grandmother, Faye.

A phone number, presumably Faye's.

"Regina, who dropped her off?" Val asked. Obviously, someone cared enough about this baby to drop her off for medical care but where was her family? Would they be coming back? Somehow Val doubted they were off parking the car.

Another shrug from Regina. "I'm sorry, I didn't get a great look at the woman. She had on dark sunglasses and her hair was tucked under a red scarf. Looked a bit like a movie star, to tell you the truth. Pretty." Regina paused, her face pinching in concentration, and she snapped her fingers in a lightbulb moment. "I did see the car. It reminded me of one of those cars from *The Fast and the Furious* movies. Very nice."

Val picked Eleanor up and gingerly placed her back in the carrier. "I'm gonna have the doc look at little Eleanor and it looks like we'll be making some phone calls. To this Faye and—"

"And the police?" Regina supplied.

"Definitely," Val answered. Something weird was going on here but that was for the folks in blue to sort out. She had an eerie feeling she might find out answers to that question on the news later.

63

L ike any well-attuned charge nurse, Val's intuition was spot on.

Every news station in town pounced on the story like metaphorical carrion birds picking at Owen and Jack's corpses. The big networks—massive vultures in neighboring big cities took flight—not wanting to miss out on the action. Nothing was better for ratings than grisly murder and mystery. Add in an (relatively) unharmed miracle baby and one had a recipe for a winning story. Casey's physical characteristics bombarded television screens and by that evening, Casey's parents held a press conference, issuing pleas for the quick and safe return of their daughter into the myriad of microphones and cellphones thrust into the air.

Casey's mother—Faye, a tearful gray-haired woman with a cardigan pulled snuggly around her frail shoulders—tearfully said, "Casey has medical problems, and just received a heart transplant. Please help get her home safely." Next to his wife—clutching Eleanor, bouncing her up and down on his hip—Casey's father's lips pressed into a thin line. As was the case with most things, he was content to let his wife dominate the press conference. Any attempts at speech reduced him to sobs. Crow's feet around his eyes deepened as he fought back his tears that came far too easily, not wanting to cry on camera for the world to see. Looking down at Eleanor, his only living grandchild, offered him some comfort: at least *she* was okay, thank God for small favors.

His daughter though?

He worried she wasn't coming back.

64

I drove Jack's 1970 blue Camaro along a back road, avoiding major highways and interstates staying under the 55-mph speed limit on the signs. No blue and red lights in my rearview mirror, thanks. It might make things a bit awkward, a cop nosing around. But I let those worries melt away, relishing the peace and quiet. How long had it been since I felt whole? Well… besides that whole killing Jack thing. That was pretty cathartic. The passing blacktop morphed into Jack sputtering a last breath, a fine mist of blood spraying from his lips, like a New Year's Eve party favor but much more beautiful and satisfying. How his muscles slackened beneath me; bristling with energy one instant, limp the next. My thighs clenched. I bit my bottom lip, nipping through delicate skin. I tasted blood and my lips curved into a smile.

Focusing on my hands wrapped around the wheel, I'd missed a spot—a dried crescent smudge ringed my knuckle. Before leaving, I'd hopped into the shower, scrubbing the grime and muck from myself. With the water as hot as I could stand it, steaming the entire bathroom, I scoured my body—first with soap, then with a loofa. Wiped the sins away—filicide and matricide. Staring at the offending blood stain—missed during my cleaning extravaganza—everything flooded back.

Love. Hate. What I was capable of. Another thought occurred to me, one that troubled me:

If I could kill my child and husband—maybe I was tainted? Maybe I was the reason Owen… was Owen? *Best pay attention to the road*, I chastised myself. But no, I didn't kill *just* to kill. I had a purpose. Eleanor. Who by now, was safely in her grandparents' arms. Hopefully her mental scars would fade in time, along with her brother-inflicted gashes. There was a gentle tug at my midsection, near my heart and my stomach flipped. Damn… I'd miss those chubby cheeks and wavy hair that almost looked permed but was au natural. Gummy smiles with the barest hints of teeth. I'd never see them grown in.

My eyes still burned, thanks to all the crying after dropping Eleanor off at the hospital. I'd been able to hold it together in the lobby, thrusting Eleanor at the startled registration lady. The second I turned my back the sadness overwhelmed me. The last time I glanced in the rearview mirror I recoiled at seeing how puffy and red my eyelids were. But things were better this way. My parents could protect Eleanor and raise her far better than I ever could. Shameful heat filled my cheeks, remembering the murderous flare of rage that seized me when Eleanor kicked me. I'd come so close. So damned close. I couldn't take her with me. What would happen the *next time* Eleanor upset me —an unavoidable prospect. Kids loved nothing more than testing the bounds of adult patience.

Rubbing snot from my dripping nose, I nodded, reassuring myself. I'd done the right thing. There was no doubt in my mind. Farmers' fields lined the road on either side—brilliantly green and vibrant against the dark splashes of rich dirt—and perfumes of the earthy growth swirled in the air. It smelled like *outside*, a nebulous scent that I knew within my heart. Like freedom. Small creeks glittered in the distance, winking when they caught sunlight. On my left, a hand-drawn sign advertised farm fresh produce. Further down, I saw "Peaches" scrawled on a piece of cardboard, solving the mystery of *what* kind of produce. A large black arrow pointed to the right, towards a bright red barn. My mouth watered, thinking of biting into a ripe peach, juices dribbling down my chin. Salivary glands cramped painfully since I had nothing to offer them. Unfortunately, I couldn't stop. I had to put as much pavement as possible between me and the Casey-of-before.

At least I was doing it in style. Oil and new car smell instead of the faint reek of vomit I'd grown used to in the van—courtesy of Owen puking Goldfish crackers into the air vents. Camaro totally trumped minivan. No contest. Plus, there was something poetic about being in possession of my husband's second love, ranked just behind Tara. I knew where I ranked: 3rd. In total, he probably spent more hours with *her* than either Tara or I. Waxing her to a shine, stroking her with more love than he ever showed me. Maybe I should be jealous of the car, but I couldn't be.

I'd also heard Jack's harsh curses when something went wrong. "Dammit, you bitch!" or a crowd favorite: "You cunt!" We were both in the same boat, mistreated by the man that claimed to love us. It didn't matter if we were flesh and blood or chrome and metal. Well… look who ended up together. I let out a chuckle. Ironic that all Jack's girls (the ones that mattered) ended up together in the end. Reaching into my pocket, I pulled the folded picture of Tara out. Without giving it a second glance, I crumpled it up and chucked it to the floormat. I'd toss it out at the next gas station. No use in leaving common trash in the car.

I adjusted the dark sunglasses obscuring my sensitive eyes—necessary thanks to how bloodshot my blubbering left them—and unrolled the window. My hair tumbled in the wind, filling the car with the scents of my green apple shampoo and the flowering trees outside. If this was how dogs felt with their heads thrust out the window, I understood. I finally felt fully alive and whole. Mostly happy and at peace, other than the deep ache of having to leave Eleanor. *It was for the best*, I reminded myself.

I filled the silence, chatting with myself. It didn't feel odd. Growing up, I always talked aloud to myself while doing homework. *Maybe you should turn on the radio and cheer up.* I turned on the radio, whirling the knob through blasts of static and voices denouncing the devil (*"Can you say hallelujah!"*), landing on an FM broadcast of local news. The standard stuff. Nurses were still striking against poor working conditions (as they should, I'd been in the ER enough to see the shit they dealt with), police brutality, and—

Me.

The Case of the Missing Casey Philips. My mom's voice pleaded, small and shriveled, like she was a husk of her former self, because, well, she was. Once she finished speaking, she let out a sob that was quickly cut off. I couldn't fight the grin that spread over my face as the radio jockey talked about the murders. They were quick to add, "At least the baby was okay!" as if it softened the blow of the story. I had to admit—it did. The radio jockey rattled off my characteristics like I was a professional athlete except I obviously was not (5' 2", petite, sickly), followed by a description of the very car I drove. With the dumb vanity plate that Jack thought was *so cool*. Too bad I'd already thought of that. I'd already procured new plates; swapping them out at a diner, a newer model blue Camaro parked (and not in the lines, typical douche behavior). Luckily, I remembered to grab a screwdriver before hightailing it. The voice whispered to me, *"grab it, just in case."*

The voice—my subconscious or whatever—was proving to be very useful.

Sooner or later, I'd have to ditch the car, but first and foremost, I needed a makeover. As a tween, I'd been completely obsessed with The Spice Girls—Ginger specifically. Red hair might look nice on me. I thrust my hand out the window, savoring the wind dancing along my fingers and palm. Blood roared in my veins, filling me with a pleasurable heat. My thighs clenched again, and a tingle rolled down through my nether regions. I let out a loud whoop and gunned the engine, shifting into fifth gear.

The vibrations of the engine rolled through me (no wonder women loved muscle cars, damn!) and the car surged forward with alarming—but delightful—speed. Weirdly enough, I'd never learned how to drive a stick shift. My dad was a major nerd, outfitted in either tweed or business casual, with wire-rimmed glasses. He couldn't pop the hood of his car without help and greasing someone's palm with cash. But when I crawled into the driver's seat—initially puzzled by the gear shift's mysterious numbers—something clicked within me. Something inside me took over and I understood. Operating the clutch and shifting gears was child's play.

I glanced at the passenger seat at my kitchen knife and reached over, patting it like one might pat the thigh of a favored child. Its blade gleamed, rinsed of the tacky blood that clung to it, and metal flashed each time it caught a sunbeam's edge.

I grinned.

And drove.

65

<hr>

The motel bathroom mirror could be better. Its edges were chipped, and the cheap overhead lighting tinted everything yellow, making my skin appear cirrhotic as I primped. The Ritz, it was not—located smack dab in "the bad side of town" as locals referred to it. It was the sort of motel where junkies ended up when desiring a safe space to shoot up and nod off. A real bargain for the price! I'd been here long enough to notice a pattern. Junkies and men.

Now the men that frequented such establishments (if they weren't washed-out junkies) sported thinning, greasy hair combed sideways to disguise pink scalps littered with dandruff flakes and odd skin growths. Jim 2.0. Not that it fooled anyone. When I wasn't reading or getting ready for a night out, I observed the comings and goings from my second-floor window vantage point—curtains pulled nearly shut, other than the small sliver I peered from. Real life was more entertaining than TV, at least, in this place.

With the deep hum of the ice machine in the background, I watched. At first the men came alone, casting furtive glances behind them as they toted a duffel bag (presumably filled with fuzzy handcuffs, Viagra bottles, and

305

copious amounts of flavored lube), then, hours later, the men came back with a guest. Most often, it was a working girl, probably saving up for a Greyhound ticket to get the fuck out of Dodge, or a twink masquerading as a pretty girl. I'd seen enough of *RuPaul's Drag Race* to recognize such things.

I gravitated to these types of motels; the ones sitting forgotten by the roadside. Somehow, they felt comfortable to me. Safe. Maybe not in my former life, I would have died before spending my time in shitholes like this. The drabbest place Jack ever booked us was a La Quinta Inn that was *light years* nicer than any of the shit stains I'd stayed at thus far. Why, The La Quinta had boasted a continental breakfast! Of course, the place I was in now had a continental breakfast if one was okay with expired, up-priced food purchased from a burnt-out vending machine. As long as you didn't mind the company of chittering cockroaches and rats with thick, naked tails.

No, in places like this—such as The Sands Motel, so named for the copious amount of sand residing in the neighboring riverbed—I could walk into the lobby and turn on the charm for the pimply boys (it must be law that they *always* employed pizza-faces who reeked of stale sweat and rotting cheese) working the front desk. Nothing more than a simple smile coupled with a glimpse of my ample, yet scarred cleavage, and I was in.

"Your driver's license, ma'am?" they asked.

Batting my eyelashes, I adopted a scared expression. Leaned forward. Watched their eyes drop from my face to my tits. Speaking in a breathy voice, I said, "Listen. I can't have a record that I was here." Pause. Then I worked up some tears, usually by thinking of Eleanor and how much I missed her. "My husband... I got away from him. Nasty man, more apt to use his fists than his words. He'll be looking for me." Cue sobs, which always made the front desk clerk incredibly uncomfortable and, in a hurry, to speed up the transaction. Stuttering, they always acquiesced. Using my real ID to book a room was a big no-no, being a "missing person" and all. But wads of bills bearing various American Presidents ameliorated *that* requirement rather easily. Who needed a credit card when I could slide cold, hard cash across the counter and into greedy, waiting hands? Especially when they thought they were helping a "battered" woman—which I was, just not in the traditional sense. Needing a heart transplant because of spousal rape certainly qualified me as abused, didn't it?

I used different names on check-in, and I enjoyed playing around with them, using such aliases as Charlize Manson or Theodora Bundy, mostly as a clever joke to myself. Another name came to me, right before I checked into The Sands Motel, in fact. A boring and sedate name: Jeannie Burke. It came to me in a flash of inspiration, and I'd felt compelled to use it, say it aloud. It came to me almost as if someone whispered it in my ear and once used, it felt *right* somehow, rolling off my tongue. It had a nice ring to it, very unassuming and bland. A name that flew under the radar.

At the first motel, The Rio, I checked in and immediately went to work on my appearance. A box of red hair dye and scissors were my dates that evening. A makeover was in order since the public was on the lookout for someone resembling Casey Philips (the news couldn't get enough of me, running segments morning and night). They weren't looking for Jeannie Burke, a fiery redhead with a penchant for murder. I'd also purchased a face mask and a bath bomb because, dammit, a girl deserved a little pampering now and then! When was the last time I relaxed? Truly? Without worrying about Eleanor crying, Owen burning the house down, or Jack drunk driving? Honestly, I couldn't remember. Now it was time to do whatever the fuck I wanted.

Or *whoever* the fuck I wanted.

The evening after completing my dye job (which turned out nice, all things considered), I went out, red hair coiffed to perfection. Deep inside me, there was a maddening itch, one I never noticed before. If it were a mere physical sensation, I would have dug my nails in and *scratched* but this one dwelled deep within me. It wanted. Needed.

Something.

So, instead of ignoring it, slowly going mad, I heeded its call. And it wanted me to go out.

Go out I did. That night with my new red hairdo, I dressed in comfy jeans that showed off my ass, a V-neck shirt with a push-up bra, and sensible Converse, and walked to a dive bar within spitting distance of the motel. Little shit stain bars and scuzzy roadside motels formed a sort of symbiotic relationship, sharing customers with predilections for raunchy sex and sickly vices.

The man at the front didn't charge me cover despite the sign that stated: Women, $4 cover charge. Instead, he leered at me, smiling a rotting grin that instantly made me disgusted. Men. They really were the worst. I took a seat in the corner of the bar and ordered a Diet Coke. As I gazed at the bar patrons: some engaged in a game of pool, others dancing to honky-tonk from the aging jukebox, more still, drank alone, I felt it. *The itch.* It grew, becoming almost overpowering. My entire body hummed, filled with unspent energy. Each inhale of peanuts and spilled beer added fuel to the fire, every time I tapped my foot or shifted on my barstool, the need increased. At first, I wasn't quite sure *why.* I didn't quite know what I wanted. A quick fuck? Companionship? What?

The answer came to me, almost by accident. I was on my second Diet Coke, humming along with *Hotel California,* nodding my head in time with the tune. My newly red hair tumbled over my shoulders, still smelling of chemicals with an undertone of apple conditioner. Next to me, a stool scraped against the wood planked floor, setting my nerves on edge. I was reminded of nails on a chalkboard and my arms prickled with goosebumps. Sipping my soda, I looked to my left to see who was responsible for the racket.

"Buy you a drink?" he asked, shooting the woman seated next to him a blindingly white smile. I'd noticed her when I sat down and judging by her hunched shoulders and wan complexion, she was going through something—anything from a hard day at work to an existential crisis. Out of the periphery of my vision, I watched the man's hands. Acting as if he were fidgeting, right hand surreptitiously removed wedding band and pocketed it. A neat trick, if not for the tan line on his ring finger that proclaimed, "I love my wife, just not tonight." Instantly, every cell within me burst into flame. Another man, another liar, stepping out on his wife at home who probably bore him ungrateful children. I imagined his wife sitting at the dinner table, one eye on the clock, hoping her husband made it home safely. I seethed. The voice inside my mind whispered, *let's watch this play out, watch what happens.*

"Sure," the woman answered, the male attention giving her new life.

His grin widened. "What would you like?" Already, he'd stood, walking halfway down the bar, and flagged down the bartender.

"Surprise me."

Two Diet Cokes and rum. Not that I heard his order, but given that there were only the two ingredients, it was easy enough to figure out. The bartender placed a maraschino cherry in each, the red fruit bobbing within the ice like debris from a shipwreck. Bills exchanged hands. I kept my eyes on the man's broad back rippling with muscle, unable to look away and thankfully, I didn't. *Watch him*, the voice said. He angled his body away from her—giving me a clear view—and I watched the same hand that removed his wedding ring dip into his pocket, remove a small bottle, and tip it over the drink on the right. *Her* drink, presumably. Several clear drops hit the surface.

I gritted my teeth and clenched my fists, ready to scream in the bar, drawing everyone's attention to the would-be date rapist.

"A drink for the lovely lady," he said, placing the tainted glass in front of her. His eyebrows knitted themselves together. "I would say your name, but I don't know it. I'm Sam." Offering her his right hand, she gripped it and shook. She murmured something I didn't hear, and I got to my feet, tossing bills on the bar top to cover my drinks and tip. Turning with far more force than necessary, I flung my elbow out, connecting with asshole's drink, upending it into his lap.

"Shit!" he exclaimed, shooting me a poisonous look.

"Oh my God, I'm *sooooo* sorry!" I said, injecting extra sugar into my voice. Grabbing a handful of napkins, I thrust them in his direction.

"It's fine," he said in a tone that negated his words. He snatched the napkins from my grip and within seconds, they were soaked. "Damn." Turning to his intended victim, he said, "Listen, I'm going to the bathroom real quick. Don't go anywhere." Giving me another glare, he exited stage right.

The second he was out of sight, I put my hand on the woman's arm and she shifted her gaze to me. Her lips were pressed into a thin line. "I don't appreciate you cutting in," she said. "He was buying me drinks."

Inclining my head toward the restrooms, I said, "That guy? I saw him put something in your drink."

"You're just saying that."

"I'll prove it." I raised my hand to get the bartender's attention. "Could you give my friend a new rum and Diet Coke? I spilled hers." I shifted her drink away. "See what happens when he drinks what he gave you. What have you got to lose?"

"I don't know what's goin' on, but I don't want any part of this."

She grabbed her purse and bolted to the door before her new paramour returned.

A minute or so later, the man reapproached the bar, and I didn't suppress my smirk as I looked at his wet crotch. "Hey, where did she go?" he asked in a haughty tone, head turning to seek out his former prey.

"I don't know. She said something about 'not wanting to be raped.'"

"Raped? Listen lady, I don't know what you're talking about."

"Sure," I said in the most condescending tone I could muster. "Drink this," I said, pushing the tainted drink in front of him.

"You're crazy. Maybe you put something in there," he said, walking away. I knew what I wanted to do—plunge the knife back at my motel room into his chest and rid the world of disgusting trash like him, but now wasn't the right time. "Choke on your lies and die; you piece of shit." With that, I left.

I knew what I had to do.

66

One trip to Walmart later, I was armed with the necessary tools. Sitting on the motel's thread barren comforter, I booted up the prepaid phone and accessed the internet. Typed in "pretty redheads" and combed through pages of photos before I found what I was looking for. Petra —according to her Instagram—lived in Croatia, and with my new hairdo, we could pass as sisters or at the very least, cousins. I remembered my stay in the hospital, still laid up with various tubes coursing from my body, and with nothing other than books and TV to keep me company, I watched *Catfish* to pass the time. Who said reality TV wasn't educational? Picking Petra's five best photos, I created a Tinder profile for Jeannie.

Spun my spiderweb.

67

"Hi, I'm Jeannie," I said, the lie rolling off my tongue easily.

"Mark," he said. The prick hadn't even bothered to take his wedding ring off, but… what did I expect? In his DM, he flat-out told me that he was married and given how their sex life had waned, he was looking for adventure that his wife couldn't give him. He was literally using his wife as the reason he was on the app.

Despite my disgust, I shot him a winning smile. "Buy me a drink?"

He leered at me, eyes unabashedly traveling down my body, lingering on my chest. "I'll buy you two."

While he ordered, my fingers closed around the glass bottle in my pocket. I hated to admit it, but… Date-Rape-Sam had the right idea, and I took a page out of his book. Finding the GHB was easier than expected… a horrifying thought.

Mark returned with the drinks. Diet Coke with rum for me (not that I planned on really drinking it) and a beer for him (based on the dark amber color, a hoppy IPA of some sort). My purse sat to my side, and I jerked, toppling it off the bar. Chapsticks, coins, and a half-spent roll of mints scattered on the grimy floor. "God, I am so clumsy!" I said, laughing. A flash of something dark flitted across Mark's eyes, there one second, gone the next. He bent over, scrambling for all the loose items. Trying to earn chivalry points he could cash in later.

As he dutifully herded my lipstick and loose change, I plonked four drops of GHB into his drink, then bent to help. Everything returned to the purse—including a tampon that rolled underneath a nearby table—we both sat up, sharing a smile.

"You're such a gentleman," I said, squeezing his bicep.

"A toast?" he asked, grabbing his glass.

"Of course!" I answered. "Let's toast to… an unforgettable night?"

Mark's eyes crinkled; crow's-feet deepened. "I like the sound of that."

Glasses clinked and we drank, Mark nearly polishing his off in one go. I giggled. "I better catch up to you, hadn't I?" I inclined my glass to him, taking a small drink. His hungry eyes remained trained on me. "Bottom's up!" We exchanged small talk after that. Neither of us mentioning marriage or children. Mark ordered another beer while I nursed my drink. Better to keep my wits about me.

Mark began spilling his "truth." How he loved his wife, but she let herself go. After the two kids, she put on 25 pounds and wasn't interested in being with him sexually. Her health problems compounded it. How hard he worked every day to pay bills, a man has needs, you know? And it didn't take long for me to realize that this could have easily been Jack at Monday Night Football, telling his friends about his bitch wife who wouldn't put out. His friends egging him on to go home and 'take what's his!' A wife home, oblivious, a total stranger in her own bed.

Mark's words began slurring, sharp consonants growing

fuzzy. His brown eyes lost their shine and eyelids drooped. When he started losing his train of thought—abruptly halting during a story about how all the girls in high school wanted him and he still chose his wife instead, his face betrayed his befuddlement—I knew it was time.

Leaning over, I put my hand on his thigh, lightly stroking it and whispered in his ear, "Hey, you look a little tired. What do you say we get out of here?"

My touch rallied Mark's adrenaline. A spark of interest. "Yesssh, I would like thhhhat." He tossed crumpled bills on the bar and stood, swaying dangerously on his feet. "Ssshit," he said, offering me a sheepish grin.

I put my arm around him, steadying him. "Let's get some fresh air, handsome."

Somehow, we made it to the parking lot with Mark shuffling down the bar's handicap entrance, because stairs were a no-go unless I wanted him to cap off the night with a head injury. Concussions and brain bleeds weren't exactly what I had in mind for him.

I'd parked underneath a massive tree whose branches drooped down, leaves almost obscuring the car's presence altogether. A nice remote location, far from prying eyes, with a conspicuous lack of streetlights—giving the impression I was up for a quick bang session.

The *itch* inside me intensified. The *want*. The *need*. I sweetly asked, "Do you want to stretch out in the back, love? More room back there." Nodding exuberantly, he lurched to the backdoor and without a single look behind him, hopped right in.

"I'm sorry about the seat covering, baby," I said. "The dog tears it up something awful, and I've gotta have it replaced."

We were totally and utterly alone as I eased in the backseat.

Men have no trouble waltzing in the lion's den without a

care in the world, because they think they're the lion. The lion doesn't preoccupy himself with the opinions of sheep because he doesn't have to listen. The lion does what he wants, when he wants, with whomever he wants.

But from the moment a girl has her first period, it's drilled into her head that lions will smell blood when they see her. She's someone to be preyed upon. And she needs to know the rules of the jungle to stay alive.

Never leave your drinks unattended.

Hold your keys tightly within a fist—a key between each knuckle—just in in case you had to fight for your life walking to your car late at night.

Don't dress like a whore, because then you'll be asking for it.

Do whatever he says so he won't hurt you.

If Mark had learned the rules of the jungle, respected the danger of the jungle and maybe, also respected his wife —things would be different. But they weren't. The maddening itch within me intensified, now positively *begging* me to scratch, and I felt my panties getting absolutely soaked.

I set my purse down, ensuring it was open. Had Mark been observant in the least, he might have seen the knife handle peeking out. But he didn't. With a forwardness that was completely unlike the Casey Philips of old, I crawled on top of him, purposely rubbing my crotch against his leg. At the first whisper of friction, his cock hardened against me. Mark groaned.

"That feelssss real nice," he slurred.

Creeping forward like a cat (the less time I spent by his face, the better), I stared into his eyes, not caring if I was giving off unhinged vibes. His eyelids fluttered, jerked open, then shut. He mumbled, "Jusssst resthing my eyes."

Fine by me. I'd wake you up when it was time. Everything around me sharpened, becoming crisp and clear.

Outside the window crickets trilled, mostly obscuring the noise of distant traffic, and inside the car I heard Mark's rhythmic deep breathing and mine, faster with a hint of anticipation. His heartbeats, slow and steady, mingled with my pulse audible within my ears. Reaching into my purse, I gripped the cool knife handle—already, it felt like an old friend—and my eyes traced the silver edge, honed by hand right before I left the motel. Itch became all consuming, sensitizing each nerve ending, readying them for untold pleasure. My skin felt too tight, and heat bloomed between my legs, Mark's leg pressing against me almost enough to incite an orgasm.

Almost.

Do it, the voice commanded. Placing my left hand behind his head, as if to tip him forward for a kiss, I hooked my fingers into his thick hair, and yanked his skull back.

Exposing his throat.

Mark startled to life with a comical snort, like a sitcom dad caught snoozing on the couch. Hair follicles ripped away from his scalp, but I kept firm hold.

"Yeah, you like it rough, baby?" he said. "HEY, what the fuck—" His mouth fell open. Pupils constricted when they focused on the knife I now clutched in my hand. His drugged eyes widened in wonder, like a kid watching a magician produce a rabbit from their seemingly empty top hat. "What—"

Before he could complete the thought, I rested my blade on his throat, just below his Adam's apple. He took a great, hitching swallow, and larynx quivered. A thin red line appeared, trickling down Mark's sternum, where it formed a small pool with each new bead of blood. The knife's edge bopped in tune with his carotid pulse. He whimpered.

"How do you think your wife would feel if she knew you were here?" I asked, applying a little more pressure. He yelped and a sanguine tributary burst forth—more than before. I let up so he could speak to his heart's content. Wouldn't want him to be offing himself before I was ready. The payoff wouldn't be *nearly* as sweet.

"Listen, I like wild stuff, but this is a little too wild for me," he said, still unafraid of the lion.

"So, your wife doesn't do wild stuff like this?" I asked.

"Who gives a fuck what she wants," he said with a rather petulant tone for someone with a knife held against their throat. "What does it even matter?!"

Spit peppered his face as I hissed, "*It matters.*" I wrenched his head back, popping something in his upper spine, inciting a pig's squeal, and just like that, he was terror-stricken again. A tingle shot down my pelvis. "Does your wife know that you're a giant piece of shit? Stepping out on her? If you tell me the truth, I'll let you live. I may even let you come."

An internal struggle waged, lasting only the barest second. His thoughts were practically projected on his face. Tell the truth? Lie and hope that I was dumb enough to believe him? Throat shuddered and he let out a low whine. Tears tracked down his cheeks and his chin quivered, reminding me of Owen when he put on an apologetic show of bullshit. He wasn't *sorry.* He was *sorry* that this was happening to *him.* My body hummed, trembling with unspent energy and I stared at the thrumming of his carotid, bobbing up and down with increasing speed. Only a thin layer of skin separated Mark from meeting his maker. He scrunched his eyes up, a sob coloring his words, "No, she doesn't know, but—"

But… the word that precedes excuses. Excuses for shitty behavior, even when their life was on the line! The word lit the fuse and with a primal scream, I slashed across his throat, skin zippering open, spraying a crimson waterfall, which petered down to a pulsatile fountain on either side of the neck. His shaking hands encircled his throat and blood oozed through his fingers. A strangled noise, like an animal twisting in a trap, escaped him and triggered something within me: an undeniable urge to make *this fucking hurt.* I whooped and plunged the knife into his chest, smack dab where my LVAD used to be in mine. Another stab, off to the right and a whistle of air shot upwards—a sure sign of a punctured lung. Except Dr. Grey wasn't here to save you. Maybe had I not married Jack and went to medical school, I could have. Of course, had I not married Jack, I probably wouldn't be stabbing a philandering man to death.

Mark twitched, guppy breathing, a watery, nasty sound, like someone afflicted with a nasty pneumonia that filled each crevice within their lungs. I smiled. If he were breathing, he was still in the land of the living. Time to really hit him where it hurt. I buried my knife to the hilt in his groin. The blade slid like it belonged, penetrating him, invading him, violating him. He violently twitched upwards, bucking, then shuddered.

Died.

I came.

The voice was right, the itching finally stopped.

After I dragged his body out of the car with the tarp into the woods, I drove back to the hotel and scrubbed everything—my body, my nails, my Tinder account. Time to head to a new town. I'd find a place to get rid of my clothes along the way. I hopped into my car, a gently used Mazda. I'd traded an impressionable teenager the Camaro for it. Thoughts of title transfers and "legalities" meant nothing to that kid, especially if he could drive around a "pussy wagon" as he called it. With a pang in my heart, I handed the keys over, knowing authorities were on the lookout for it. They talked about the car enough on the news, although coverage of my case was waning, especially as new disasters sprang to life.

Where to next?

Maybe a bigger city? I considered. I'd always wanted to visit Chicago—see The Bean, eat their famous cheesy caramel popcorn, and explore—and from what I heard on the news, the police were too busy with gang violence to notice little Casey Philips strolling around. Getting on the Interstate, due East, I frowned and thought of last night. The pain I caused. The pleasure I received. How I saved a woman from the same fate I had suffered or even worse. Maybe she can fulfill her needs now. I will keep satisfying mine. Already, the itch was back, very low and mild but present.

And I knew it would grow.

Ridding humanity of its trash was a noble way of quelching the thirst too.

I thought about how I'd come to after my intense orgasm, staring at Mark's face, ragged X's marking his cheeks, X's I didn't remember making.

69

Rows of arcade machines lined the back wall—obnoxious noises, and flashing lights that would make an epileptic pitch a fit. Two college-aged boys, half-drained craft brews in hand, watched their friend wind his way through the Pac-Man maze, avoiding ghosts and gobbling fruit. Despite being at a brewery, I sipped a Shirley Temple while I waited for Tom. We'd exchanged a few messages and within that short timeframe, I learned Tom was recently engaged, but was "exploring his options" as he put it. He would do nicely. Lazily, I surveyed the room.

I gulped, 7-UP bubbles scorched my esophagus, and my cheeks flushed.

Wow.

A young auburn-haired woman bent over a pool table, exposing a gravity-defying butt, jeans perfectly molded to her derriere—no wonder men went wild over nice asses. Her hair bounced as she tossed her head back, unleashing a fine, tinkling laugh that made my stomach clench. I ran my fingers through my own false red locks, brighter and more artificial than the woman's gorgeous auburn hue. Chicago's moniker as The Windy City hadn't disappointed, so I'd pulled a black stocking cap over most of it, having learned the hard way that the wind coaxed my curls into a massive rat's nest.

My eyes trained on the beautiful stranger, I fluffed my hair like a male peacock preening and prancing for a potential mate. I'd never been into women. Not the Casey of *before*, anyway. But more and more, I noticed one beautiful woman after the next. The city was filled with them—all nationalities and colors—and I found them hard to ignore.

Men now existed for me to sate my hunger—the way a lion would suddenly care about a sheep. And whenever I was hungry, there were plenty of sheep dressed as lions on Tinder, the hunters who realized they were prey a second too late. It was as if a lion could shop for whatever they wanted at a supermarket. Maybe it was all too easy. The lion needs the chase to stay sharp. To stay alive.

I directed my attention back to the pretty little thing near the pool table. She grasped the pool stick in her hand; fingers wrapping around it in a way that felt erotic. Brilliant green eyes flickered up, meeting mine and the auburn-haired woman's face broke out in a beaming grin. A pulsing warmth bloomed between my thighs and my new heart hammered against my ribs. I barely felt the sinister cold within my chest, more focused on the overwhelming arousal roaring within me. I thought of the nightmares—the dreams —where I chased that gorgeous auburn-haired woman. How glorious it felt when I caught her, wrapped my hands around her throat and *squeezed.*

Had that been a premonition? I searched myself for the itch but couldn't find it. I couldn't taste the blood. Instead, I felt the urge to be with this woman. To nurture her, not dominate her. To treasure her.

But what if she's luring me in? What if I let my guard down? Maybe it wouldn't be the worst thing in the world.

Something about her felt right. It made my heart feel right.

And I knew there was *nothing* wrong with a little change of heart.

ACKNOWLEDGMENTS

A few years ago, I found a bucket list I made during college. There were a few checkmarks; run a marathon (glad I got that out of my system!), graduate med school, climb a 14er, amongst others. Number one on the list? Write a horror novel.

Getting it published? That was the secret dream I'd harbored since falling in love with the horror genre.

And I couldn't have done it alone so thank you.

To my biggest cheerleader, my wife, Ashley. I'd started writing in secret, but after I came out to her about my author aspirations, she bought me a Moleskin notebook for my ideas and gifted me a book for Christmas: *Before and After the Book Deal.* She always believed in me even when I didn't believe in myself.

Fraley, my work wife, who read countless rough drafts and provided insightful feedback, even though she's terrified of such tales and had to sleep with a nightlight afterwards. One might say she is *cool for the summer.*

My fellow wordsmith, Shadrin, who understands the necessity of creative pursuits while working in healthcare—providing Sprite to all.

My Mom, who immersed me in the horror genre at young age. I still remember the first-time watching Ripley kick Xenomorph ass *while* saving the ship's cat (my primary concern as a child). Once I'd exhausted my YA books, she tossed Stephen King tomes my way thus completing my education. Let's not forget Dennis, my darling stepdad, who reads my stories even if he doesn't read much else. Thanks for always laughing at my terrible jokes and being there for me.

To the family I married into—I'm one of the lucky ones that loves their in-laws. They've been unfailingly amazing, snatching up everything I put out. Sherry and Terrie—you guys might be my biggest fans, hopefully not in an Annie Wilkes way! Chip, thanks for the jokes—check's in the mail. Chip Jr. who buys all my books and will read them one day.

ER fam. You keep me sane (relatively) while we go through hell together, saving lives and cracking jokes. You give me plenty ideas too!

To the Twitter-verse, where I've met amazing people, some within the writing, horror, and medical world as well as generally good humans. Ya'll are weird as heck, and I love it. Thank you for your support!

Speaking of Twitter, without the bird app and #PitDark, I wouldn't have matched with my editor, Michael Dolan, who believed in my story and took a chance on a girl with a dark, twisted tale. He's my Kris Jenner always telling me, "You're doing amazing, sweetie!" I'm so proud to be part of the Winding Road Stories crew.

My grandpa, who nurtured my creative side from the beginning. I think of you every time I put pen to paper.

My cattos who hang out with me while I write: Nico, Epic, Theodore, and Cat Bane.

And thank you, dear reader, for buying my book. I hope you enjoy it (and if so, please leave a review!) and if you don't… I'm sure there's medicine for that.

ABOUT THE AUTHOR

N.J. Gallegos is an Emergency Medicine Physician who enjoys horror, medicine, and wicked women looking for revenge. Put all three together? Now we're talking! She lives in Illinois with her wife and two cats. In her spare time, she enjoys binging reality trash tv, brewing beer, and running while listening to EDM so she can drink said brewed beer. She is the author of two novellas: *Just Desserts* and the chapbook *Only You Can Prevent Forest Fires*.